Finders, Seekers
Losers, Keepers

Finders, Seekers
Losers, Keepers

Heather J. Rolland

Mill City Press, Inc.
212 3rd Avenue North, Suite 570
Minneapolis, MN 55401
612.455.2294
www.millcitypublishing.com

ISBN - 1-934937-43-6
ISBN - 978-1-934937-43-3
LCCN - 2008939818

Cover Design and Typeset by Tiffany Laschinger

Printed in the United States of America

Acknowledgements

The author wishes to acknowledge the assistance of many friends, neighbors, acquaintances, and, of course, family members, without whom this project would have been difficult or impossible to complete. While many people in the town of Dover, NY, were supportive and helpful, Town Supervisor Jill Way deserves special mention for her warmth, enthusiasm, and passion for Dover, and her kind friendship to me. Jim LaPierre went above and beyond, protecting me from overzealous landscapers when I was new to the neighborhood, and calling his contacts in Keeseville for local information. I fondly remember all our chats.

Many friends helped with childcare during my years as a single mom – I am grateful to all of them. The Pitera family tops this list.

Thank you, Jennifer Tillotson, for providing information regarding the New York State seventh grade science curriculum. More power to middle school science teachers. Warm thanks to my editor, Bethany Saltman. She nailed it – the issues, the quandaries, the big picture and the details. Thank you to Kurt and Cynnie Boyer for friendship, meals, inspiration, and community. Rest in peace to Black Bear Hollow – she was well-loved.

Thank you to Julie Bennett of Julie's Antique Prints: http://stores.ebay.com/juliesantiqueprints?refid=store for providing the Baedeker map used on the front cover. This map is from Karl Baedeker's 1909 guidebook entitled *The United States With Excursions To Mexico Cuba Porto Rico And Alaska. Handbook For Travellers,* and is used with permission from Verlag Karl Baedeker.

My family - old and new, step and bio, of origin

and of choice – has been there for me all along, from the idea stage straight through the publication. My mother and my daughter were true collaborators – they made me believe it was possible and their ideas made the story work. Iske was my constant companion, my rock, my alter-ego, and my "dog double." I am grateful to the powers that be that she was sent to me.

Thank you, thank you, thank you – Tom, Flammeus, Minister of Strong Coffee. When it's right, it's right, and all we can do is get out of our own way. You are a brave man to follow where love leads; you are a wise man to know that there is no other destination worth seeking. So what took you so long???

Dedication

For Anne and Maya – the two bravest, strongest, most beautiful women I know. You are my role models and my inspiration. I am truly blessed to be mother and daughter to you.

drinks

alizarin smoke: blueberry juice, cassis, seltzer, ice

black and blue: cassis, blueberry juice – no seltzer

concussed dog: pomegranate juice, ice, and someone to keep an eye on you for 24 hours

loup garou: mayan style hot chocolate – dark chocolate with smoky chilis

melting sun: mango sorbet, vodka, lemon zest, ice – blended smooth

virgin lizard: blueberry juice with seltzer

the blue eft

nellie hill road   dover plains, ny

Chapter 1

"If I'm sleeping then I'm not getting up," Halia stated. She considered the level of liquid left among the ice cubes in her drink, and decided against tipping her glass all the way up to get the last sip. It was not the stain the cassis was bound to make on her silk blouse that she wished to avoid, but the anticipation of the cold and wet impact on her nose that swayed her decision. The noise level in the bar was not loud enough to prevent conversation, but Halia used her teacher voice as much out of habit as out of necessity.

Grace actually understood what Halia meant by her contradictory statement. She opened her mouth, reviewing her options – a) whine in protest or b) attempt to cajole her friend into getting up early. After a moment she thought the better of both options, shut her mouth, and grinned. Halia was just Halia – as usual, she made no effort at social lubrication. She just blurted out the truth as it unfolded with no intent to hurt or disappoint. Halia might get up early and meet her as they had discussed; she might not. Close friends for decades, Grace knew Halia better than to fret over the potential rejection.

Of course, Grace herself thought nothing of getting up early on a Saturday morning and driving the hours it would take to reach the eagle-watching appointment at the Shepaug Dam; the lure of nearly any opportunity to observe wildlife was hard to resist for this young veterinarian. However, she was well aware that her enthusiasm was not shared universally, and that Halia, unattached, childless, and prone to insomnia, did not always pop out of bed on the weekends ready to leap into action. And, she admitted to herself, six a.m. was pretty early to be up and out on a Saturday. She accepted Halia's response diplomatically, and offered a way to remain noncommittal right up to the moment. "Tell you what: if you wake up in time, call me and we can meet at the bottom of the hill. Maybe leave one car in the library parking lot? Ok?"

Halia nodded.

The two women were enjoying their end-of-the-week ritual – a drink, or perhaps a meal, at The Blue Eft. A neighborhood pub occupying the former lawn mower repair shop on a quiet side street in Dover Plains, NY, The Blue Eft sat two doors down from the house Halia moved to after her divorce, and just around the corner from the animal hospital where Grace spent her days. The weekly meetings started years ago – during a different phase of life for both women. They honored their friendship by continuing to meet through the proverbial thick and thin that life seems to hand women during their twenties and thirties. Now both facing forty, their weekly meetings were full of the sundries of life being dealt with and set aside for an hour, if they could spare that much. As often as not, Grace's cell phone would twitter and Grace would tele-parent from her table at The Eft.

From drinks to entrees to live music, the theme at The Eft was black and blue: black currants and blueberries were scattered throughout the menu, and blues blared from the sound system or makeshift stage. Transforming the garage into an inviting space required heroic measures – years of oil and grease and smoke (both cigarette and engine) stained the floors and scarred the walls. Louise, the owner and substitute bartender or chef, was up to the task. Inspired by the décor in a Finnish tea room in Great Barrington, The Blue Eft was delightfully dark, cozy, eclectic and relaxed. Artfully mismatched tablecloths and napkins sported black and blue plaids, stripes, polka dots, and a few solids, ranging in shades from aqua to cerulean. Similarly, the lighting from a combination of candles, table lamps, and wall sconces, was Louise's own personal collection, scrounged from estate sales and antique stores over the past ten years. The overall impact, heightened by the presence of sofas and oversized armchairs in the pub, and warm wool rugs strewn here and there, was that of being in a tag sale addict's home. And yet, somehow it worked. So well, in fact, that the restaurant reviews The Blue Eft garnered regularly mentioned that under Louise's guiding hand, the collectique aesthetic was elevated to upscale heights. Comfortable, personal, and inviting, there were times when Halia wondered if she did feel more at home here in The Eft, as it was affectionately referred to, than in her own home.

Halia and Grace sipped alizarin smoke – a concoction Louise created involving cassis liquor, blueberry juice and club soda – and relaxed into a comfortable silence.

For a Friday evening, the bar was quiet: only a smattering of regulars, haunting their habitual tables, and a few misplaced members of the horse crowd, brandishing their drinks (all either created or renamed by Louise, the current menu featuring concussed dogs, melting suns, black and blues, and the loup garou) as if to announce their charter membership in the Bohemian avant-garde of eastern Dutchess County. Halia surveyed the scene discretely, as Grace gestured in greeting to an immaculate couple in their 50's, wearing riding britches and boots.

"Patients of yours?" Halia murmured.

Grace nodded, her long blond hair working its way loose from its hastily gathered bun. Halia consumed the couple with her eyes, taking approximately three seconds to complete her research. "King Charles Cavalier spaniels," she declared matter-of-factly. Grace didn't ask how Halia knew, nor did she congratulate her friend on being correct, once again. She did acknowledge the correctness with a nod, pulling the black nylon hair-tie out of her hair. It was a game they played - a game that Halia had yet to lose. The first 50 or so correct guesses over the first few years of their friendship, way back in junior high school in Bergen County, New Jersey, had resulted in astonishment and the demand for an explanation. However, each time Halia told Grace what she had seen, heard, smelled or felt, Grace saw that the combination of encyclopedic knowledge and observation of minutiae added up to a complete lack of guesswork for Halia. To her, each animal (or whatever the specific situation involved) clearly left its calling card, there for all to see. Halia just seemed to know where and how to look. Really the game was more like calisthenics for Halia's brain, her personal version of sudoku.

Halia, for her part, smiled at Grace's ability to remember human owners and their pet counterparts despite years of running a busy veterinary practice in a land populated by weekenders. If Grace and Mrs. Spaniel meet in the ladies room later, Halia mused, Grace would be able to ask after the dogs by name. And she would honestly care about the answer. Halia watched Grace gather up her hair, finger-combing loose strays back under control, twirling the long, slippery tresses back into an unruly pile on the back of her head. Halia's smile broadened.

"What are you doing this weekend?" Grace asked Halia. She lifted her chin to look down at her, then added, "besides sleeping through an appointment with eagles?"

Halia's eyes flicked over Grace, measuring meaning behind her question. Satisfied that Grace was purely playing at the barb, she let it go with a shrug.

"I have my list." Halia paused, twirled her straw between her fingers and shrugged. "I have some grading I should get to … and lesson plans… I'd like to do some exploring in Ulster County this spring – you know, the Gunks and Rosendale… I'll just have to see what the weather does," Halia sighed, "and how adventurous I feel." Her eyes failed to sparkle quite as playfully as Grace's had as she added, "And how late I sleep."

Grace ticked off her various chores, errands, and appointments filling the weekend, more a review of her list than as part of the conversation. She sighed too. "I wish my weekends were determined by whim and weather."

"Whim and weather – that would make a great name for -"

"Travel accessories? Camping supplies? A new boutique in Kent?" Grace set her drink down on the table. "I'd shop there."

"Hmmm … maybe when I retire, I'll create the Whim and Weather franchise."

"Maybe Aunt Joann would help you fund this new venture. She may want to be your silent partner."

"Thank you for reminding me." Halia began rummaging through her purse, if one could call the portable cavern Halia toted such a dainty name. She came up with an envelope, the back nearly covered with her own neat print. She removed a pen from the front pocket. "I need to send Aunt Joann a check when I pay bills. I'd better add it to my list." As Halia wrote "check to Jo" at the bottom of the long list, Grace couldn't help but notice both the length of the list and the unpleasant nature of many of its items.

"You're busy." Grace's tone had changed slightly. No one but Halia would have noticed the concern in her voice.

"Busy is good." Halia replied.

"Busy is good when it includes fun," Grace continued to strive for a tone that did not reveal her worry, nor her criticism. She strove to keep her tone lighter than her content, but Halia was not fooled for a moment. She met Grace's eyes and allowed herself to be studied. Her unruly, thick, brown hair hung in shaggy bangs, shading enormous brown eyes and grazing her shoulders.

She sat up straight, which made her appear taller than her 5'2", and held herself upright but not tense, as if in yoga class. At times she looked younger than her 37 years of age; her olive skin was wrinkle free and her not-straight-not-curly hair was without the silver sparkles that bespeak age. And then there were times, like now, when her emotional distance made her seem quite ageless. Halia aimed for unremarkable in her physical appearance, with her preference for shapeless and colorless clothing. Halia worked hard at flying low under the radar, and often failed – her huge eyes and confident movement drew attention and admiration, despite Halia's desire to observe without being noticed.

"Busy is good for me now." Halia spoke matter-of-factly.

"I think you're addicted to being busy. You never seem to want to hang out and just fuck off." Grace frowned as she spoke, as if the words were distasteful. She didn't curse often. The effort wasn't in eliminating vulgarity from her repertoire – it was in knowing how to use it judiciously. "Why won't you let yourself enjoy life a little?"

Halia considered Grace's question. Grace sighed inwardly, realizing that intellect, not emotion, would govern Halia's answer. If she wanted Halia to open up, Grace decided, she would need to surprise or annoy her.

"I'll have to think it over and get back to you." Halia, uncannily astute when others were concerned, appeared to be at a loss, as if she'd been asked by one of her seventh grade students about a subject other than her own. The question gave rise to serious, thoughtful contemplation, but she was truly unable to provide an answer.

"I mean, I know you have your own ways of enjoying life," Grace hastened to remind her that she hadn't forgotten who Halia really is. "But I don't know if you realize just how 'blah' you've been acting for a while now. You used to have fun in your own weird way." Grace's delivery, complete with rolling eyes and fake Valley Girl accent, was a little over the top, but sweetly so. "These days you just work constantly. I don't believe that your lesson plans need to be that OCD perfect. You don't give a shit about him." Grace referred to Bones. Halia's frown was an autonomic response. "And you're not lonely. So why the hell are you moping around? You need some real recreation. Y'know, recharge your batteries. Relax." Grace's eyes crinkled up with self-deprecating mirth. "What do the kids all say these days? Chillax?"

Halia didn't join in laughing. She considered providing her Human Body Lecture in which she points out that batteries are not included, but decided against it. She knew Grace was motivated by genuine concern; Grace had known Halia during her darkest days, both recent and distant. Halia was used to Grace, she tolerated Grace's devoted friendship, she loved Grace, and she trusted Grace. She had come to believe that Grace understood her, perhaps better than anyone ever had. But pep talks like these stretched Halia's patience thin.

Relax? Have fun? Halia felt like Grace must have had a momentary lapse. Grace's expectation that Halia would somehow, post divorce, perk up and become "normal" was unfair – Halia had never been the type of normal Grace seemed to be hinting at, and she knew it. It was the pressure to be something other than she was, to make her parents or her few friends feel comfortable, that led Halia astray in the first place. Halia realized that these thoughts had her clenching her teeth, and tried to relax her jaw. Her marriage to Bones and its demise lived in her mind as a shining example of her own greatest folly – a profound error, generated by allowing herself to a) try to act like other people and b) make those around her happy by faking it. She had given it a try because... Halia sighed, not wanting to rehash that episode, and then realized she uttered the sound aloud and checked Grace's face. Grace was waiting for her response, and by the looks of it, anticipated her train of thought. It was precisely because Grace seemed to understand her that Halia thought she should know to leave her alone.

Grace was unsure how to interpret Halia's silence, uncertain if she had said too much. "'I'm sorry Hali," she tried again. "'I just don't buy it that it has to be this bad. I'd like to see you happy. Genuinely happy."

Halia nodded, her lips glued together, making a perfectly straight horizontal line. She didn't want to argue about her own happiness, or lack thereof. To her, at this point in her life, it didn't seem very important. To be honest, Halia couldn't remember a time in her life when her own happiness felt important to her. Not that she sought out discomfort or misery – not at all. Halia just focused on other things – her passion for observation, or her satisfaction with ticking items off a list, for example. Back in high school, her eccentricities had shown themselves in high relief. Her parents had dragged her off to a psychiatrist because she didn't want to go to the mall or hang out and get high, like other kids. Ok, Halia chided herself, be fair. She didn't act like other kids, and it wasn't just the lack of interest in shopping or substance abuse. It was lack of interest in society, in intimacy, in other people's opinions, in grades… it was Detachment, and her parents were normal enough to know that it wasn't normal. The doctor told her parents that she had "sub-syndromal schizoid personality disorder." In other words, she was a loner. Clinically speaking, that is.

Halia had been more than a little freaked out back then, worried that there might be some bizarre, tortuous treatment in store, but eventually, when the appointments stopped, and her parents left her alone, she began to relax about it. It wasn't until after her divorce that Halia developed an interest in her quasi-diagnosis and after a modicum of research, decided there may be more than a little truth to it. *I might not be a full blown schizoid,* she had told herself, *but there are days when the shoe sure seems to fit.*

Grace watched Halia slip into and out of her visit with memories, guessing where Halia's thoughts had gone and remembering those days herself. Halia had been part of her entire life – her next door neighbor from the day Grace was born – and Grace loved her as the sister she'd never had. Halia was always there – embarrassing as the nerd-girl that sat with her on the bus, patient and generous when Grace needed calculus tutoring, full of oddly provocative opinions as they touched base during the college years – so Grace had witnessed the entire Bones chapter start to finish. Grace did understand Halia's response, but she couldn't resist wishing that with the elimination of Bones from her life, Halia would magically turn into someone who looked happier on the outside. That Halia was still Halia, plus all the post-Bones anger and hurt, was hard for Grace to take.

The two women let their silence settle around them

while the sounds of the pub filled in the gap in the conversation. It was Halia who spoke a couple of minutes later, after both of them had let their thoughts wander in different directions.

"Three dogs in post op tonight?"

Grace nodded. "I need to check on them before I go home." Grace almost slipped and asked how Halia knew it was three dogs post operative before realizing she had written owners' cell phone numbers on the back of her left hand – the list of status report phone calls to make before she went home for the night. Grace occasionally had afternoon surgeries and if the technicians stayed late, she passed the time at The Blue Eft waiting for the animals to recover from the anesthesia. She would check back in at the animal hospital on her way home, and call owners with the news update once their pets were no longer woozy. Grace knew that Halia would have known how many, and quite possibly what breeds even if she hadn't provided such an obvious clue.

Grace was used to Halia's non sequitur observations, as eerie as they could be, but not quite comfortable with being so transparent to her friend. Those who knew Halia well enough to have witnessed her in action had nicknamed her Holmes, but Halia felt that the compliment exaggerated her ability. She would know – Halia had damn near memorized the complete works of Conan Doyle. Remarkably, Bones never knew about Halia's knack for observation á la Holmes, and had never been the subject of her studies. Perhaps Halia intuited enough to know that where Bones was concerned it was best not to know.

"Eagles in the morning?" Grace gathered her wallet and keys and stood up.

"Perhaps." A smile played around the edges of Halia's lips.

Grace reached around the table as Halia stood up to receive and reciprocate the hug Halia offered. Grace was off. Halia moved from her table to a barstool.

Louise, tending the bar this evening, had her back to Halia. When she turned around, her long black braid swayed pleasantly. She gestured toward the sign she had just posted behind the bar: Free Kittens, Ask Louise.

"You need a pet," Louise stated firmly.

If Halia had been a dog, she would have growled.

"You need a man." Now she was joking. This time Halia simply shook her head.

"Well, what do you need?" Louise asked, playful exasperation minimally masking concern. "You seem restless. Bored? Underchallenged at work?"

Halia laughed out loud. "No … none of the above." She smiled, her eyes remaining thoughtful. "I think I need a problem." Both women laughed. "No really," Halia persisted. "Something to puzzle over, to figure out. Something real."

"A crossword puzzle?" Louise teased.

Halia rolled her eyes and pushed her glass toward Louise. "A virgin lizard this time – I have to walk home soon." As she located her wallet and counted out the bills, she added, "Have you thought of creating and marketing black and blue ice cream?"

"Thanks," Louise placed the drink in front of Halia, picking up the neat stack of singles. "Black and blue ice cream," she mused. "It would probably come out grey, like blue corn bread."

"Not if you make the ice cream part vanilla, and just add tiny wild blueberries in it, with a cassis swirl."

Halia laughed. "Not that I've given this much thought, of course."

"Can I borrow your ice cream maker?"

"Sure. I never use it any more." Ice cream-making had only briefly been part of Halia's culinary repertoire, and the oaken bucket with a hand-crank sat gathering mildew in Halia's damp basement. Content with the notion of the machine being put to good use, Halia relaxed into a reverie that involved package design and marketing strategies. The Blue Eft's Black and Blue ice cream … a hypothetical project and the imaginative exercise of working out the kinks provided Halia with the mental rest she needed after the weekful of labs and quizzes and science fair preparations.

Louise busied herself serving Rob Desman, one of the regulars at The Blue Eft. Single and a touch peculiar, Rob's free time was absorbed by his plant breeding efforts to create a blue currant. He held onto his day job - a landscaping business that catered to the residents of Quaker Hill (the more-money-than-sense crowd) – ever hopeful that his big plant breeding break was right around the corner. Having pressed Rob's drink into his soil-stained fingers, Louise swept past Halia, graceful and efficient despite her bulk, to wipe the recently vacated corner tables.

Halia finished her drink, this time taking the last sip and allowing the clunk of ice against lips to occur. She stood up.

Rob noticed and tipped an imaginary cap at her. "Evening, ma'am," he drawled. Halia squinted at him, her lips pursed to one side in an expression of mild and friendly disdain. Rob caught the look and laughed. "Lighten up," he suggested, as she made to leave. She laughed too, and swung her purse up onto her shoulder.

Louise waved a purplish blue tea towel at Halia, then flicked her braid out of the way as she headed back behind the bar. "G'night, Hali," she called.

"'Night, Halia," Larry, the evening bartender coming in to take over from Louise, bade her goodnight.

The walk home was short and sweet. The night air carried the scent of wild white roses in bloom, and Halia gulped it in large breaths.

The house – Halia's house – a recently renovated 1890's stucco saltbox – had green trim. Not a subtle, tasteful, or muted green. Not an exterior house trim color at all. The previous owner, a Caribbean islander who clearly missed the sight of anole lizards, had chosen grass green, lizard green, and damn near fluorescent green for the turned porch supports and trim. Several different shades of crayon box greens and "you've got to be kidding" greens. Halia, typically unmoved by the visual qualities of her surroundings, had grown attached to her insane green trim. The combination of thick textural stucco swirls (rather like marshmallow fluff spread on the walls) accented with vivid green poked fun at all the gentrified renovations up and down Nellie Hill Road. Not upscale, Halia admitted, and shrugged.

Halia's house offered a feast for the eyes beyond the texture of the walls and the color of the trim. Her raggedly mowed lawn, her half collapsed garage with yard long weeds growing in the gutters, her semi circle gravel driveway and its increasingly vague start and end points… Halia's neighbors shook their heads and occasionally wagged their fingers, or tongues, at how Halia could allow the place to look so run down. It was true that these things did appear to escape Halia's notice. They certainly escaped her To Do list. In truth, an eye such as Halia's took in everything and a mind such as hers processed it all at a glance. Most commonly, if it appeared that Halia was oblivious, the truth was just the opposite. Notice had indeed been taken, and judgment concluded with the briefest of glances. The height of her lawn and the condition of her garage (beyond repair when she bought the house) were deemed trifles and relegated to the realm of the cosmetic. Halia didn't believe in wasting her time on trifles, and keeping up appearances definitely met Halia's criteria for being trifling.

She was awakened the next morning by the raucous jeering of crows. Jerked roughly from sleep, she was briefly disoriented. Slowly time and place settled into neat categories, dream and reality's boundaries clearly reestablished. She checked the time and felt a twinge of regret. Grace and the eagle watching appointment... Halia took cold comfort in remembering she hadn't made Grace any promises. Halia felt strongly about honoring commitments and keeping promises.

Halia paid the bills over breakfast, and composed a brief, polite note to Aunt Joann, her check slipped inside the notecard. Balancing proper business etiquette with heartfelt warmth for the older woman was something Halia attended to carefully.

The school week came and went with all the usual drama. Tuesday set the tone for the week when the usual suspects hid Halia's planbook and refused to give it up. Halia had tolerated benign practical jokes all year from them, but the refusal to 'fess up and hand it over crossed a boundary. Halia felt compelled to write them up. As the week wore on and administrators and parents became involved, Halia considered some of the adults' behavior even more inappropriate than the students'. There were times when Halia felt at a loss, disheartened that no amount of enthusiasm for the material, nor any number of conferences or workshops on positive discipline for teachers resulted in lasting peace in the classroom. Halia's memories of her own middle school years were no help, as she had been labeled "brainiac" as far back as she remembered. She had always longed for deeper and richer content in all her classes, and had always been frustrated when she realized that the material had been "dumbed down" for public school consumption. She couldn't relate to her peers back then, and she worried that she didn't relate well to her students now.

Despite the extra paperwork Tuesday generated, Halia found herself somewhat less busy this week: a combination of good fortune and good planning. She enjoyed more than a few moments sitting on her front porch watching people pass by. Families, delighting in the gorgeous early spring weather, took bike rides in the late afternoon, people walked dogs past Halia's house on their way to the park, or to the cemetery, and the exercise-obsessed woman from the blue house on the corner ran by at least once each day. Halia brought grading outside several evenings in a row and on Thursday finished early enough to stroll over to The Eft to visit with Louise.

A spirit of celebration pervaded The Blue Eft for no apparent reason. Halia saw Rob at the bar chatting with Anne Marie, the woman who ran an ecotourism business out of a small office in town. Her bicycle tours of Dover included lunch at The Eft, as a stop in between the Stone Church and Nellie Hill. She was always a welcome addition to the evening crowd. Her enthusiasm and energy seemed boundless. Halia often thought of her as a psychic twin to the woman from the blue house – both single moms, both athletic, both enthusiastic and totally besotted with Dover. Almost begrudgingly Halia's enjoyment and appreciation of her new hometown grew consistently, but for the most part, she did not show it.

This evening, it was a friendly crowd at The Blue Eft and Halia's appearance in the doorway elicited happy greetings called across the room.

"How veddy nice to see you here tonight," Rob affected a formal British accent. "And not even a weekend. You must have finished all your lesson planning?"

"How many melting suns have you consumed?" Halia asked, laughing.

"How could you possibly know what I've been drinking?" Rob looked around for evidence and saw none. No telltale empty glass sat on the bar in front of him. And Anne Marie held a concussed dog in her right hand. No clues there. "And what makes you think I've had more than one?"

Louise patted Rob's arm and said, "Don't ask. Halia saw the wet circles on your napkin. It's the size and shape of the bottom of the glass - I don't use the melting sun glasses for any other drink."

"Besides that," Halia waved the unveiling of her observation aside, "you only tease me after achieving a certain blood alcohol concentration. Had you not consumed two melting suns, you would have greeted me very differently."

"Correct, again," Rob sang out, his volume indicating that he was getting a bit tipsy. "Two melting suns. I'll have to start busting your chops before I take the first sip, just to throw you off."

Halia ordered alizarin smoke and joined Rob and Anne Marie at the bar. The restaurant was bustling; the bar was nearly full. The weather, Halia reasoned. People have been cooped up all winter. This taste of warm weather has people crawling out of their caves, yawning and stretching and taking full advantage. Memories of the tough winter they had all just survived were fresh in most minds around Dover.

Lukey Jane joined them. She ordered a virgin lizard and launched into a treatise on deer fencing. She and Rob, both avowed plantspeople, often commiserated over drinks at The Eft. Lukey Jane, officially Lucinda Jane Noyes, was responsible for the community garden and park across the street from The Blue Eft.

"It was the first time the town board had to look at a proposal that un-did development! Instead of building, we were taking stuff down. We were building open space!" Lukey Jane had a loud, opinionated and boisterous way about her, and she looked like a horse, but she had done a great thing for Dover. When she bought the Country Squire apartments and the unnamed apartment building next door, they were an eyesore. Lukey Jane encouraged her tenants to leave by paying them a month's rent on their move-out day, and helped many of them find new homes in town. She also offered them free space for the first year in the community garden, and many took her up on it.

After the last to leave left, demolition of the buildings and the creation of an incredible park happened at Lukey Jane's breakneck pace. What she couldn't do herself, she could afford to hire out, but it was a common sight to see Lukey Jane behind the wheel of some piece of heavy equipment, waving like mad to passers-by, shouting unintelligible greetings drowned out by engine noise, and often laughing uproariously at some harrowing near miss she had just avoided. When Lukey Jane's name came up, most folks around Dover would affectionately refer to her as an accident waiting to happen, and thank Dover's lucky stars that Lukey Jane neither smoked nor drank, as it was feared that either one would make her that much more of a hazard.

Halia recalled meeting Lukey Jane for the first time. Lukey had joined Hali, Rob and Grace at a table at The Eft, striding over, bellowing a greeting at Rob, and rounding on Halia. She had shoved her hand into Halia's yelling "I'm Lucinda Jane Noyes – you say it noise, but you spell it no-yes. Call me Lukey Jane."

Halia had responded "I'm Halia Frank. You've recently returned from Oklahoma, I see."

Lukey, half Irish, half Apache, hailing from Oklahoma, had regarded Halia as something of a shaman since then, and tried to tone it down a bit in her presence. She tried hard to organize her long limbs, long hair, and large personality onto a bar stool without shouting in Halia's ear or accidentally knocking over drinks, chairs, or any of her friends. Rob, Anne Marie, and Halia absorbed her into their circle gracefully.

The conversation centered on problems Lukey Jane faced at the park. Lukey's vision had bloomed into a living work of art and education. The garden areas were divided among the community garden, the demonstration perennial garden, the composting area, and a shady lawn with picnic tables. The trouble was that the half of the park – a recreation center with basketball courts and a skateboard half-pipe – had received bad press of late after several injuries were reported.

"The trouble is," Lukey Jane boomed, "the kids aren't hurting themselves. It's the darned old fogeys! The come over to work their gardens and get all interested in the skate park. The next thing ya know it's 'hey sonny, let me try out your board!' and we've got gramps out there, no pads, no helmet, zipping around like some danged fool!" Lukey Jane tossed her head and Rob and Anne Marie lunged to steady the drinks. "We got a 48 year old with a broken wrist and a 62 year old with a broken hip. I think the kids are getting pissed that their skate park is getting all famous for the wrong reasons!"

Halia listened as Rob and Anne Marie brainstormed with Lukey Jane regarding various solutions. She let the conversation flow around her without becoming engaged. She had actually been hoping for a more quiet, introspective evening at The Eft. Louise's company, or lack thereof, as Louise was often too busy to chat, was serene and relaxed. In fact, The Blue Eft itself had a calming effect on Halia. Louise had created an environment that knew what it was and declared itself confidently. Halia had been surprised in her first year as a homeowner by the number of decisions she had to make on a regular basis and by how few of them could be made purely rationally. She was haunted by notions of style, taste, and preference, and often chose to avoid the whole issue by escaping to The Blue Eft. The one thing that did occasionally vex Halia was her inability to predict or control who else fled to The Eft seeking solace, companionship or an audience on any given evening.

Feeling a little bit torn, and just a touch foiled in her attempt to have a quiet evening with Louise, Halia bade her friends goodnight and headed home. After all, she reminded herself, she would be back at The Eft tomorrow evening for dinner with Grace and Eddie.

Eddie and Grace were filling each other in on their respective days when Halia arrived. On her way to their table, she overheard a strange phrase, and greeted the couple with a question. "Grace, have you heard of the Philmontian coati?" Halia's voice rose with surprise as her eyebrows disappeared behind shaggy bangs.

"Sure." Grace grinned at Halia's incredulity.

"A what? Is that a hazelnut flavored koala?" Eddie was laughing at his own joke. Halia's face was more puzzled than amused, and Grace rolled her eyes at Ed.

Halia squinted at Grace, her lips pursed. "Philmont, NY... but coatis are South American..." her face softened as her confidence returned. "Was there a zoo escape?"

"Well, sort of," Grace began. "'On the other side of the river, there's a collector outside of Albany, somewhere near Latham. This collector, a fairly young zoologist – I don't remember her name – was pretty passionate about central and South American mammals. She kept an agouti for a while, as well as a few capybaras." At this point Eddie was making low flying plane gestures while Grace studiously ignored him. She had hit her stride, enjoying holding court on her favorite subjects: unusual mammals and urban (or non-urban in this case) legends. Halia listened intently, also oblivious to Eddie's goofing around.

"Apparently, some of her coatis mated, and she had a litter. After they were weaned, the story is that while the zoologist – I wish I could remember her name – I've met her a couple of times at conferences -" Halia's face showed some impatience, and Grace hurried on with her narrative. "While Dr. Whatever-her-name-is was teaching a workshop at Cornell, one of the young ones escaped. Some people say it was her husband who let the baby's out to play, and was a little sloppy about counting how many got back into their cages, but I don't know if that's true. Anyway, about 3 years ago, outside of Latham, a single female coati went AWOL. Maybe 4 or 5 months later, the wildlife biologists at the DEC started getting calls from people in and around Philmont, NY reporting sighting of an animal that look like a cross between a groundhog and a raccoon, with a long tail. The sightings are all unconfirmed; no animal has been caught or even sighted by a DEC biologist, and after the first few, there have only been one or two sightings a year. But sure," Grace smiled at Halia's level of interest, "I've heard of her. Why do you ask?"

"There are some people at the bar talking about it – sorry, her. I overheard them as I walked in."

Grace's head swung around to look, but the people Halia mentioned were no longer there. They sat in silence for several moments, each savoring different elements in Grace's story. Eddie had watched Grace closely and looked captivated by his wife's enthusiastic glow. Now, he slid his hand over hers, and when she met his eyes he smiled. "You look beautiful tonight," he leaned in and spoke in an undertone, his low voice adding to the overall susurrus in the bar.

Halia's brow knitted together as she pictured the young animal swimming across the Hudson River and making her way east to Philmont. Philmont, of all places, Halia thought to herself. "Personally," Halia couldn't resist, "I'd have gone to Stuyvesant Falls instead."

Eddie and Grace chuckled and nodded, then Grace gestured to Halia to turn her attention back to the bar. The man they referred to as Freecycle Sam was talking with a much younger unfamiliar man.

"He must have asked 'what is freecycle?'" Grace murmured.

Eddie looked from Grace to Halia for an explanation.

"Freecycle Sam is the name we gave him." Grace's voice was low and Eddie had to lean in to hear her. "His real name is Jim or Josh or Jordan or something. Anyway, he's kind of a bore. Always going on about his latest treasures, and how he's such the freecycle expert, always ready to initiate the uninformed. We've witnessed him talking a few people into a corner enough times so that Hali and I could practically write the script."

"'Some people say the best things in life are free, but I say that the free things in life are best.'" Halia repeated Sam's line with such accuracy that Grace became helpless with giggles. Eddie flicked his eyes over to the bar where Sam continued extolling the virtues of freecycling, unaware of his additional audience. Eddie put an arm around Grace tenderly before shushing her.

They continued to chat, Eddie and Grace switching from alizarin smoke to lemon tea. Halia nursed her loup garou, both hands wrapped around the mug, absorbing the heat. The cayenne warmed her from the inside out, the steaming mug taking care of the extremities. During a lull in the conversation, Halia couldn't help but overhear Freecycle Sam, with a new "victim" now, reporting his latest find.

"An older woman, probably in her 70's or so, was getting rid of tons of stuff. I couldn't believe it. Why she didn't have a garage sale is beyond me." Sam verbally underlined the penultimate word in every sentence. Halia wondered if that was what irritated her about him. "I had to drive all the way to Kerhonkson to get this stuff, but you know, when I have the time, I check listings for local groups all over New York, Connecticut and western Massachusetts."

"What did you get from this woman? Antiques?" Sam's listener evinced concern for an elderly woman along with envy over a great score.

"I got." Dramatic pause. "An entire set." Now Sam emphasized the final word in each phrase. "Of Partridge family memorabilia: the lunchbox with the original thermos, gum cards, cigar bands, magnets, posters," Freecycle Sam summarized triumphantly: "You name it."

Halia stopped listening.

Grace and Eddie left in time to catch the late movie in Millerton. "We're taking full advantage of Andrew sleeping over at a friend's house," they said. Rob joined Halia at the table soon after, looking bedraggled and excited, and regaled Halia with tales of plant breeding mishaps. Halia was grateful for the diversion, not yet ready to go home to the laundry and lesson plans.

As Rob began winding down, the woman Halia had seen around the middle school – Anne Marie's psychic twin - walked in. She looked embarrassed and hesitant. Halia immediately felt compassion for her and wondered if she and Rob should invite her to join them. Halia swiftly decided against it, realizing that despite all their demographic similarities (age, marital status, recent buyers of older homes on this quiet side street, employed by the local school district) they really had nothing in common. After all, the woman had a daughter of mall-rat age who lived with her part-time. And Halia saw this woman exercising almost daily, with a dog at all times. An exotic dog at that. Halia wasn't being critical or judgmental, just truthful. They just had nothing in common. Really. Still, Halia watched her head for the bar tentatively, and continued to feel aware of her presence even after turning away.

"Louise is introducing her to Joe, the actor." Rob followed Halia's gaze and read her thoughts. "She's doing some sort of club for elementary kids – a Shakespeare thing. She met with Louise about it earlier today and Louise wanted her to come back and meet Joe this evening."

Halia nodded, taking it in: the story, the woman's appearance, the manner in which Louise, then Joe, greeted her. Observe, store, file. You never know when you might need it again. Decades of indulging in this habit meant that Halia was now so expert in this type of observation, she could do it in public without risk of rudeness – she had mastered the art and science of the fleeting glance.

Rob left as abruptly as he had arrived, the nervous energy of a long hard day wearing off and exhaustion setting in. Halia contemplated leaving also. The woman at the bar had ordered an alizarin smoke, and her awkwardness seemed to be wearing off – going up in smoke perhaps. Halia overheard her ask Louise about the history of The Blue Eft, and Halia waved to Louise on her way out without interrupting the animated response.

Halia walked home, getting the mail on her way in to the house. She tossed the small pile of bills and catalogs onto the kitchen table and headed up the stairs, mulling over all she had seen and heard this evening, along with what the weekend had in store for her. She went to bed without noticing that topping the stack was an envelope addressed in her own handwriting. It wasn't until the next morning when she sat with the mail and her coffee that she realized it was the envelope containing her monthly check to Aunt Joann, stamped "Return to Sender, No Forwarding Address."

Chapter 2

I know why people pair up. Why they mate – for life, or if that doesn't work out, for life again with someone else. It's physics – the Observer Effect. We don't feel real unless we're witnessed. Observed. A shared life is an observed life – and being seen, truly seen, changes everything. Somehow, no other observer really does the trick. Friends, colleagues, ex-spouses, children, parents, siblings. Nope. Seems like it needs to be a partner – a lover – a true mate to bear witness to the mundane and profound, the daily, weekly, yearly sums of experiences that add up to a life. Without that – without being witnessed, observed, received – we don't feel real. We know, in our hearts, that this fancy notion in physics holds the truth – the emotional, spiritual, and literal truth of human existence. And we, those of us who are un-coupled, know the bizarrely empty feeling of being un-real, of failing to exist, of having entire days go by without being held or heard. Loneliness is this feeling's punky kid sister – the emptiness makes loneliness look simple, gawky, immature. Feeling unreal goes so much deeper.

It can make you do strange things. Laughing out loud at words you haven't spoken, for example. Or pouring your heart out to a stranger who hasn't asked. It can twist you up into a version of yourself "the coupled you" can barely recognize. And it can make you very, very sad.

Children who grow up unobserved become so hungry to be coupled, so hopeful that indeed a mate will fill the hole childhood created that they may choose poorly out of desperation or longing. Halia Frank grew up alone, an only child of aloof, intellectual parents. Yet despite all their long, dry conversations over dinner (usually "take out" as neither one of them cooked) Halia could feel a current between them – a bond that each respected and enjoyed. They made each other real, and somehow in that forest of words they all lived in, even Halia felt her presence acknowledged.

Living alone seemed like the most natural thing in the world to Halia after her divorce from Bones. Alone inside the house with the stop-and-stare green trim, Halia felt as close to "home" as she ever had. It was the coupling that felt strange – a visit to that foreign country of Coupledom. She was dimly aware, even during her visit, that she was a tourist and that as native as she could go, one day she would return home. Even during the good times, there were nights when she would lie stiffly in Bones' arms, and take cold comfort in knowing that one day this foray into Coupledom would end. For Halia solitude equaled – equals – solace.

But Halia is an anomaly – the exception that proves the rule. She would gladly tell you this herself, but she never really considers the matter. She won't even talk about her marriage to Bones, and doesn't think about it except when unavoidable. She appreciates her friends, but doesn't need them. She is bonded to no one, and feels deeply at home in that state of not disconnection, but unconnectedness. Perhaps no man is an island, but Halia Frank is no man.

Grace and Eddie drove home from the movies, singing loudly and off-key to Bob Dylan songs on the pick-up's cd player. The laughter and lightness stayed with them as they transitioned back to being parents, homeowners, and small-time farmers arriving back home after a long day. Grace took care of the animals as Eddie performed triage with the answering machine messages. They met up in the bathroom, boxer shorts on and toothpaste in hand.

Eddie finished first and collapsed on their bed, listening to Grace complete her bathroom ritual. She came to bed, long blond hair loose, and snuggled against him.

"You lit up like fireworks when you were talking about that animal being sighted up in Columbia County." Eddie looked at his wife, admiring, appreciating, enjoying. She is so beautiful, he thought. He reached for her hair, just to feel its texture in his hands, and pulling her close, tickled her gently. She pushed him away laughing. He asked her, "Do you really think that's the escapee?"

"The winters make me wonder. There are a few coatis at that little zoo at the Millbrook School. Maybe I'll stop by sometime and ask how they manage in cold weather." Grace, sleepy during the car ride home, perked up at the topic.

"Do you think it might mate with local animals?" Eddie wondered out loud. "Maybe its offspring have been sighted – not just the original jail breaker."

"Well, it's possible," Grace allowed, "but they wouldn't be fertile." Grace paused, imagination and intellect waltzing around the subject.

"It would make a great scientific paper, wouldn't it?" Eddie suggested.

Grace nodded, the wheels turning in her mind. "You'd need some real evidence – photographs, scat, footprints, even DNA samples… and the right angle." Grace's eyes sparkled – her whole body seemed to buzz.

"Do you think it, or they, could be trapped?"

"DEC permits … and I'm just a suburban veterinarian … I should probably see if anyone from any of the universities is already looking into this… although I doubt there is much grant money available for zoological urban legend hunting." Grace sat up, swept her hair off her face with her forearm and pounced playfully on Eddie. "Let's go for a bike ride on the rail trail with Andrew this weekend. The Bash Bish section is not so far from Philmont. Maybe we can just drive around a little … at dusk?" Grace smiled an intentionally charming smile at Eddie.

"That's not necessary," Eddie said, referring to the extra charm. "It sounds fun. I'll make sure the batteries for the camera are all charged up. But let's enjoy tonight too." Eddie pulled Grace down next to him and resumed tickling her. This time she did not push him away.

It rained all weekend, a steady soaking rain that delighted gardeners throughout the Hudson Valley. Bike rides and all other outdoor activities were summarily ruled out. Malls and movie theatres up and down Route 9 were filled to capacity with pent up children and their parents bucking cabin fever, memories of being snowed in last winter all too fresh in their minds. In the Harlem Valley, the Ten Mile River rose steadily, and the convergence of the Swamp River and the Ten Mile flooded the small island separating the two. Louise, visiting friends at the craft village, marveled at the high water from the safety of Tilly's Boutique on the south bank, while Grace and Eddie took turns playing chess with Andrew at their farm on top of Wingdale Mountain. The stream behind Halia's house swelled to the point of transforming the western quarter of the backyard into a shallow pond. The long pale grass waved and swirled under the water, with no one there to appreciate it, save the crows.

The returned letter sat on the kitchen table awaiting Halia's attention. Discipline and organization meant that Halia would address items on her list in order, and Halia did not deviate from her list unless circumstances were dire. Halia felt the letter disturb her, tug at her sleeves, distracting her from the tasks at hand, but she refused to be derailed. When I'm ready, Halia told herself, it will be there.

Saturday was consumed by schoolwork – grading a written assignment that involved writing about a rock in the first person, and a quiz on the hardness scale. After that, Halia updated her webpage and worked on lesson plans for the coming week. As was her habit, she did so in silence, spending hour after hour seated at her kitchen table without radio, television or any other human source of aural input. The rain pattered steadily, creating a blanket of white noise that enveloped Halia.

She did not speak aloud all day, and the silence was thick and palpable.

By Saturday evening, Halia felt chilled to the bone from lack of sunlight and dampness. Even piping hot borscht with horseradish failed to warm her adequately, and she went to bed ill at ease.

The rain invaded her dreams. Upon waking, the image of caves, with dripping stalactites, flitted about the edges of her conscious thoughts.

After breakfast, she ventured into the basement without a specific errand in mind and instantly regretted it. Rain had seeped in from several areas around the foundation and nearly an inch of water covered the entire floor. Instinctively, Halia thought of Bones. Dealing with a House Problem, especially if it involved the attic, basement, garage, plumbing, electricity, appliances, gutters, or anything structural, called the notion of Bones to her consciousness almost against her will. In this instance it made her even more angry.

"Why?" Halia asked herself. "Why think of him?" It was true that a House Problem should not automatically conjure up an image of Bones-the-Husband. Halia had handled the lion's share of problems when she and Bones shared living quarters. Despite initially resenting the intrusion upon her time, Halia ultimately enjoyed using her skills at observation to pinpoint the issue, and creative problem solving to come up with a solution. It was only when brute strength was a critical component that she was foiled, and even then she was deceptively strong and tough, outstripping what most would imagine given her slight frame.

Halia wasn't sure which annoyed her more: the fact that her basement was flooded, or that Bones had found his way back into her consciousness. She fumed as she rattled around the house, puttering, tidying, all the time weighing alternatives regarding how best to dry out the basement.

By late Sunday afternoon, the rain had stopped. Halia was wet through, but triumphant: The basement was free from standing water. Her face wore the set expression she reserved for those occasions when irritation mounted beyond the tolerable mark. Her sense of humor, in short supply anyway these days, was utterly absent. When the phone rang, Halia had just enough self-awareness left to pity the person on the other end.

Grace was actually calling to invite Halia to Easter dinner at her house, but she held off, hearing the tension in Halia's voice. They discussed the flooded basement, and Grace immediately offered to come over with her husband, son, a sump pump, a shop vac, and a hot meal.

Realizing that the flooded basement was truly no longer an issue, and that Halia didn't feel much better, Grace asked, "What else is on your mind tonight?"

"My check to Aunt Joann came back on Friday marked return to sender, no forwarding address." Halia paused, reaching across the kitchen table, and noticing her own grubby fingernails as she did. She held the envelope up and re-read the original postmark. "My March check. I just mailed the April check last week."

"Maybe the post office made a mistake?"

"Maybe."

"Have you heard from her at all this month?"

"No, but I usually don't. We exchange cards at Christmas, and not much else."

"Have you tried calling her? Do you have phone numbers for her?"

"I haven't had the opportunity to address this yet. I've been busy all weekend." Halia remembered her chat with Grace the week prior, at The Blue Eft. She re-pressed a self-recriminating smile hearing those words. She decided not to add that she had spent all day both days performing less than pleasant tasks and ticking items off her list.

"Oh, sorry." Grace remembered how the phone call began. "Your basement, of course. Next time call me as soon as you can. You know we'd come down and help."

"Thank you," Halia said, and she meant it. "I know you would. I appreciate it."

"Hey, I almost forgot," Grace remembered her original intent in calling Halia. "Would you join us for Easter? My mom and Eddie's sister will be here, and we'd love to have you."

"Sure. It'll be nice to see your mom again." Grace's family held that sacred place in Halia's heart – close enough to share history, but enough distance to limit the baggage. They finished the conversation, and Halia hung up the phone, envelope still in her hand. She shook her head as if to clear all the half-formed thoughts, feelings and ideas out of her brain.

Start simple and obvious, Halia told herself, as she reached for the small leather notebook she kept near the phone that held all her phone numbers.

Aunt Joann's home phone number yielded another disturbing result: a recording informed Halia that the number was no longer in service.

Still seated at the kitchen table with the envelope in her hand, Halia shook her head once more, slowly this time. Elbows on the table, she propped her forehead in her hand, pushing her bangs out of her eyes and staring at the returned envelope. Visually it disturbed her to see her own handwriting, intended for different eyes. It felt wrong, disquieting, perhaps almost rude – looking at the envelope now, after it "belonged" to someone else. It reminded her of the anxious twinge in her stomach attached to eavesdropping or trespassing.

The post office could have made a mistake, Halia allowed. Yes. That was possible. The phone company could also have made a mistake; Halia knew that happened occasionally. The coincidence of both happening at once seemed unlikely. More than unlikely, Halia thought.

Well, not necessarily simultaneously, Halia reminded herself. The envelope's postmark showed that it left the Mid-Hudson Valley on February 27. "Today is March 29," Halia murmured, thinking aloud. "When did the Keeseville post office start returning Joann's mail?"

Almost before these thoughts became conscious, Halia was on her feet pulling a piece of paper out of her recycling bin and a pen from the drawer in her kitchen table. She began immediately: the list of phone calls to make. Joann's former workplace, the post office, the phone company ... what next?

Family. Halia's heart sank, realizing that there was someone she could call right away to seek information. Bones. Halia inhaled deeply and exhaled slowly, disliking the inevitable task that lay before her. As much as she might argue with herself – that Bones won't know anything anyway – it was futile. She knew she had to call him. He would know who else to call in Joann's extended family. Halia gritted her teeth involuntarily.

Bones. Most of his friends didn't know his real name, and if Bones was to be believed, only Halia knew the true origin of the nickname. Not much Bones had told Halia during their 10 years together held water with Halia now. The unveiling of the truth of their marriage exposed so many lies Halia felt as if everything he had ever told her – from the names of his childhood pets to whether or not he'd sold the house out from under her – was suspect. Bones lied about where he was, what he did, and who he spent his time with as a matter of course. But he would be able to at least provide a name or two and phone numbers for other members of his family.

"Unless he lies about having any phone numbers," Halia thought. But Halia held onto a strong sense of right and wrong, and she believed it was right to try to find out what was going on with Aunt Joann, if for no other reason than to continue to pay her back. Money – that might motivate Bones to be truthful – if he thought he might benefit from Halia finding Joann, he might be more cooperative.

As Halia thought it through, she picked up the phone again. Bones' phone number – her former phone number – was memorized by her fingers rather than her brain. Halia glanced up at the kitchen clock as she listened to the phone ring. 7:30 p.m. She willed herself not to picture what she may be interrupting and mentally rehearsed an answering machine message.

"Hello?" Bones picked up on the fourth ring.

"Bones, this is Halia." She spoke crisply, as if clipping off the words would minimize contact.

"What can I do for you Hali?" It was Bones-the-Charmer who answered. He used his sweet and mellow voice for Halia. She ignored his bedroom tone.

"I am looking for someone to contact to find out what has happened to Joann."

"Joann Grant?" he sounded genuinely surprised.

"Yes." Halia explained the situation, and Bones made her hold the phone for several minutes while she heard scuffling and banging. Bones returned to the phone with two names and phone numbers: Joann's uncle, John Grant, who was living in Pottersville, NY, and her brother Justin, for whom Bones had only a work phone number and no address. Halia thanked Bones as briefly as possible and hung up. She considered disinfecting the phone before catching herself and shuddering.

It was getting dark – twilight but not quite gloaming - but Halia felt the urge to walk with every fiber of her being. Perhaps it was walking away from contacting Bones, or just the need to be under the sky after an unpleasant day indoors, but Halia moved swiftly – almost urgently –throwing on battered sneakers and a sweatshirt, and banging the front door shut behind her.

She walked past Mrs. Cutlow's house, into and out of the pool of streetlight, past the impeccably kept old saltbox on the corner, and between the stone pillars into the cemetery. She didn't slow down, or actually notice her surroundings until she reached the northern end of the dirt track and had another decision to make. After a moment's hesitation she turned west, and sought out the stone that stated "Fell at the battle of Loral Hill." That inscription rarely failed to halt disparate thoughts and capture her imagination. The words spoke of romance and valor to Halia, despite her intellectual commitment to pacifism. She found those words profoundly evocative and could not resist, each time she read them, wondering about that day. The battle, the men who fought (those who survived as well as those who did not), the families back home … Halia was not a romantic or sentimental person, but she did find herself drawn to this stone and these thoughts, especially when she needed to clear her mind.

She stood in the deepening darkness, knowing the words rather than reading them, for only a few moments before continuing to walk west, along the path, towards the newer section of the cemetery. She had allowed herself to mentally leave modern day Dover and visit another time and place. The vacation, albeit brief, calmed her.

She heard a jingling before she could make out the shapes clearly. A person and a dog approached. The dog was moving fast, loping towards her in the darkness, metal tags tinkling rhythmically. Halia stood still. Between the available moonlight, Halia's excellent eyesight, and her mental rolodex containing holographic images of every animal in the neighborhood, Halia was able to recognize and identify the dog, and thus the owner, while still some distance away. She moved away from the overhanging trees to where she could be seen, hoping to avoid startling the dog or the woman.

The dog reached her first. Tentative and alert, the dog stopped several feet away, and circled her once, sniffing. Halia spoke softly to the dog and waited for its owner to catch up.

"I'm sorry." The woman from the blue house on the corner snapped her fingers and the dog returned to her side. "I hope she didn't startle you."

"I heard her collar and tags before I saw her."

"We don't usually walk in the graveyard at night,"

the woman started explaining, "but after all that rain we really needed to get out, and it's cleared up to be such a beautiful night."

Halia nodded, and then realizing that in the darkness it would be better to speak, she said, "I'm Halia Frank. I've seen you at superintendent's conference days."

"I'm Asha Jackson. I'm the social worker at the elementary school." She paused, looked down, and added, "This is Brulee."

"I've noticed her before too. There is something intense and unique about her. She's not like other dogs."

Asha just said, "Yes, I feel that too."

They walked in silence, continuing in the direction Asha and Brulee had been heading. Halia noticed that she was not irritated by the intrusion upon her solitude.

Brulee, a medium-sized dog the color of perfectly done toast, with black singe-like markings on her face, jogged in front of the women. Halia concentrated on the dog's movements, observing closely. She was undeniably feminine in her gait and carriage, and yet athletic and confident. Halia found herself wishing she could teach her seventh grade girls to be feminine, athletic and confident all at once.

"She's something of a role model," Asha said, breaking into Halia's thoughts. "She was terribly neglected and mistreated as a puppy. It didn't prevent her from forming a relationship with me, though. Sometimes I use her story in my counseling."

Halia didn't feel the need to respond. It was really more like Asha had given voice to Halia's thoughts than as if she had sought conversation. They were approaching the stone pillars, and Asha called to the dog. Brulee was at her side in a heartbeat, wagging her tail and sitting at the sight of the leash. Halia watched the way the dog and the woman interacted.

"She's very motivated to please you," Halia observed.

"It's a hallmark of the breed." Asha smiled, white teeth catching the streetlight. "I'm willing to put up with a lot, but I require strict obedience." Halia waited but Asha did not elaborate.

In the absence of an explanation, Halia absorbed Asha's words, watching her connect with the four-legged animal. "It looks like more than obedience to me. More, or maybe just different. I've seen well-trained dogs before, but the way she responds to you feels different. It's like you give her a choice and she chooses to comply."

"Yeah, I think that's the way things are between us. I don't ever attempt to train her. I just build and deepen my relationship with her by spending time with her." Asha laughed a happy, gentle laugh: "My daughter trains her to jump over logs in the backyard." Halia laughed too. "Pearl is totally horse crazy – I guess Brulee is the next best thing." Asha shrugged. "I'm just glad Pearl is playing outside and paying attention to the dog."

Halia didn't feel the need to answer. She walked alongside Asha and Brulee and let her mind wander. Another species. Halia enjoyed becoming fascinated with that concept, taking only the most tentative baby steps in the direction of wondering what her criteria would be for a pet. It was a stretch to consider any pet at all for more than a fleeting moment, but, Halia reasoned, *I am in the midst of a thoroughly out-of-character experience, so why not make it complete? I'm* out for a walk (Halia never exercised on purpose), I'm in a graveyard at night, and I'm with a person I choose not to spend time with, so why not consider owning a pet? It was ever so slightly less outlandish than entertaining the notion of dating, but decidedly less distasteful.

"How long have you been divorced?" Asha's question caught Halia off guard.

"Uuuhhh," Halia did the math in her head. "Two years in August."

Asha didn't respond immediately, but walked on, Brulee matching her stride to allow slack in the blue nylon leash. Halia waited, then asked, "Why?"

"You don't have a dog." Asha couldn't see the confused look on Halia's face, but anticipated it and hurried to explain. "You were out, alone, walking in a graveyard in the dark. It's a little unusual. A dog is a good excuse for such eccentric behavior."

Halia found herself wanting to explain her day to Asha, and for the third time since leaving the house, felt taken aback by her inclination. Suddenly awareness fell into place for Halia – she had been uncharacteristically obtuse. Asha is a social worker. Of course I feel comfortable opening up to this woman, or even just being in her company, Halia realized. She's a professional. Halia laughed a short, percussive laugh out loud. She explained her situation clearly and succinctly -- the basement, the apparent change of address for Aunt Joann, the need to contact the ex-husband, and her visceral reaction to speaking to him. By the time she had finished they were standing outside Halia's home. She checked her watch. "Would you like to have a cup of tea on the porch?" Now that was downright friendly, Halia thought. I hope the Self I recognize shows up soon.

Asha's polite refusal convinced Halia that Asha possessed the ability to read her mind. Either that, or it was simply the fact that it was getting late on a Sunday evening. Asha walked home with Brulee, and Halia went inside alone.

The house felt different. Halia wished for a moment that she was the type of person who kept cedar smudges handy for removing all trace of Bones from the very air. As if his voice, through the phone lines, infected her whole house like a virus. Halia settled for filling and running her dishwasher, and, after changing into flannel pajamas, washing all the clothing she had been wearing.

Monday, she thought, is an 'A' day. I'll have my prep 3rd period. She collected all her school things into a neatly packed canvas bag with folders, lesson plan book, accordion files, water bottle, and refilled bottle of ibuprofen, all ready to grab on the way out. She sat down with her list regarding Joann: two more phone calls were now added – John and Justin Grant. She hoped she would have enough time to make all the calls, then caught herself and wondered for a moment – what was it that she was hoping? That she would clear up the mystery and find Joann right away? Or that she would have enough time to search thoroughly? She remembered joking with Louise about needing a problem – have I got a good one now? Is this the problem I ordered? Halia sighed audibly, a forceful exhalation, as if to reject the notion of taking pleasure or satisfaction in Joann's apparent disappearance. This is ridiculous, she decided. I'm just trying to pay her the money I owe her – that's all. No analysis required.

As Halia got ready for bed, a brief feeling of dread

popped up: what if Bones has caller ID? Halia's stomach churned at the thought of Bones having such easy access to her phone number, but she pushed the thought out of her mind fairly easily. He won't put any effort into calling me, she reasoned. He's sure to be busy with other conquests. Besides, he doesn't need to use caller ID to find me – I'm not hiding from him. My number is in the phone book, for crying out loud. Despite his sleazy charm on the phone today, he's as glad to be rid of me as I am of him. Of that I have no doubt. Halia slipped off to sleep confident that the anti-Bones forcefield she created and diligently maintained had not been breached.

Upon waking, she was aware that Brulee, Asha's dog, had dominated her dreams. Brulee and a beautiful black cat with metallic gold threads running through her coat. She thought maybe there had been a blond child in the dream too – a girl? Halia wasn't sure. The amount of time she had to indulge in cultivating her awareness of dreams was limited to her shower, and even then she often needed to use her shower time to think about other things. It was Monday – time to hit the ground running.

During the school week, Halia saw Asha, either running in the afternoon, or out walking with Brulee and her daughter, nearly every day. Because Halia felt strangely bonded to Asha after last Sunday, she felt compelled to acknowledge or greet her. Asha seemed to sense Halia's reticence – or perhaps guarded her own solitude – as she did not stop or chat despite numerous opportunities. This careful tending of the boundaries suited Halia well. Between her school days, her half-hearted attempts to maintain the house and yard, and her minute amount of free time now consumed by telephone calls regarding Aunt Joann, Halia was wholly unable to embark upon the cultivation of a new friendship. There just wasn't time.

As usual, busy or not, Halia entered The Blue Eft at 6 p.m. Friday evening. Grace was not there yet. The restaurant was crowded, the pub even more so. Halia seated herself at the far end of the bar in front of the cash register. She planned to move as soon as a more preferable spot opened up.

Halia enjoyed watching people in the bar – many were people she knew somewhat, from school, or from around town. She saw people she recognized from the library, the owners of the hardware store, the couple who ran the auto parts store, Wingdale's post mistress, even the man with the shuffling gait who whistled incessantly was at Louise's tonight. It took Larry, Louise's bartender and right hand man, longer than usual to find Hali in her corner.

"Alizarin smoke," she ordered. "Busy evening."

"Yeah," Larry poured the drink with all the necessary care and flair, and Halia acknowledged his efforts with a grateful nod. "Nice," she indicated the sinking swirls. Larry winked a brotherly wink and moved off to serve some overdressed strangers who had just walked in.

"What is the name of that drink?"

The deep, rich, heavily-accented voice from behind her made Halia jump involuntarily. She turned to face a man holding an antique knobby cane. His height was of such proportions that Halia, despite being seated on a barstool, had to crane her neck to see his face. His thinness accentuated his height, giving the impression he was even taller than his six plus feet. His perfectly smooth skull shone as if polished, and his eyes gave

Halia a chill. The overall impression he gave was of age – profound, distinguished, fragile.

"Alizarin smoke," Halia repeated slowly, loudly and clearly, projecting her voice towards his ear as she hopped off the barstool and offered it to him.

"No thank you," he shook his head at her gesture to take her seat. "Louise will bring me a chair from the restaurant. I need a hard seat with a firm back." The accent was Hebrew, Halia decided. "Alizarin," he repeated. "What is that?"

"Alizarin is the name of a reddish purple pigment – the color the blueberry juice makes when it gets mixed with the cassis. When you pour them into the club soda, they look like wisps of smoke as they sink." Halia explained.

The man nodded. Louise appeared with a chair.

"Mr. Beckerman, I see you found Halia." Seeing Halia's blank expression, Louise continued, "Halia Frank, allow me to introduce Mr. Sidney Beckerman."

"It's a pleasure," Halia extended her hand. "Your recording with the Gil Knight trio – the 1956 sessions – it's just perfect."

The old man's eyebrows lifted slightly as he appraised Halia. "You are a connoisseur of the obscure to know about that." He did not look pleased or flattered, but instead seemed somewhat wary.

Halia had not been trying to flatter the elderly gentleman. She chose not to react to Mr. Beckerman's cool response, and was unmoved by his suspicious air.

"Can I get Larry's attention for you?" she offered. "Would you like a drink?"

"Thank you." He began moving off toward a sofa, leaning alternately on his cane in one hand and the straight-backed chair Louise brought in the other as he pushed it across the floor. "A loup garou, please."

Halia ordered the drink and delivered it to Mr. Beckerman, placing it carefully on the end table next to where Mr. Beckerman had parked. There were no additional chairs nearby, and the sofa was full of university types, so Halia returned to the bar. Mr. Beckerman looked as if he didn't mind being left to his own devices – in fact, he looked quite content in his public aloneness. Halia knew that feeling well and let him be.

It was 6:45 when Grace arrived. She signaled Halia from the doorway to come outside. Halia followed her out and Grace led her to her pick-up truck, apologizing and talking way too fast. Halia began pulling together known facts, ready to figure out what was up with Grace if the information was not forthcoming, but her process was interrupted midstream by Grace's explanation. "'I'm late because," Grace opened the cab door, and there in a cat carrier was a small pink...

"What is it?" Clearly a baby something, the lack of light made the huddled form difficult to identify.

"A pharaoh hound puppy." Grace was reaching into the cab, and the wrinkled pink package huddled deeper into the carrier. Grace gently extracted the animal and cradled it against her body. "She's not quite 5 weeks old and I can't leave her in the hospital over the weekend. She's coming home with me." Grace seemed entranced, cuddling the puppy tenderly. "Could we hang out at your place for a while? I want to hear what's going on with you, but I don't want to leave her alone."

"Sure. Let me just run in and pay Larry. Do you want anything?" Halia peered into Grace's face after studying the rose-beige velvet infant.

"No thanks."

Halia disappeared into The Eft and returned moments later. The two women walked to Halia's. Once they passed under the railway bridge, Grace set the puppy down in the tall grass of Halia's front lawn. Her ears flopped comically as she stumbled after Grace.

"Does she have a name?" Halia asked.

"Bezef," Grace replied.

"Is she ill?"

"No," Grace scooped Bezef up, the purpose of her release having been served. "The breeder was concerned about her rate of weight gain. She seems to not have much of an appetite, and is just a little lethargic." Grace paused as Halia let them into the house, looking at Bezef carefully in the front hall light. "The breeder was really smart to bring her in. These little guys can get very sick, very fast. I'm not sure why Bezef wasn't thriving at home, but she's doing ok with the amount of attention we're giving her. She hasn't lost any more weight, anyway."

"Does she need anything right now?" Halia headed into the kitchen.

"I'll get her some water." Grace knew her way around Halia's home as well, or perhaps better than Halia, as she had helped Halia move in and basically set up her kitchen. Halia put on water for tea and sat down at the table. Grace filled a bowl of water, set it on the floor, and offered it to Bezef. The puppy drank, and Grace left her on the floor while she joined Halia at the table. The women began to talk, Bezef's tiny toenails clicking on the tile floor as she explored the kitchen, sniffing.

"I don't have a lot to tell," Hali was saying. "I called Joann's home number a couple more times, just to make sure. When I called the phone company, all the information they could give me was to confirm that Joann terminated service as of March 15. When I called the Keeseville post office, they told me the same thing: moved, no forwarding address, as of March 15."

"Hmmm." Grace frowned in concentration. "Ok, so she moved. Why wouldn't she leave a forwarding address?"

"I don't know. I thought maybe her family would be able to tell me what's going on, but so far I have yet to speak with anyone. I left a message at Joann's uncle's number, but no one has called back. The number Bones gave me for Joann's brother is a taxi company in Nyack. I left a message, but who knows … I don't have a lot of faith that I'll get a call back from him either." Halia bent down and picked up the wandering Bezef. She stroked the puppy thoughtfully.

"Does she work?" Grace asked.

"She retired last Christmas." Halia shrugged. "I'll call her old office next week and see what I can find out. Maybe someone there stays in touch with her."

"It's odd." Grace's eyes rested on Bezef, sprawled on her back on Halia's lap. "Did you and Joann ever discuss this kind of thing – like if one of you moves, or what happens at the end of the loan?"

"I'm a little less than one year into paying her back. I've still got more than 9 years left to pay. And we only really talked about what happens if I sell the house and move. Not what happens if she moves." Halia shook her head again as she came to the same unsatisfying stalemate. "I thought she wanted the money, so I never really thought about her being out of touch or hard to track down." Bezef wriggled, and Halia set her down on the floor again. "She clearly made a decision to move, planned things out and left. There's no indication of anything else happening," Halia said firmly. Grace nodded sympathetically. "The whole thing just doesn't sit well with me." Grace nodded again.

The women finished their tea and took Bezef out into the back yard. It was a cold, clear night, bright with stars. Bezef romped playfully, chasing leaves and sniffing the deer trail across the yard with great interest. Halia and Grace crossed their arms against the chill and blew steam into the night air.

"What will you do next?" Grace asked.

"I don't know," Halia replied. The indecision seemed to anger Halia, and she added a taut, "yet."

"Whatever you need," Grace reached out and laid a hand on Halia's arm. "You know I will help in any way I can.'"

Although Grace's gratitude was heartfelt, Halia couldn't stop herself from responding stiffly. The emotion and affection was just too much for her, and she felt herself freeze up. Had she thought about it, she would have realized that Grace was the only human being who had touched her at all in the past two years, but Halia wasn't keeping track. All she knew was that any touch – even Grace's – made her shrink away internally. Her emotional shield experienced all touch as a direct affront, but Grace knew that the cool response her kindness elicited was just Halia. Well, Halia, plus the last remaining remnants of post traumatic stress disorder her marriage to Bones and the revealing of his infidelity brought upon her. Slightly schizoid or not, faced with the enormity of deception and betrayal and the need to reinvent herself, Halia had responded by doing what came most naturally – shutting down. There was no one but Grace, and not much besides work, these days, to attach to and gain meaning from. Perhaps the most frustrating part for Grace had been Halia's apathy about her own happiness. Although, Grace admitted to herself as she drove home, it felt good to see Halia get angry about wanting to find Joann.

Later that evening, as Halia locked up downstairs, she found herself anticipating Bezef – listening for the click of toenails on tile, and walking with awareness as if to avoid stepping on paws. Halia's knowledge – a result of her own research and training, as well as practical knowledge absorbed via her friendship with Grace – resulted in a moderate level of concern for Bezef. Failure to thrive at this age could be serious. Halia caught herself hoping Bezef would rally over the weekend, and quickly transformed her wish into a rational prediction based on her observations of Bezef over the course of the evening.

On Saturday Halia made the trip across the Hudson to visit Rosendale and meet with the town historian. Halia was trying to arrange a field trip, corresponding to the rock and mineral unit. The Widow Jane Mine would excite even the most devoutly bored, and the natural history of the area would work well with the ecosystems unit. Despite the hour drive each way from Dover, Halia felt that armed with the information from the town historian, and the ridiculously low cost of admission, she would be able to convince her academic team to support the field trip. She indulged in a visit to New Paltz on the way home, hitting all the required New Paltz hot spots: she bought cheap socks at the Groovy Blueberry, and grabbed a catfish taco from

Mexicali Blues, and ate it sitting on a bench in Sojourner Truth Park. New Paltz appealed to Halia; it was an easy town to be alone in.

During her drive home, Halia's mind wandered pleasantly. She found herself thinking about the puppy, and remembering the texture of her fur. Halia wondered about massage for failure to thrive puppies, and made a mental note to ask Grace about it.

She made another mental note to call the anthropology office at SUNY Plattsburgh, to see if any of Joann's former colleagues could shed any light on her current situation. Halia felt herself frowning and tightening her grip on the steering wheel, and made a conscious choice to lighten up. She reminded herself that she had no evidence that anything unpleasant had occurred, and considered worry to be a total waste of energy. Stick with the facts, she told herself, and pursue facts, not fantasy, until you lay bare the whole story. That attitude restored a semblance of a smile, and Halia drove the rest of the way home at ease.

Chapter 3

come morning,
dreams flicker at the sky
gentle sad and soft
sleep on, sweet soul mate
haunting me with a smile
music to my heart
rise joyful, laughing
a wedding ring shall caress thy finger

Bones had proposed in writing, a poem that Halia later suspected was not original. It was a strange time in Halia's life – a moment bounded on both ends by something she recognized much more clearly as her own. It was a hiatus, island-like in its uniqueness. It was a colossal mistake, in Halia's opinion, and she paid for it. Quite literally, in that Halia paid her lawyer's fees with the last of her inheritance, leaving her nothing left for a down payment on the green-trimmed stucco palace. It had been Bones' distant relative, his offbeat, never-married-no-children, archeologist-professor Aunt Joann who had offered to provide Halia's down payment at generous (and thus financially plausible) terms. When Halia asked Joann why she was doing this, Joann had simply said that money should never be an impediment to moving forward. Joann acknowledged that Halia had deep regrets about her connection to Bones – courtship, marriage, and divorce - and had chosen to offer advice after the closing. A letter arrived the first week that Halia lived in her new home, imparting enigmatic words of encouragement: "We all make mistakes. Some of us live them out – we let them become our guideposts along the way, and in avoiding them, we cling to them. I don't want to see you do that, Halia. If buying this house moves you forward, then it's right. Each time you send me a check, I'll think of it as one more step forward. Keep moving forward, Halia. Don't stand still. Don't stagnate."

I'd like a slice of pie, Halia thought as she drove home from work. It was Tuesday, 3:40 p.m., and Halia was hungry. Halia's desires often showed up in this manner – factual rather than passionate. Rational desire – Halia had to smile at the oxymoron she created to describe her hankerings. Hunger = fruit pie. Skiff Mountain pie, in fact. It was inescapable, not romantic or sensual. Halia drove past the turn for Nellie Hill Road, and headed into Kent.

She did not think "This unscheduled event will

wreak havoc with my schedule for the rest of the evening." She did not wonder "What if Strobles doesn't have Skiff Mountain Pie today?" She did not calculate the number of calories in a slice of Skiff Mountain pie. She did not reconsider several times, chiding herself about choosing to indulge in eating out when she had plenty of food at home or about spending money, time, or gas on non-essentials. Once her decision to respond to her physical sensation of hunger with Skiff Mountain pie had been made, her mind was free to address other concerns.

Joann Grant's whereabouts was foremost in her thoughts. Today during her prep period, Halia had called Joann's uncle again and this time she reached him. He sounded spry and lively for a 90 year old. His failure to call Halia back, he apologized, had been due to a trip, gambling at a casino way upstate, from which he had just returned. He said that he got in late last night – too late to call, but that he had indeed received her message. He confessed that he thought it a little odd for Joann to apparently move without leaving a forwarding address, but then, he remarked, the Grants could be an odd bunch. He described Joann's brother as a "strange bird" and was about to launch into family stories when Halia interrupted him. Her prep period would be ending soon, and she felt a distinct desire to avoid hearing personal stories about Bones' extended family.

Halia's interruption had reminded the elderly gentleman of her relationship to his family. "Well, yes, of course, Halia, you're a strange bird yourself." He may as well have winked over the phone, his elderly voice rich with unspoken meaning. "And you were married to Bones. Enough said."

Halia couldn't have agreed more heartily. Too much said. But any real information about Joann was absent: no, he hadn't heard from her, his most recent address for her matched Halia's, he didn't have any idea why she'd move, or where she'd gone. He did make the de rigueur jokes Halia expected about having Hali send the monthly check to him in her absence, but he was unable to actually shed any light on her current location.

Halia had also tried Joann's brother, Justin – the "strange bird." Again, the answering machine for Bud's taxi in Nyack, NY was as far as Halia got. She left a second message for Justin Grant, and hoped her voice sounded more neutral than she felt. Time ran out before Halia was able to call the SUNY Plattsburgh archeology office. Halia placed an asterisk on her list to indicate that phone call's position as next.

It was too chilly to sit outside and eat, so after buying herself a slice of Skiff Mountain pie, Halia drove north on route 7 to Kent Falls, and ate her pie sitting in the driver's seat of her car. For most observers, it would be difficult to say whether or not Halia enjoyed the pie – indeed it would be hard to discern whether she tasted it at all. The satisfaction of her desire appeared to be as matter-of-fact as the decision had been. I want it, I got it, it's done all happened for Halia without attachment to any of it. The eating of the pie held the same emotional charge as putting gas in the tank. She ate neither slowly nor quickly, and stared nearly unblinkingly at the waterfall.

She chose to look with a layman's, not science teacher's, eye. The recent rain, coupled with the heavy snows of last winter meant the falls were roaring. The music of the falls lulled Halia into a reverie – she thought about the phrase she'd heard used in a yoga context – something about moving into stillness. She watched the movement of the water and the movement became constant – a blurred version of stillness. She looked at the falls, ate her pie, and sat, not thinking, not feeling.

Last winter – it hung on in folks' memory, and haunted the dimly lit corners of damn near everyone's consciousness at this point. It was the record-breaking number of days in a row that snow fell in Dover that would remain noteworthy – like the summer of '86, when temperatures hit over 95 degrees (with over 95% humidity – or at least that's what it felt like) for 42 days in a row. From December 6th until January 18th, at least some flakes were spotted falling everyday. And like clockwork, every fourth day, a sizable dump occurred, hindering traffic, closing schools, wreaking havoc with schedules, and sending families scurrying up to Catamount or down to Big Birch for skiing. That is, those families that ski or board... the rest of the folks in and around the Harlem Valley holed up and waited it out. It was a long winter for Halia, new to the neighborhood, and new to home ownership. The gutters, hanging just below impressively green fascia boards, committed suicide under the weight of combined snow and ice. Halia found them lying on what would have been her foundation plantings, had she planted any. The neighbors watched and shook their heads as Halia picked up the bent and twisted metal and dragged it off to the swaybacked garage. It was a beautiful, awesome, expensive winter, and folks around the Harlem Valley were only just beginning to heal.

Halia took a circuitous route home, passing the huge rocks along the Housatonic, just south of the

Indian princess's grave. The narrow ephemeral water-falls cascading down the rocks reminded Halia of long straight hair – a narrow shock of hair hanging down someone's back. They too were full with snowmelt, and roaring. She arrived home and unloaded the car, bringing in and dumping on the couch the canvas bags filled with homework to grade, conference request forms to be filled out, and the remains of her lunch.

The pie served as dinner and grading absorbed the remainder of the evening. The rest of the week followed a similar pattern minus the pie diversion: despite efficient use of her prep period, grading and preparing for the next lessons consumed the lion's share of Halia's evenings. The weather held, and by the end of the week, mowing the lawn asserted itself as a contender for the weekend to do list.

Grace begged off Friday's meeting at The Eft, as Andrew had caught a cold and she wanted to stay home with him. Halia went by herself, intending to stay only briefly and get to bed early.

She had no sooner walked in than Rob was at her side. He began midsentence, it seemed to Halia, and the words failed to match the tone of voice. Halia caught only bits and pieces of his tirade (she thought it was a tirade, as his tone clearly smacked of complaint, but the content of the monologue appeared to be much more benign) between her own internal distractions, the noise level in the bar, and her snap judgment that Rob was now sounding off rather than conversing. Hence she took on the role of audience rather than participant, and gave Rob only the top third of her conscious attention.

Suddenly Rob's tone and demeanor changed. Halia felt the difference with every sense – she was sure his very aura changed color. Halia looked around, searching for the source of the shift, and found it, she thought, in the form of Asha Jackson. Halia couldn't help but notice a hopeful blush on Asha's dark cheeks as she scanned the bar. Halia increased the already platonic distance between she and Rob, and awaited Rob's invitation to Asha to join them. When it came, and Asha greeted Hali and Rob with much more enthusiasm than Halia felt she deserved, Halia made polite excuses and headed back to the corner to pay Larry and leave.

Lukey Jane and Anne Marie were deep in conversation at the bar, discussing the recent negative press coverage the skate park had received. Both signaled to Halia to join them, but she declined. Lukey Jane shouted something after her about needing her advice, and Halia hesitated, then gave in, glancing at her watch. She wanted to call Grace, partly to see how Andrew was feeling, and partly, she admitted, to see how Bezef was doing. Well, if it gets too late to call, she decided, I can call in the morning.

Lukey Jane reached for Halia, as if to clasp her hand or pound her back in greeting. Halia braced herself for the blow. Anne Marie asked, "Where's Grace tonight?" Halia reported Andrew's illness and both women made sympathetic noises. Then Anne Marie explained to Halia that she was concerned about the injuries at the park. She told Hali that her business might suffer if Dover and the skate park received continued bad publicity, but that she and Lukey Jane weren't sure how to do damage control.

"You said the kids were annoyed about the article in the paper, right?" Halia asked.

Both women nodded.

"Can you get the main users of the park to meet with you? Both the gardeners and the skateboarders? They've coexisted pretty peacefully until now, right?"

Lukey Jane looked thoughtful.

"They've never had a problem with each other as far as we know," Anne Marie answered.

"Well, what I would try," Halia advised, "is getting together all the 'stakeholders' – the boarders, the gardeners, your maintenance crew – to brainstorm with you. See what they come up with."

Lukey Jane was nodding enthusiastically. Anne Marie moved their drinks out of reach. "Yeah,'" Lukey seemed to enjoy the idea more as she mulled it over. "Get everybody who really spends time there together and let them figure out what to do. It makes sense.'"

"I'll talk to the crew," Anne Marie offered. "And I'll be there too since I have a stake in what happens."

Lukey Jane and Anne Marie began to talk about specifics and logistics. Halia edged away. She caught Larry's eye and he extricated himself from Freecycle Sam to meet Halia at the register. She paid for her drink and went home.

It was too late to make a telephone ring in a house with a sick child in it, Halia decided. She sat outside on her front porch, reviewing what she had learned so far about Joann's ... departure? Disappearance? Halia realized she had reached the point where she had to name the topic in her mind. That isn't a good sign, she thought. The next task on her Joann list was to call Joann's former workplace, to see if anyone there knew anything. Halia decided she could try tomorrow – sometimes people were around University offices on weekends, even if the offices weren't technically open.

It's worth a try, Halia thought, as she allowed her gaze to fix lazily, unfocused, upon the silhouetted horizon east of the ridge. Anyone at the University office on a Saturday will most likely be pretty devoted to the program. Maybe even one of the professors, and if anyone there had kept in touch with Joann, it would be one of them. It was getting late, and getting chilly, so Halia went inside and readied herself for bed. I'll call in the morning, she promised herself.

Saturday dawned gently, clouds and drizzle slowly giving way by 10 a.m. to another gorgeous spring day. Halia tried Joann's former office, and was not surprised to hear the phone ring away unanswered. She hung up after the 10th ring.

Her next call, to Grace, yielded more fruitful results. Andrew was feeling well enough to ride his bike on the rail trail with Grace and Eddie, and would Halia like to join them? Halia declined politely, and asked after Bezef. In reply, Grace held the phone about two feet from the floor and cooed "speak." An explosion of barking erupted in Halia's ear.

"She's gained some weight and is a fast learner," Grace laughed, "but the breeder is not keen to take her back. She's looking like she's going to be pet quality – conformation flaws, undersize, you know, not up to their standards. For now, they're happy with taking a wait and see approach. In the meantime, they think she's doing better with me than she would with competition from all the other puppies for food, so I'll hang onto her a while longer."

Halia was silent a moment too long, and Grace intuited that Bezef had somehow insinuated her way into Halia's heart. Grace had an idea. "Listen, if you're not going to come for a ride with us, would you be willing to keep an eye on Bezef for me? She really should have some attention and a meal while we're gone." Grace continued, gathering steam. "I could drop her off at your place – we're driving right past."

Couched as a favor to Grace, Halia was able to agree to puppy-sit for the afternoon.

Saturday afternoon passed pleasantly, Halia doing school work at the kitchen table, Bezef napping in a pool of sunlight on the kitchen floor. As the afternoon gave way to evening, Halia fed the puppy and took her for a walk in the graveyard.

The names on the stones matched some of the names in her classroom. Bensons, Dutchers, Dingees … it seemed like many of the founding families of Dover never left. Halia wondered what that would be like – she was far from home, and her parents also spent their adult years far from any ancestral place. The ideas of connection – emotional or spiritual – to people or places fascinated Halia. She denied any experience of such connections, but watched it happen in others. Grace was a transplant, Louise a transplant once removed. Asha … Halia wasn't sure if she was old Dover stock, or a recent arrival. Both seemed equally plausible. All three women, Asha, Louise, and Grace, seemed ready and willing to use the word home – to become attached to Dover. Halia realized that she was being non-committal. She also realized that, at least for the moment, there was no question about being any other way.

Halia succumbed to the compulsive habit of calculating ages or dates (whichever was missing) from stone after stone. She noticed a series of exceptionally long-lived Bensons, and began to wonder about life expectancies in the 1700's and 1800's. She wondered if anyone had studied comparable small communities around New England (or perhaps compared New England with settlements of the same age in the South) to see if there are places that lend themselves to longevity. Halia thought about water quality, fertility of the land, relations with native peoples, genetics, and wondered. For Halia, this was an amusing diversion.

The intense blue of the sky was bisected by a long narrow vapor trail with ladder-like rungs that reminded Halia of snowmobile tracks. She watched the trail, headed for Stewart Airport by the looks of it, fade and distort, and allowed the memories to surface. Walking on snowmobile tracks as a child, she had marveled at the firmness of the snow beneath her, the walk-ability of the track compared to the difficult wallowing her short legs necessitated as she struggled through in the deep soft stuff beside it. She had walked in the woods, breaking trails of her own, and walked on the snowmobile tracks alongside the road, and had compared the two, wondering about the different textures, and enjoying the comparative ease of motion on the snowmobile-packed snow as only a seven year old could. She remembered and felt a twinge – she had always been alone.

Without siblings, and her parents always inside reading or writing, Halia was permitted to go outside if she so desired. Permitted but not necessarily encouraged, nor accompanied. Nor discouraged, for that matter – in some ways it felt like one adult interacting with another adult – permission was simply not a part of the interaction. Even at that age, the Drs. Frank parented Halia as if they were entertaining a visiting scientist – they treated her with the courtesy and slightly distant kindness typically reserved for a peer. Halia's father would look up from his work and smile a slightly shy smile, and after making eye contact he would duck his eyes back behind the book – the whole interaction having the emotional quality of passing a stranger on the street. There was the necessary acknowledgement of their existence, but more was somehow deemed inappropriate. Halia would come back in from her snowy forays, and her mother would ask after her outing. She would offer hot chocolate if she remembered that children liked such things, and make it with the same cool efficiency she showed in the laboratory. She seemed to care whether or not Halia wanted it and enjoyed it, but not so much as a loving mother nourishing her child - more like a tourist watching some foreign ritual.

Halia had long since forgiven her parents for being freaks. It took a little longer, but she had also forgiven them for their role in making her a freak. She knew they cared about her – with hindsight, she ultimately came to that conclusion. They cared about her but were quite clueless about parenting. And really, they didn't do too bad a job, all things considered. There was food on the table, predictably and at meal times (well… sometimes meal times got a little vague and Halia would have to remind them, especially if a deadline loomed for one or both of them). Halia was supported in her interests as they developed, and respected as an individual – not expected to be just like her parents in thought or deed. It was that particular insight, in fact, that helped them to help Halia understand herself and her social "issues" as they began arise. It was their self awareness of their own oddity that actually empowered them to be the best parents they could be.

After the whole Bones fiasco, Halia was determined to be as freakish or normal as she was, and refused to care about what anyone thought or said. Attempting to appear like other people, to want what they wanted, to act as they did, had contributed to the disaster, Halia thought, and she had no desire to fall into that trap again. Halia had fooled Bones with her efforts to pretend she was like other women, but then again, Bones didn't care much about who Halia really was anyway. Halia hadn't fooled anyone else, much less herself. Much more so than being angered by Bones' betrayal, or hurt by the ultimate rejection, Halia nursed regrets that she had ever strayed from her true nature. She felt that she had betrayed herself first, long before Bones had ever played out his Bonesian melodrama, by acting the part of a woman in love, a woman open to partnership, a married woman, half of a couple. Halia was ill prepared for such roles; she hadn't done the research. Now, post-Bones, she experienced the homecoming of a returning to Self, and she welcomed it. That is, as much as Halia ever indulged in that sort of thing anyway.

Finally Halia turned around and headed home.

After Grace picked the dog up, Halia found herself once again looking for Bezef during the evening – listening for her footsteps, or hesitating before rustling papers or shifting her position, aware that the sound could startle Bezef, and forgetting momentarily that she was alone. The awareness of another being in her house was novel and tiring – somewhat like having company. Bezef was not fussy or difficult in any way, but Halia felt she could not relax completely with a live creature dependent upon her, under the same roof. She wondered, as she caught herself seeking Bezef for the third or fourth time that evening, what becoming a parent would be like, and imagined that it would be emotionally exhausting simply to no longer feel alone. She pressed her lips together disapprovingly at such thoughts.

Louise spent the day with her parents at Stonecrop, a botanical garden about an hour south of Dover. Leaving The Blue Eft for a full day was not a cause of anxiety for Louise, as she was lucky to have a staff that was both talented and dedicated. While Louise didn't spend much time away from The Eft, she knew she didn't have to worry when she did.

It was a beautiful spring Sunday, a perfect day for admiring the immense trillium, bloodroot, and hepatica collections Stonecrop boasted, among the other early spring woodland blooms. Louise had thoroughly enjoyed strolling, chatting, and letting her mind wander in the company of her two favorite people. It was Halia's idea – black and blue ice cream – that had captured her parents' imaginations, and ended up playing a leading role in the day's conversation. Louise's mom took up the recipe aspect, and mused aloud about the ingredients involved in a cassis swirl. Louise's father produced a small memo pad and pencil, and sketched label designs during their picnic lunch. It had been a fun and creative afternoon and all three of them returned to Dover with renewed enthusiasm for projects old and new.

Now, with Larry taking care of the bar, and the Benson brothers running the kitchen, Louise had time to sit and reflect upon the day, and chart her course for the next few weeks or so. Thinking about the ice cream project turned her thoughts to Halia. I need to ask her about the ice cream maker, Louise reminded herself. Louise wondered briefly if asking Halia would add undue stress, as Halia had been looking rather drawn and taut lately. She knew that her friend was trying to track down a valid address for her ex-husband's whatever she was – a distant cousin or something. Louise knew that many people would accept the woman's change of address without looking into it very deeply at all – if she's gone without a trace then I can't send her a check – Oh Well. Louise also knew Halia well enough to know that she would never simply accept a situation at face value if it made no sense, and so far, no one had been able to make much sense of this woman's situation.

Not that it was all that widely discussed, for that matter. It had been Grace that mentioned it to Louise, and just last week Halia had been talking about it with Rob and Asha, but somehow all who heard the story felt Halia's tension and did not pry.

Well, asking to borrow an ice cream maker isn't going to overtax someone like Halia, and it certainly isn't prying to check in and see how Halia is doing. With that resolved, Louise picked up the phone to call Halia. Then, for some reason, she reconsidered, phone in hand, waffling. I'll walk over there, she decided, and carry the ice cream maker back here with me.

Louise's knock brought Halia to the door, looking disoriented, with a pencil in one hand and a whisk in the other. Louise followed her back into the kitchen to find lesson plans, and student work spread out on the table, and Halia whisking together salad dressing ingredients at the counter.

"Multi-tasking?" Louise asked.

Halia answered without stopping her rhythmic movement. "I got hungry in the middle of grading. It was most inconvenient, but it wouldn't be fair to the students if I grade papers while I'm hungry. Hunger affects my judgment."

Louise, realizing Halia was completely serious, asked about the ice cream maker. Halia, now preparing the salad, gave Louise explicit verbal instructions for retrieving the ice cream maker from its storage spot in the basement. When Louise returned, Halia was seated at the table, a schoolwork-free island around her large salad bowl.

"Would you like some?" she offered graciously.

"Thanks." Louise, seeing avocado and smelling the fresh herbs in the dressing, couldn't refuse. They sat together at Halia's table, noisily crunching. Louise asked if any news about Aunt Joann had come to light.

Halia finished her salad, and placed the blue glass bowl, along with all her prep utensils, in the dishwasher before answering. She sat back down at the table, and sighed heavily.

"No news." Halia looked piercingly at Louise, as if she might hold answers woven into her long black braid. "I have one or two threads left to unravel but I'm not exactly hopeful there will be answers. I'm heartened by the fact that there's nothing to make me think something bad has happened to her, but I'm just not coming up with any real information about what has happened to her."

"Well, can you file a missing persons report?"

"I don't know whether or not she's actually missing." Halia tried hard to keep the frustration out of her voice, as she appreciated Louise's company and interest. "I guess I could call the police and see if they'll take a report." With that she reached across the table and extracted the "Joann list" from a pile of papers. "Call to office" was at the top of the list. "Call police" was added just underneath. Halia paused, tapped her pen against the chipped enamel table top, and then wrote "call brother again" at the bottom of the list. "The payments I owe her are going to start adding up. It seems like maybe she's not interested in the money." Halia seemed to be talking to herself as much as to Louise. "How could someone forget about that much money coming in? Or just not need it? I wonder if something has happened to her ability to think clearly and make sound decisions. Most people don't sell their house and move, all of a sudden. Do they?"

"Asha's the expert on who does what and why," Louise spread her hands. "But most people do leave a trail. It's almost like your aunt doesn't want anyone to know where she is."

"Hmmm. Does she want anyone to know where she is?" Halia repeated Louise's insight, murmuring it to herself and not bothering to correct Louise about the relationship between she and Joann. She looked up at Louise after writing something on her list. "I hadn't really entertained that thought – at least not thoroughly. What if she doesn't want to be found?"

Louise could see that she had set something in motion in Halia's mind, and that it was time for her to go. Halia walked her to the door, and held the screen door open for her, as she awkwardly wrestled the bulky ice cream maker through. Halia stepped out onto the porch and leaned against a green (yep, plain old green this time) column, watching Louise manage the cumbersome box as she strode north, back to The Eft. Halia stood there for some time in the gathering gloom, working out possible scenarios. Finally, she went back inside.

Over coffee Monday morning Halia double-checked her schedule for the week. A team meeting today would steal time she could otherwise use to make phone calls, and necessitate entry into the faculty room. Halia remembered the aura the faculty room held when she was a little girl: the inner sanctum, the private realm where teachers dropped their guard and were human. Back in the 1970's, faculty rooms smelled of cigarettes and coffee, and Halia remembered feeling almost as if she's rather not enter, lest she see her idols fall from their pedestals.

As she trained to become a teacher, she thought of the faculty room as a potential place to belch and fart (both literally and figuratively) away from prying student eyes. Her teaching experience soon proved her wrong. In the two districts she'd experienced, one as a student teacher and the other here in Dover, she found that the faculty room all too often gave way to being a gossipy clique-ishly unpleasant place, painfully reminiscent of the seventh grade lunch room. The "popular" crowd among the teachers, in Halia's opinion, were extremely concerned with the pursuit of excellence in teaching, often to the detriment of their actual classroom performance. These were the darlings of the administration, who attended conferences and returned ready to implement new techniques. The problem was that they were much more interested in their own excellence – creating it, maintaining it, and promoting it – than in connecting with their students. Halia had met many truly excellent teachers at Dover, but she discovered early on that they were not generally to be found in the faculty room.

Halia arrived for the team meeting on time, and found only Sue Sasko, the math teacher, there. They exchanged polite pleasantries and waited for the rest of the team to arrive. Sue, like Halia, spent as little time as possible in the faculty room, and seemed equally uncomfortable there despite her veteran status.

They made it through the team meeting without being nauseated by Excellent Teachers, crowing about new Excellent Methods. Halia wondered if Peter Gabriel's song Excellent Birds had been written with public school teachers in mind. Today the puffed up chirping was blissfully absent and the field trip to Rosendale, among other items of business, was dealt with matter of factly. Halia found herself with five minutes to spare at the end of the period, and dialed information on her cell phone as she walked down the hallway back to her classroom.

"Keeseville, NY, police department," she spoke clearly to the computerized voice.

After to speaking to a human operator, discussing the lack of a specific Keeseville police force, and did Halia want the Essex county sheriff's department or the local state trooper barracks, or was this an emergency, Halia finally found herself speaking with a desk sergeant from Troop B, zone 1 station in Plattsburgh, NY. Halia checked her watch. In 194 seconds she would have seventh grade company.

"I need to find out about filing a missing persons report for an adult who has moved without leaving a forwarding address." Halia spoke as quickly as she felt she could and still be understood.

"Typically missing adults are not a police matter, ma'am. Depending on circumstances," he added politely. "Is this a tenant who has skipped out owing rent money?"

"No," Halia went for the quick and blunt explanation. "This is someone to whom I owe money. I'm trying to find her to pay her back, but she seems to have moved and left no forwarding address."

"I'm sorry," the officer sounded genuinely sympathetic. "This doesn't sound like something we'd investigate because it sounds like there's no suggestion of a crime" - his pause was filled in by Halia's noise of assent – "and this is a person who can function independently? No need for medication? Not disabled?" Again, Halia mmm-hmmmed. The seventh graders were entering the room and Halia had twenty-three seconds before the bell. "Try an internet search," the trooper suggested. Halia thanked him and hung up with six seconds to spare. The fact that her mind was still in a trooper barracks in Clinton County meant nothing to the twenty four pairs of eyes upon her – it was time to get to work. She slipped her phone into her blazer pocket and dove into the lesson, trusting the material and the students to bring her back to Dover. It was going to be a long afternoon.

Easter break was staring them down, students and teachers alike. Easter fell late this year, and the week off felt long overdue. As it approached, the hallways buzzed with excited talk of vacations and other plans. On Thursday, school let out at 11:15 a.m., and soon afterwards the parking lot was empty. Halia headed straight to The Eft, an idea distilling into a necessity with each passing moment.

Halia entered The Blue Eft at lunchtime, and was immediately confronted with two mildly disturbing facts. First, there was the music. Louise was a creature of habit or routine, and perhaps even a touch of superstition governed her consistency with details. Her establishment was a near magical success, despite impressive local competition from The Power Plant (the new brew pub located at the Wingdale train station) and Gordy's. In spite of, or perhaps due to Louise's quirkiness, The Blue Eft had made it. The Eft had several themes, from décor to menu to music, and if there was music playing at The Blue Eft, it was blues. For Halia, musical preference was not an issue – she listened as part of the overall practice of observation, not as a connoisseur, nor as a lover. But observe she did, and after two years of regular observation, the sound of reggae being played in The Blue Eft was a jarring, glaring error. A disjuncture, a rip in the fabric of reality. A symbol? Halia considered and dismissed that notion. A symbol of what, she asked herself.

The second source of Halia's distress was the table near the open garage door. Several tables pulled together, actually, filled with teachers. Halia chose her companions carefully, and her haunts more carefully still. She found the social company of many of her colleagues unpalatable, despite the fact that many of them were quite nice individually. All strove to do their jobs well, but even Halia laughed when a veteran teacher from the art department (forgiven, tolerated and expected to be eccentric) labeled this crowd "overly caffeinated." They seemed to talk too much, too loudly, and too often about what others (parents, students, other teachers, and the administration, for example) should be doing. This busybody bean-counting had informed Halia's opinion about this particular group of teachers several years prior. She continued to await a significant challenge to her original judgment.

She sidled into the bar, nodding a tactful greeting to those who looked her way, and perched on a bar stool, looking for Louise.

Pretty Rose Brown from across the street emerged from the kitchen. "Oh hi, Hali," she beamed, a huge smile creasing her face. "Can you believe I found some Bob Marley cds in the kitchen? I thought it was strictly blues around here, but someone must have left these." Rose chattered in her upbeat, slightly hyperactive way, her hands wiping, straightening, tidying, while her eyes roamed the room. "Louise asked me to come over for a while. She went over to her parents for something. I think it had to do with a painting her dad is doing for this place." Rose trailed off, trying to read Halia's expression.

"I'm leaving to go upstate next week," Halia stated. "I just stopped by to talk to Louise about a date for the ice cream event she's planning. I offered to help her with it, but I've been somewhat unavailable lately. I'll be in tomorrow night with Grace but I thought Louise might be too busy to talk then. I understand Beckerman will be playing, too."

"Yeah, isn't that amazing? I mean, he's got to be, what? 90? At least..." Rose shook her head and whistled in admiration. Then she shifted into neighbor mode.

"'Would you like me to bring in your mail while you're gone? Do you need me to water plants of anything like that?"

Halia accepted Rose's kind offer to take care of her mail and they arranged details - hidden keys, cell phone numbers, etc. Halia hoped Louise would return before they finished sorting things out, but she did not. Rose returned to the kitchen and a waitress appeared soon after to deal with the chattering flock of teachers Halia avoided.

Halia remained seated at the bar, her back to the dining room, her eyes resting on the terrarium on display behind the bar. Grace had made it as a just-for-fun project with Andrew, but when Louise opened The Blue Eft, all agreed that the only appropriate home for the terrarium and its red eft inhabitant. Thus prominently displayed at Louise's new hot spot, Spotty Justina (as she had affectionately been named) came to live at The Blue Eft, her woodland home gracing shelves that once held lawn mower belts and chain saw lubricant. Even Andrew agreed that she was an essential element in making The Blue Eft what it was.

The Blue Eft was not Louise's first establishment. After finishing her undergraduate degree in biology at Smith College, Louise stayed in Northampton and opened The Braid and Bonnet, a women's pub. Wildly successful from the start, Louise had played her cards well, riding the wave of the real estate upswing such that she was able to sell The Braid and Bonnet to a couple from Park Slope, Brooklyn, for a pretty price. She returned to Dover with enough cash in hand to buy the mower shop with the house next door and renovate them both. Within a year she opened The Blue Eft.

Dover wasn't quite ready for a place as bohemian and offbeat as The Eft, but Louise was prepared for a few slow years. She had banked on staying power, her family's support, and the changes in Wingdale to give The Eft the boost it would need before the money ran out, and she had been right. Louise was rightfully credited with being there for Dover's birth as a tourist destination. With Dover firmly in its youth as such, Louise's Blue Eft holds a position of respect and seniority, as the place that heralded the boom. From the glorious bead shop, art supply emporium, and antique and second hand stores lining Market Street to the extension of the Rail Trail along the Ten Mile River; from the independent movie theatre housed in the former delicatessen, to the funky renovated houses and trailers tucked away on the side streets; and perhaps best of all the surprise transition plan for the former state psychiatric center creating the campus of SUNY at Wingdale and the north branch of the Metropolitan Museum of Art – Dover had come into its own. Finally, Dover was experiencing a time when it was being compared favorably with its neighbors – both Pawling and Kent, CT, and even the Grand Dame of pleasant tourist strollability: Rhinebeck. Dover had arrived, but Louise's Blue Eft, with its quirky themes and offbeat sensibility, held an important place in Dover's appeal, as a destination all of its own.

Halia lost herself in Spotty Justina's world, thinking about Louise's success and all that was involved in the process of a place like Dover (said with disdain) becoming a place like Dover. A voice beside her broke into her reverie.

"Who put Bob Marley on?" Louise's voice was both surprised and amused.

"Rose found it in the kitchen. She was delighted," Halia replied.

Louise considered, head tilted, listening as the words to Three Little Birds filled the bar. She shrugged. "Doesn't exactly sound blue to me, but maybe some history of music professor from down the road can explain how reggae is really the blues of the islands. Or something like that." Louise headed for the kitchen singing to herself. She stopped in the doorway and turned on her heel, quickly enough to send her black braid helicoptering around behind her back. "Can I get you something, Hali?"

"A virgin lizard, please," Halia checked her watch. Louise returned and filled a glass with ice and seltzer. Halia added, "I'm leaving to go upstate on Monday. I need to talk to people where Joann worked, and see where that takes me."

"Can't you just call them? Or email?"

"I have tried to call a couple of times, without success. It just doesn't seem right to email the department about Joann – it isn't tactful. I don't know enough to know who to ask, so I can't email any one person individually. I never knew Joann really well, so I want to be respectful and courteous since I am pursuing something that perhaps she'd prefer I left alone." Halia had thought through all of this already, knowing that her decision to drive at least six hours to talk to people in person who may not know anything anyway would be viewed in this age of computerized communication as unnecessarily archaic. "Besides all of that, there is a certain amount of following a scent that can only happen in person. And," Halia's face changed, her eyes widened, and for a moment looked dangerously full. Her voice cracked with innocence and honesty. "I need to go. I can't even explain it to myself. It's one of those things that I have to accept, despite the irrationality of it."

Louise chose not to remark upon the obviously irrational basis for Halia's decision. "Are you heading straight to Keeseville, or will you stop on the way?"

"No, I'm going straight there. I think I should arrive before nightfall."

Nightfall, Louise repeated silently, repressing the urge to shake her head in disbelief. No one talks like Halia, she thought.

Halia was absorbed with calculating hours: breakfast, packing, and time on the road. Although she thought she would arrive too late to accomplish anything on Monday, Tuesday would be a productive day.

Louise was asking her something. Halia divided her brain into sections, and allotted just enough of her awareness to continue the conversation with Louise, reserving the rest for finishing her internal train of thought.

"How long will you be gone?"

"I'm not sure..." Halia wondered what she would find out and how long she would need. She'd never done this before, so she had no baseline. "I only have the week off, so I can't be gone longer than that."

"Will you stay in contact with Grace?" Louise wanted to know.

"Yes. And Rose offered to take in my mail, so I'll also call her if my plans change. And you too, Louise. I'll call you if I find anything out," Halia sighed a barely perceptible sigh, "and if I don't."

Louise shook her head at Halia, her braid swinging in s-curves behind her back. "You couldn't look much lower if you were sitting in the shadow of a shipwreck," she spoke sympathetically. Nice metaphor, Halia thought, her critical appraisal of Louise's colorful words lifting her spirits a touch. Louise continued, "don't doubt yourself. It's a total waste of energy."

Wasting energy on negative emotions was close to abhorrent to Halia. The mini-pep talk helped. "Y'know, I came here today for something else." Louise lifted her eyebrows and Halia continued, "I promised to help you with the unveiling of the black and blue ice cream at the ice cream event." Louise's face relaxed into a laugh. "Have you set a date?"

"Let's wait until July or even early August – blueberry season. We'll have to have several test batches between now and then – and" Louise's brow furrowed somewhat, the corners of her mouth turning down, "I know what the end of the school year is like for middle school teachers. Don't worry – just focus on one thing at a time. By the beginning of July, I think we'll both be more ready to nail things down."

Halia left The Eft, the trip to Keeseville already taking shape in her mind.

"A road trip?" Grace sounded skeptical as they chatted over drinks on Friday evening. The crowd was thin as it was Good Friday, but Mr. Beckerman cast a long shadow on the room, sipping his loup garou despite the unruly April heatwave. "You will have Easter dinner with us? Go on Monday or Tuesday, but stay here for this weekend, ok? You can find out when the office at the University is open and aim for then."

"I already did. It's posted on the archeology department website. I'm driving up on Monday – they're open on Tuesday. I'm staying at Ausable chasm – it was the cheapest motel I could find in the northern part of Keeseville, so it's right in between Joann's old house and her office in Plattsburgh." As to be expected, Halia was thorough, precise and swift in her planning and decision making, her time spent well Thursday afternoon. She changed the subject. "What can I bring on Sunday?"

"Well, between Andrew's pickiness and Eddie's sister's Atkins diet, and my mother being a vegan, I know I won't please everyone." Grace ticked off these special needs as if everyone routinely accommodated this level of short order cooking when they entertained. Halia's eyes widened. "My plan is to do a vegan spread for the main course, with this phyllo dough Easter pie that one of the techs at the hospital swears by. And then I thought we'd have tons of rich desserts available for the animal fat crowd." Halia glazed over, counting her blessings that she was divorced, childless, and an ersatz orphan. "Can you make one of your fabulous chocolate cheesecakes with the ginger snap crust?"

"Sure." Baking, more a science than an art to Halia, appealed immensely. "I'll make something vegan too."

As they talked, Louise and Larry arranged furniture in the corner of the pub until a makeshift stage took shape. Mr. Beckerman, trumpet in hand, made his slow and careful way over to Louise.

"Would you be so kind…?" He gestured to his music stand, and Larry fetched it. The sparse crowd began to take notice, and Grace and Halia adjusted their chairs to improve their view.

"Have you heard him play before?" Grace asked.

"Only on recordings. I have a couple from the 1950's."

"He's as great now as he was then." Halia cocked her head skeptically at Grace's emphatic statement. "I heard him here, about 6 months ago. I hope the same bass player plays with him. It was really something."

As if Grace had summoned him by speaking her hopes, a man much younger than Beckerman, but equally tall and equally bald, joined Louise, Larry and Beckerman in the corner with an upright bass.

"Apparently he's from Woodstock. He put out an album that was recorded in that abandoned mine you're taking the kids to on your field trip next month." Grace explained with just a little too much enthusiasm. Halia noticed and let it go. Were she less distracted by her upcoming trip to Keeseville she would have subjected Grace to a thorough dose of teasing about schoolgirl crushes and being starstruck. Instead, she noted her friend's condition without comment. She didn't even wonder what it would be like to have such emotions herself, so distant and remote were they.

Beckerman and Levine, the bassist, played beautifully together. Both Grace and Halia listened, rapt. There were moments when the hush of deep listening consumed the bar profoundly, and even Larry held still, eyes closed, transported. Halia realized at one point that she was "seeing" the music, the melody like an animal snaking around the furniture and audience. It was an evening both Grace and Halia would wax nostalgic about for the rest of their lives. Like the first kiss from the love of one's life, the chemistry of all involved on that warm April night was just perfect. The stars lined up and for the hour and a half that they played, Halia was truly without past or future, with neither diagnosis nor symptoms, nobody's ex-wife, and without a search for Joann underway. Happiness, however it might be defined by Halia, was observable in her quiet hands, smooth forehead, and half-closed eyes.

Halia slept deeply that night, and did not recall even a shred of a dream upon waking.

Saturday stayed warm and pleasant. Halia spent several hours taking care of school work, uncertain if her stay in Keeseville would be extended to the point of interfering with accomplishing items on her to do list. Finally, after a late lunch, Halia considered her progress sufficient and headed out to the front porch to experience the day.

A little cloudier and a little chillier than would earn the epithet glorious, the early afternoon sun did invite outdoor activities, as opposed to insisting Halia turn right around and head back to the kitchen to make desserts for tomorrow.

After standing on the front porch, blinking, for several minutes, Asha and Brulee pulled up in Asha's ancient, battered pick-up truck. Asha's openness to a friendship with Halia seemed to have increased in proportion to her time spent at The Blue Eft. Newer to the neighborhood than Halia, it seemed Asha was figuring out her new life on Nellie Hill Road, and she had begun to let Halia know she'd like her to be a part of it.

"Hey!" Asha called to her. Halia waved. "Wanna come for a walk? We're meeting Rob at the river road in Kent."

Halia considered briefly. "I need to do some baking for tomorrow. How long do you plan to be out?"

"I need to be back by 4 at the latest – Pearl's dad is dropping her off at 4:30, and he's surprised me by being early in the past." Asha fiddled with the car keys, then checked her watch. "Let's go! It's a great day to be outside. I'll pick you up in five minutes." She began to drive the truck away, calling over her shoulder through the open window, "Just change your shoes!"

Halia looked down and a sideways grin crept across her lips. She was wearing fuzzy pink slippers Grace had given her as a joke, with her paint splattered sweat pants and green and black Buffalo plaid flannel shirt.

Five minutes later Halia was seated in the front seat of Asha's Volkswagen, Brulee curled up in the back. Halia's appearance was no longer comedic, as she had thrown on her weekend uniform of levi's, t-shirt, sweat-shirt, and sneakers at an astonishing speed. She ran her fingers through her hair, realizing she hadn't brushed it since waking up. She was in like company, though, as Asha was also more concerned with the activity at hand than the clothing it involved. Both women eschewed make-up, hairstyles, and shoes with heels without a second thought, and yet both women were frequently surprised to find themselves on the receiving end of wolf whistles or the more modern equivalent.

Rob's knowledge of local flora, and Brulee's wild animal grace-in-motion combined for a pleasantly di-verting walk in the woods. The three friends compro-mised intuitively, Asha slowing her athletic pace and Rob speeding up his slightly attention deficit infused meandering. Halia found the result a comfortable speed that allowed them to cover the entire section of the Ap-palachian Trail from trail head to trail head in the time allotted.

The two women were mostly silent, and Rob played the role of tour guide. Halia was impressed with Rob's

breadth of botanical and ethnobotanical knowledge –
he was so obviously fond of the plants and their stories.
Halia couldn't help but notice that Asha seemed equally
impressed with Rob's tousled long hair and 5 o'clock
shadow, and Rob was obviously fond of Asha and her
dog. Slowly Halia realized that this walk had become
the way to announce the existence of Rob-and-Asha as
a unit to her. As it dawned on her, Halia smiled slowly.
She felt an unnameable twinge for a split second, and
hoped they'd be good to each other. They seemed off to
a nice start.

Halia was aware of all that awaited her, both tasks
and concerns, but visualized her day as neatly compart-
mentalized, rather like a daily pill dispenser – and in
choosing to be in the afternoon stroll compartment, she
felt it acceptable to enjoy this place and this moment.
Her next compartment – baking for tomorrow – would
come complete with opportunities for multitasking,
including turning her attention to her trip to Keeseville
and her search for Joann.

The evening was a manageable flurry of activity for
Halia, shopping, baking, and planning. She was looking
forward to her visit to Keeseville, inasmuch as she believed she would discover whatever it was she needed to
know about Joann Grant. She was also looking forward
to spending time with Grace's family, as she so rarely
even saw what was left of her own. She thought it was a
good way for her to have a family – to get absorbed by
Grace's for a holiday. The conversation could be trusted
to be stimulating and Grace and her mom were both
wonderful cooks. Halia had spent her share of holiday
meals at Grace's with her own parents throughout her
childhood, as Grace's mom loved to share, and kind of

"grokked" what Halia's parents would have wanted to provide for Halia, had they the ability to do so. Grace's mom was there, ready and willing to step in and do the traditional holiday things that Halia's parents just couldn't quite figure out.

By the time Halia was actually driving to Grace's on Sunday, she had put forth an impressive effort, creating a superlative version of her cheesecake, a technicolor fresh fruit salad, and a strawberry rhubarb crumble (two out of three items vegan for Grace's mom), and even dressed in non-weekend clothes, as her way of thanking Grace for the lending of her family.

She was greeted at the door by Andrew and Bezef – both of whom it seemed had doubled in size since Halia had seen them last. Bezef barked at Halia, Andrew yelled at Bezef, the Taresius family cats, Gusto and Pesto, came running to mount an escape attempt, and Halia had to dash in around 14 legs threatening to become a plate of spaghetti at her feet. She managed to get the desserts safely to the kitchen and sat down, Bezef appearing at her side moments later. She chatted with Andrew about 4th grade and petted Bezef.

At one point during dinner the talk turned to Halia's trip to Keeseville. Grace and Eddie were bustling about in the kitchen and returned to the table to find Halia politely fending off questions from Eddie's sister and brother-in-law. Grace's mom listened pensively, and eventually broke into the conversation.

"I wonder if she doesn't realize she is missing." Halia met the older woman's eyes and nodded slightly. "Maybe she believes she has taken care of all her loose ends, and just doesn't realize she's left you out of the loop."

"Seems odd to simply forget about that kind of money." Halia's voice was soft, considering rather than challenging.

"Maybe she has something else on her mind. Something compelling…" Grace's mother also spoke with a quiet intensity, as if she were addressing something other than Halia and her missing aunt. Eddie's sister and brother-in-law, feeling the pall of introversion creep up on the table, excused themselves to assist in the kitchen. Halia and Grace's mother sat across the table from each other, comfortable with the silence, contemplating each other's words.

The delivery of dessert shifted the small talk to Grace and Halia's enjoyment of Beckerman and Levine's performance the previous Friday evening. Halia, poker-faced as always, chose to reenter the Easter dinner compartment of her day and play the role of the charming guest, once again trusting that she would have time to fully concern herself with Grace's mother's words (those spoken and those left unsaid) on her long drive upstate.

Bezef spent the afternoon and evening alternating between chasing the cats, playing raucously with her toys, and sleeping at Halia's feet. Grace took note but refrained from mentioning it.

"Why is she still with you?" Halia asked. "She seems perfectly fine now."

"They are letting me hang on to her. They kind of have their hands full with her littermates. I mean, they'd take her back, but this informal vacation for her seems to be working out well for everyone. I guess they'd like to sell her eventually, but she's not their priority at the moment."

Halia didn't ask how much Bezef would cost.

Later, Andrew gave Halia a sleepy hug, and Eddie wished her well as he walked her to the front door. Halia drove away, her belly full, her mind already navigating the northern reaches of Route 9 and rehearsing conversations. Halia decided to watch a movie before falling asleep – to keep from focusing too intently on her trip – and planned to get up early to finish packing, write down last minute thoughts, and finalize her route. Halia did not believe she could be overly prepared.

Chapter 4

I don't know why it ends. Why some couples uncouple and some don't. A therapist friend said to me once that there was no difference in the marriages, just differences in the people: some decide to end it and some decide to tolerate it. The moment of that choice, that secret solo decision that swiftly snowballs from that first inkling ("I could leave") into the inexorable need ("I must leave in order to survive") separates the golden anniversary set from the multiple marriages set. I don't know…

Sometimes when you hear people talk about getting into relationships they talk about momentum, although usually, they are talking about getting in too deep too fast – what if I decide I don't really want to link my future with his, but I've already given him a spare drawer in my dresser? Momentum involves speed – regarding intimacy, too much too soon. Once a relationship starts to gather its own momentum, it's bloody difficult to go backwards. It is easier to just be there, half satis-

fied (and half enraged) than to interrupt the slide down the slippery slope.

The formal definition of momentum (mass times velocity) also references resistance to slowing down. A movement in a given direction that just gathers its own steam and becomes its own reason for existence, resisting the inevitable, could either be the reason a relationship fails or the reason it perseveres. People certainly talk themselves into embarking upon astoundingly foolish relationships (been there, done that, got the t-shirt); perhaps they also talk themselves into remaining in relationships – the sales job being more the thing than the actual thing. Momentum being the operative force – until friction overcomes the forward motion and you stall.

Friction – now there's a concept we all know well. He chews with his mouth open, she snores, he leaves his socks on the living room floor, she pronounces words incorrectly, he leaves the cap off the toothpaste, she rattles my cage, he messes with my feng shui... All the little niggling annoyances that were utterly and amazingly absent during the first blush of passion (lust) pop up like daisies telling us friction is at hand. Do we choose to forgive? Ignore? Plot revenge? Friction is inevitable – physics tells us so, but what do lovers do with all this newfound irritation where fascination and desire once lived? Depends – like I said before – some just grit their teeth and stay with that goddamned oaf/bitch. Some leave. Some forgive the flatulence and sloppiness, and love on. I'm sure I don't know.

Grace crossed the living room, collecting up the flotsam and jetsam of family life – an accordion pleated sock, abandoned colored pencils, a half chewed stick

– as Eddie helped Andrew stay on task during his bed-time ritual. Andrew called down to his mother when he was ready for bed.

"I'm on my way," Grace called back up the stairs.

Eddie kissed Andrew goodnight, and embraced Grace warmly as they passed each other in Andrew's doorway. Andrew watched his parents speak quietly to each other and kiss briefly before his mom entered his room. He heard his dad's heavy tread on the stairs, and the sound of clinking dishes and running water soon wafted up from the kitchen.

"Did you have fun today?" Grace asked her son.

"Yup." He grinned at her. "I made you something." He tossed the covers back and popped out of bed. He padded barefoot across his room and opened a folder on his desk. He returned to his mother seated on his bed, paper in hand.

Grace gazed at the drawing, speechless. It resembled a child's rendering of every description she'd ever heard of the Philmontian coati. "Tell me about your picture," she managed to squeak.

"Well, remember that day we rode our bikes to the big waterfall?" Grace nodded. "After, we drove home the long way. I was getting really bored. You and Daddy got into a big conversation about houses and front porches, and stuff like that." Again, Grace nodded. "I was looking out the window while you were talking, and I saw an animal on the side of the road. It looked like it was half groundhog and half raccoon, with a long pointy nose. So while you were busy cooking today, I decided to make a picture of it for you." He finished by giving her a quick hug and saying, "Happy Easter, Mom."

Grace took the drawing, held it carefully, and examined it closely. "This is really special, Andrew. I'm going to treasure it forever. Thank you so much, honey." She snuggled Andrew back under the covers and kissed his forehead. "Hey, Drew," she added casually, "if Dad and I took you back to that road, could you find the spot where you saw this animal?"

"Sure, Mom. I didn't put it in the picture, but there's a green and white little sign with numbers on it -" he reached out and indicated a spot on the drawing, "right there."

"Great. Maybe if there's a nice day this week, we'll take a ride up there, ok?"

"Ok." Andrew closed his eyes, settled down, and asked "Can Bezef sleep with me?"

"No sweetie, Bezef sleeps in her crate. Good night."

Andrew drifted off to sleep, listening to his mother's voice, excited and breathless, talking to his father in the kitchen.

Halia was on the road by 10 a.m. The Northway was smooth sailing – traffic free, and bone-crushingly boring. Halia listened to music from the cds she brought with her: lively upbeat music designed to provide respite from the monotony. She stopped for lunch just north of Lake George, and hurried through the meal.

Halia found herself approaching the outskirts of Keeseville from the south at about 4 p.m., and the advent of the end of the long drive roused her from the road buzz stupor hours on the Northway can induce. Her thoughts came in layers. Her conscious mind was occupied with logistics – she scouted for a place to eat dinner, keeping her eyes peeled for the motel. She thought about Joann's daily life in this town – where might she have spent her time? What was her Sunday morning routine? Who might she have chatted casually about retirement plans with, and how would Halia find those people? At the deepest layer, partially formed nagging questions lurked. Halia was self aware enough to feel the doubt and the foolishness of this trip, and experienced the quiet insistence (I need to do this) as frustrating and confusing.

Halia pulled over suddenly. The sign, peeling black letters on an ancient looking sandwich board, read "Jogue's antiques." Halia felt herself succumbing to a force other than rationality – she could not explain to herself why she was stopping here. Halia regained control momentarily by choosing to regard intuition as an acceptable guide (especially in the absence of reason). She decided that if she relaxed, perhaps the reason would present itself. She entered the shop with an indecipherable expression on her face.

A young teenager appeared from behind a mirrored vanity. "Is there something I can help you with?" His Quebecois accent sent shivers down Halia's spine. She stared openly at him, taking in his pale skin, black hair, and slight frame, and yet appearing not to see him at all.

"I don't know why I stopped here." Halia relied on a blunt statement of fact to guide the encounter.

The boy regarded her equally without discretion. "I'm Jacques," he said. "This is my grandmother's store. I just help out sometimes."

Halia nodded. She tried to observe, to think, to marshal reason and logic to regain a sense of purposefulness, without result. She just stood there, looking at 15 year old Jacques Jogue, and feeling like she had entered a trance from the moment the car stopped.

"Perhaps you stopped here for Buffalo china?" The boy started across the store and Halia followed numbly.

"Buffalo china," Halia repeated.

"The kind used in diners. They are thick, heavy, and white, sometimes with a green stripe around the edge. Some people collect it." Jacques picked his way across his grandmother's shop, stepping carefully over piles of dusty books and magazines, boxes of lamp parts, navigating coat racks and lobster pots and ancient headless mannequins adorned with elaborate Edwardian costumes. He stopped at the tableware area against the far wall. Halia felt the debris of so many lives wash over her and she nearly gasped for breath. Her usual composure had deserted her entirely and in its stead was uncharted ground. She wondered for a moment if she might pass out.

"My Aunt Joann collects it. Collected it." Halia listened to the words she spoke. "No. Not my Aunt Joann." She trailed off.

"She was here." The boy informed Halia.

"Here? When?" His words broke through her confusion and for a moment Halia thought she really was dreaming. This was a little too bizarre, but Halia jumped at the chance to finally receive some news about Joann. She also welcomed the jolt back into her familiar role.

"Two, maybe three months ago. She sold us quite a bit of her collection. They are still here." Jacques began unloading the china from a milk crate, unwrapping newspaper and setting coffee cups and saucers on top of a cardboard box. Halia picked up a piece of newspaper Jacques had tossed aside, and noted the date. February 20 – well, at least that didn't contradict what Halia believed she had already pinned down as the date of departure being March 15. But it did indicate that Joann was packing up and paring down in preparation for the move in late February.

Halia picked up one of the cups Jacques had placed on the box. Turning it over, she ran her fingers over the embossed buffalo. Jacques continued to unwrap pieces of china and set them neatly on top of the cardboard box. For a moment, Halia felt as if she and this boy were preparing to play with the china, like a child's tea party.

"How did you know my -" Halia hesitated, then began again. "What makes you think these pieces came from the woman I mentioned?"

Jacques, crouched on the floor, looked up at Halia over the staged china. He raised his eyebrows, his face an unreadable mask of teenage blankness. His expression was the extent of his reply.

Halia found herself going on. "Did you see her?"

Jacques nodded. "I was here that day. Grandmother was in Montreal, at a wholesale auction. I was the one who helped your aunt."

"Did she say why she was moving?"

"No."

"Did she say where she was moving to?"

"Not in so many words. She said that she was moving to a place that had no address."

Halia looked at him intently, her eyes narrowing to almost a squint. She realized she was about to start chewing the insides of her cheeks, and made a conscious effort to relax her jaw.

"I offered that we could mail her a check if she left her china on consignment. That's when she said that where she was going had no address."

Halia set the coffee cup down and picked up a tiny pitcher. She turned it over in her hands and then held it to her nose, wondering if it smelled like Aunt Joann's house. "Are all these pieces from her?"

Jacques nodded.

Halia set the pitcher down, looking at the small collection on the box. "What was she like, the day she came in here? Happy? Nervous? What kind of mood was she in?"

Jacques appraised Halia before offering his enigmatic response. "If her tongue caught fire, she wouldn't have opened her mouth."

It was Halia's turn to raise her eyebrows as a response.

Jacques grinned, lessening the tension. "It's an expression. I mean she was not about to tell me her secrets."

"What makes you think she had secrets?"

Again, Jacques looked at Halia, his face clearly readable this time, and the best translation for his expression may have been: "What do you take me for? I can read a face better than most in two languages." Aloud he said, "Sometimes I just know things. My grandmother knows things too."

"How much do you know about Joann?"

"Not very much really." Jacques was relenting, melting under Halia's combination of persistence and concern. "She was happy, but she was trying to keep her mouth closed over her big smile." Jacques paused and cocked his head at Halia. "Do you know what I mean?"

"I think so."

"She didn't care about the money. I told her she could have gotten more for her china if she left them on consignment, or sold them herself. I couldn't give her very much for them." Jacques gaze turned inward and he shrugged. "I told her, but she said she didn't want to do consignment because it might take time. She said she was moving and needed to wrap things up quickly. So I bought the best pieces in her collection from her at wholesale price and she seemed happy with that." Jacques lifted his gaze back to Halia. "She was happy, madame. I can say that for sure. She was happy, and there was something she was not saying."

The rest of Halia's afternoon passed without incident. The sign at the motel indicating that check-in was at a campground a quarter of a mile away was a surprise, but the motel room was as she expected. The evening meal in town was also as she expected, and she couldn't help but smile a small wry smile of recognition and familiarity as she recalled Marisa Tomei, in "My Cousin Vinny," predicting that the local Chinese food would be sub par. Certain areas in upstate New York, Halia knew, have not yet experienced the impact of gentrification, yuppification, dinkification, or whatever other socio-cultural process leads to the rise of fashionable eateries.

Her head still spinning from her dreamlike interview with Jacques Jogue, she completed all her preparations for the next day. Finally, lists in order, maps and clothes laid out, Halia slipped into an uneasy sleep.

The next time Halia looked at the cheap plastic alarm clock on the bedside table, it read 1:45 a.m. It was very quiet in the motel room, and no sound entered through the open window. Halia thought of Holmes – his ability to travel in apparent comfort, or his complete lack of concern for his own physical discomfort. Halia found Holmes to be comfortingly and utterly himself, at home and abroad. He did not rely upon his digs, nor familiar settings, to support his identity in the least, and Halia admired that characteristic. She also aspired to be like that, despite the ridiculousness of modeling oneself upon a fictional character, and was somewhat disappointed by her apparent insomnia. To need Home, on any level, felt like weakness, and was an inconvenience Halia felt she could ill afford. Besides, it simply did not mesh with her cut and dried approach to life – her own comfort, be it physical or emotional, was not on the week's agenda, so it was pointless to descend into self indulgence of this sort. As Lukey Jane remarked from time to time, when Halia was particularly oblivious to an apparent illness or injury, "You sure ain't no Taurus, girl!" Halia smiled to herself bitterly, frustration with her wakefulness gritty between her teeth.

However, Halia was equally disinclined to indulge in denial. She was awake, at least for the moment unable to fall back asleep, and fed up with herself. She swung her bare feet to the floor and stood up stretching and reaching for the light switch. She fished a paperback out of her suitcase and scanned the table of contents. The Disappearance of Lady Frances Carfax would hit a little too close to home, she decided, so she went with The Adventure of the Bruce-Partington Plans.

An hour and ten minutes later the light clicked off and Halia returned to the cheap motel bed, still not sleepy but resigned to spending the rest of the night there. The black-haired boy figured prominently in her restless dreams. She awoke well into second period according to her middle school adjusted internal clock and started, disoriented, before regaining her bearings.

Halia showered, dressed, and loaded all her "tools" for the day into her day pack. Breakfast was a bagel and coffee purchased at a gas station on Route 9, on her way to the SUNY campus.

The secretary for the division of social sciences needed no help in placing Joann Grant.

"Of course," she smiled at Halia. "Our resident archeologist. Always going to such interesting places, and finding fascinating things on her digs. She retired at Christmas time, didn't she? We threw a lovely party for her, over to the catering place." The woman paused and sized Halia up carefully. "Are you one of her students?" The woman sounded doubtful.

"No, no," Halia hastened to explain why she was standing in front of this woman's desk. "Do you have a current address for her?" Halia asked, tense in her awareness that the entire "mystery" could evaporate in the next five seconds.

"Sure, honey." The secretary didn't look old enough or old fashioned enough to call her honey, but she let it go. The woman tapped Joann Grant into her faculty and staff database, and the Keeseville address that Halia already had appeared on the screen.

"That address is no longer valid," Halia informed the secretary. "Apparently, Joann moved last month. I'm trying to get an address more current than that one."

"Oh." The secretary looked crestfallen.

"Is there anyone here – someone Joann was friendly with, perhaps – who might have her current address?"

The secretary suggested she speak with Dr. Nase

or Dr. Barker and directed her down the hall. Halia stopped at Dr. Nase's door first and read the neatly printed sign indicating office hours during Easter break. Halia checked her watch. Dr. Nase would be in after lunch – that gave Halia several hours to kill. She continued down the hallway to Dr. Barker's door.

The door was open, revealing a small office crowded with books, plants, artifacts, and clothing. The occupant, presumably Dr. Barker, was standing on her desk, a rolled up catalog in her hand. "I'll get you, my pretty!" she crowed, and whacked the de facto swatter against the upper left corner of the window.

"And your little dog too," Halia answered from the doorway.

Nimbly, the sixty-ish grey-haired Dr. Barker scrambled down, more gracefully than Halia thought possible, given her portly frame. Red-faced and puffing, she approached Halia and energetically pumped her hand in greeting. "Joy Barker," she stated.

Halia grinned to herself. She could see how Joann, or anyone else, would come to be friendly with this positively jolly person. Halia was forcefully reminded of Lukey Jane when Dr. Barker shook her hand. "Halia Frank," she replied, "I'm here hoping to find a current address for my -" Halia faltered, uncomfortable. Joann wasn't a family member, nor a friend, and "ex-husband's father's cousin" would lose even this kind woman halfway through. "For my aunt," Halia decided on. "Joann Grant."

"Joann Grant?" Dr. Barker sang out the name loudly. "You want to know where Joann Grant has gone?" Dr. Barker looked confused but a spark of interest lit up her cherubic face. "Who are you? Who is she to you?" Dr.

Barker waved away the notion of Joann being Halia's aunt with a laugh. "I know Joann's nieces and nephews – Justin only had a couple of kids. But Halia … I know that name. You're-"

"Bones' ex-wife." Halia finished the sentence for her. Halia adopted a sheepish expression and explained, "Ex-husband's father's cousin just seemed like a bit of a mouthful."

"Well, come in," Dr. Barker grabbed Halia's wrist and then dropped it. "I change my mind – let's go out. I'm being driven crazy by a fly in here. Would you like a cup of something? Tea? Coffee? Cocoa? We can go to The Other Side – it's just a little snack bar here on campus. We can sit and talk there."

Halia agreed and they walked together past the secretary and out of the building. Halia chatted politely with Dr. Barker about their mutual appreciation of maps, powdered ginger drink mix (with calamansi) and collecting heart shaped rocks. The campus snack bar was only a short walk from the social sciences building, and the genial conversation lasted easily until they were seated.

Halia's tea sat on the formica table top, steaming in its paper cup. Halia ignored it so completely it may as well have been back in Dover. Dr. Barker's information was Halia's sole concern. She waited silently while Dr. Barker removed the plastic lid, blew on her drink, replaced the lid, and took a sip.

"Look, I'm going to be up front with you," Joy Barker began. "I don't know where she is. I know that she moved, but I don't have an address for her."

Halia sat silently, patiently, making no move to touch her tea. Dr Barker fiddled with her tea bag and the plastic packet of honey. Halia waited and eventually Joy continued, "We were friends. Maybe not terribly close, but we did have a real friendship. She confided in me lots of times, but in the last year, as her retirement got closer and closer, I could tell there was something happening in her life, but she never came out and told me the whole story." Joy tilted her head as she spoke, first one way, then the other. "She seemed like maybe she wanted to talk about something – like sometimes she would wait to walk to the parking lot with me, and there were hesitations – you know, pregnant pauses? But I guess she always decided against opening up, because she never did. I figured I could be patient and just wait until she was ready. But after she retired, I heard that she was moving, and then before I got a chance to talk to her again, she was gone." Joy Barker blinked, her chubby face looking serious and sad. "I think eventually she might get in touch with me. I will certainly let her know that you've been looking for her." Joy smiled a kindly smile at Halia. "Perhaps you'll hear from her before too long."

Halia shifted in her chair. Joy interpreted the movement as discomfort, and immediately began apologizing. She reached for Halia's hand across the table with the intent to comfort. Instinctively Halia steadied her tea with one hand before allowing Joy to take the other. The similarity between this woman and Lukey Jane Noyes seemed quite limited, but with hot tea on the table, Halia was taking no chances. Halia murmured her first words since sitting down. "It's ok. I'm not taking any of this personally," she assured Dr. Barker. "I just need to know that she's safe – and I need to pay her back."

Dr. Barker nodded and released Halia's hand. Halia slipped both hands around her tea and contemplated taking a sip. Dr. Barker regarded her for a moment. "You're putting a lot of time and effort into looking for Joann. You drove all the way up here from Dutchess County." It was hard to tell if the comment evinced incredulity at foolishness or admiration at the level of effort. Both, Halia decided.

"It seems like the right thing to do."

"Is this about doing the right thing?" Joy asked. She didn't give Halia time to respond, but continued. "There is someone here in Plattsburgh that you might want to talk to. Joann saw a therapist for a few months last year. I have her name here somewhere." Dr. Barker produced a business card from her purse with surprising speed. "You know how therapists can be – she'll probably cite confidentiality and avoid providing any real information, but you're here … I think it's worth a try."

Halia took the card and thanked Dr. Barker. Halia decided that she would need time later to replay this conversation, slowly, when she had time to observe and catalog every nuance. She had learned much, but she suspected that upon analysis, there would be even more to glean from what remained unsaid.

"I think I should get back to work," Dr. Barker said.

"You have a fly to kill," Halia smiled at her.

"Will you be in Plattsburgh long?" Joy asked.

"I'm actually staying down in Keeseville, near the road to Port Kent. I should be here a couple of days, I guess … depending on how things go."

"Well, be sure to tour the chasm," Dr. Barker took on the role of tour guide for a moment, "and if you're looking for a breakfast place, try McLean's. Joann and I used to go there on the weekends sometimes, before a day of sailing."

"Sailing? I didn't know Joann went sailing," Halia considered the proximity to Lake Champlain and realized sailing was a natural choice of activity.

Dr. Barker was laughing. "Tag sale-ing."

Halia laughed too.

Dr. Barker said her goodbye and left Halia at The Other Side, drinking warm tea and contemplating her next move. Try the therapist, she thought. She wondered if she could convince the therapist to speak with her at all, considering the circumstances. She dialed the phone number on the card.

Rachel Zimmerman, LCSW, had an outgoing answering machine message that indicated that she checked her messages frequently and would attempt to return all phone calls the same day. Halia left her cell phone number for Ms. Zimmerman and hung up.

She was loathe to head back to Keeseville to her dreary motel room, but equally loathe to waste time touristing around Plattsburgh, Burlington, or Montreal when she could be more gainfully employed. She checked her watch and decided to mull over the past two conversations she'd had, call Grace and Louise, and head to Joann's old house in an hour. On her way, she thought, she'd swing by the archeology department once more to see if Dr. Nase had decided to come in early. And perhaps, between now and then, the therapist would call back.

Louise sounded tired and busy, but happy to hear that Halia had safely arrived. She was intrigued by Halia's description of Jacques, and agreed with Halia that things were not becoming any clearer yet. They had to hang up quickly, as Louise was at The Eft, receiving a produce delivery from the CSA at Listening Rock Farm.

Halia tried Grace, but was only able to leave a message. She hung up, checked her watch again, swigged the now cold remains of her tea, and pulled a notebook out of her bag.

She wrote the sentence Jacques Jogue had said on a sheet of paper and studied it. There is no address for where she's gone. Halia considered it a puzzle, a riddle. What places have no address, she asked herself. And from what Joy Barker indicated, it was a place that Joann would either return from or move through in some way. Halia decided to create a list of such places later, perhaps over dinner.

Both the boy at the antique store and Joann's colleague had referred to a secret. Joann seemed to have had a secret – a delicious secret was what Jacques had hinted at – perhaps she shared this secret with at least one other person. Halia found herself too intrigued to be relieved: it was becoming more and more clear that Joann was intentionally missing, but Halia was not ready to sit back and wait to be contacted. A couple more steps down this path, she told herself. Let's just see where a few more steps down this path takes me.

It took Halia a moment to recognize the ring of her cell phone, muffled in her day pack. She flipped open the phone and examined the unfamiliar number on the screen. The area code was wrong for it to be the Plattsburgh therapist. Halia answered as she placed it: Westchester or Rockland County.

"Is this Halia Frank?" a pleasant older man's voice asked.

"Yes."

"This is Justin Grant. You've left a couple of messages for me at the taxi office."

"Oh, hello Mr. Grant." Halia shifted gears seamlessly from her internal musings to being ready to conduct an interview. "I was calling you because I'm trying to find an address for your sister, Joann. I sent her something, but it got sent back to me by the post office, and they don't have a forwarding address for her. I was wondering if you did."

"Last I knew she was way the hell upstate. She worked in Plattsburgh and was living in some tiny little town right around there. I'd know the name of it if you said it."

"Keeseville, New York?" Halia asked.

"Yep, that's it." He seemed pleased with himself, and Halia could almost feel him anticipating being thanked. She ignored the pang of guilt she felt as she informed him as gently as she was able that Joann had retired and moved. "Funny, you know – she didn't mention it."

"You spoke to her?" Halia heard her voice rise with surprise.

"Yep. I bumped into her at the graveyard – you know, Oak Hill. She told me she was down to see the grave and take care of some loose ends here in Nyack." He paused, then continued, half hurt, half suspicious. "She didn't mention moving. Or retiring for that matter."

Halia wasn't sure what to say. She knew she was close to receiving quite a bit more information about Joann, and where she had been recently. She also knew she was perhaps equally close to alienating this man, and that he was key in gaining the next round of leads. Halia decided to risk another question. "When Joann visits the grave, does she stay with you?"

"No, she usually gets a room at one of the motels on Route 59." Justin paused, as if he were thinking something over. He relented. "Joann and I aren't that close. In fact, some years we only talked at the holidays. I guess we each dealt with losing Jesse in different ways."

Halia's mind raced. Jesse. She searched her mental rolodex at top speed, but came up dry. "Who's Jesse?" she asked.

"Bones never told you? Well, I guess that doesn't surprise me." Justin Grant sighed a long deep sigh. "Where are you now? You still live up by Bones? Up by Poughkeepsie somewhere?"

"Yes," Halia replied. "I live near Bones, in Dover Plains."

"Well, that's not all that far from Nyack. Why don't you come down here – we'll talk face to face. It's a long story, all about Jesse and what happened, and I'm not much for talking on the phone."

"Thank you, Mr. Grant," Halia moved swiftly, telephone carefully balanced under her chin, one hand locating a pen, the other removing her calendar from her day pack. "I'd like to meet with you and talk more. I'm actually in Plattsburgh right now, trying to learn more about where Joann is by meeting with her former colleagues. I'll be back in the Hudson Valley in a couple of days."

There was a long pause on the other end of the phone. Halia wondered if Justin Grant had hung up or if they had been disconnected. Then she heard a long measured exhalation.

"You're worried about her." Halia had trouble discerning the emotion behind the gruffly spoken words.

"I owe Joann money," Halia stated simply. "I plan to pay her back."

"You drove all the way to Plattsburgh because you owe her money." He didn't try to keep the sarcasm out of his voice. "Ok." He paused again. Halia waited him out. "Well if you'll drive way the hell up there, then you may as well drive here when you're done. Meet me at The Runcible Spoon on Friday, at 10 o'clock." Halia was scribbling down the name of the restaurant when she realized Justin Grant had hung up.

Halia snapped her phone shut and replaced it in her day pack. Almost immediately, it rang again. Halia checked the phone number before answering, and, as she anticipated, it was Rachel Zimmerman, LCSW – Joann's former therapist.

Halia explained her situation as briefly as she could, ending by asking if she could meet with Ms. Zimmerman since she was in the area, to discuss the situation.

"I do offer free single session consultations," Ms. Zimmerman sounded professionally kind. "I can schedule you in one of those appointment times. Tomorrow morning … can you come in at 11 a.m.?"

"Yes. Thank you," Halia, poised once again with her phone held between shoulder, cheek and chin, took down directions to the woman's office.

Phone calls are temporarily completed, Halia told herself, putting her phone away for the second time. She looked at her scrawled notes and decided to start a new list. Dr. Silas Nase topped the list, followed by a notation to look up the Runcible Spoon on the internet and get directions. Summarize new information was next, with a sublist of the sources of this new information: Joy Barker, Jacques Jogue, and Justin Grant. Come up with a list of questions for Rachel Zimmerman, LCSW, was the last item on the list. Even Halia's lists referenced lists. She thought those tasks would fill up the afternoon nicely.

Halia then took stock of her current situation. She was not especially hungry but it was lunchtime and The Other Side was beginning to fill up with faculty and staff. Halia decided to pack up, swing by the social sciences building to speak with Dr. Nase (if possible), then head back to Keeseville.

As she replaced her pen and notebook in her day pack and gathered her fleece jacket under her arm, she heard Joy Barker's voice calling out to her. Halia turned to see Dr. Barker heading her way, with an athletic look-ing man of about 60 years of age at her side.

"Ms. Frank," Dr. Barker positively hollered from across the room. "This is Dr. Silas Nase." Her voice took on a more conversational tone as she reached Halia. "I bumped into him on my way back to my office. He wanted to meet you." She added in a stage whisper, "He has something to tell you."

"Oh, now Joy, don't make it sound more important than it is," Dr. Nase's firm handshake and Montreal Expo's baseball cap contributed to Halia's positive im-pression of him. "Since the young lady is clearly wor-ried about Joann, I just thought I should tell her – tell you" he looked from Joy to Halia "what I noticed about Joann last semester."

Halia, who had gained her feet before Drs. Barker and Nase approached, sat back down and gestured with her open palm to the other chairs at her table. The two professors seated themselves. Halia sought eye contact with Dr. Nase, and upon gaining it, he continued.

"Joann Grant worked in the same department as Joy and I for more than 15 years."

"More than 20," Joy broke in.

Dr. Nase shot her a pained look, then continued.

"Joann and I worked fairly closely for the past 5 years on the same project for at least half of that time. I got to know her is what I'm trying to say. I saw her moods, I saw her approach to life. We talked about things … sometimes the conversations got pretty personal, you know. After years of getting to know someone that kind of happens." Not always, thought Halia. Some people are careful to avoid that, but apparently not Joann. "Anyway, we talked about retirement – both hers and mine – and our plans. Well, what I wanted to tell you," Dr. Nase leaned toward Halia and lowered his voice, "is that Joann would never say what her plans were. It was clear that she had plans, I could tell that plain as day, but she'd just smile that Mona Lisa smile of hers and sit there looking like the cat that ate the canary." Halia wondered if Dr. Nase always peppered his speech so liberally with idioms. He continued without any verbal encouragement from Halia, her body language sufficient indication that she was riveted. "I don't know where she is, why she sold her house and moved, nor why it all happened now. But I do know this." He paused and Halia leaned in involuntarily. "I saw a change in her after Thanksgiving."

"What sort of change?" Halia asked.

"Well, it's hard to pinpoint, but if I had to sum it up I'd say she looked like she'd fallen in love."

Halia's eyebrows disappeared under her bangs.

"I know the signs. I recognize the glow. She never said a word, even when I asked her straight out, but that's what I saw."

Halia turned to Joy, eyebrows remaining hidden.

"I cannot confirm or deny his diagnosis," Dr. Barker spoke seriously but her eyes twinkled merrily.

Realizing that Halia might misinterpret her gaiety, she explained, "For women our age, the idea of falling in love – that breathless, nervous, can't eat or sleep, can't wait to be with that special person … it can't help but make me smile to think of Joann in such a state." Joy tossed her short grey curls around and jutted her chin out in a mock defiant gesture. "I hope it is true. I hope she did find love. She certainly deserved it."

Halia nodded. To her, the notion of falling in love was a distant and academic one. She understood why Joy looked ready to celebrate, vicariously enjoying even the possibility of her former colleague entering such a state. Halia did understand, she supposed, but she did not share the feeling. Bones had really given love a bad name.

Drs. Barker and Nase left Halia to her thoughts and lists and disappeared into the cafeteria. Well, ok, Halia thought. She fell in love, did she? Big change since Thanksgiving of last year, she reminded herself. Halia did not believe Dr. Nase at face value, but she was ready to consider any reasonable hypothesis. This one would get thorough consideration.

She drove back to Keeseville in silence, allowing her thoughts to wander around superficial topics. She noticed the place Dr. Barker had suggested for breakfast on Route 9: McLean's Dairy Bar. Odd, thought Halia. I definitely would not have guessed that would be the breakfast place of choice. Thinking of Grace's need for goat cheese and balsamic reductions to be featured on a menu (and the word café or bistro to be included in the name), Halia made a mental note to tease Grace mercilessly by describing the specials du jour available in her best faux upstate New York accent.

She slowed down as she drove over Ausable Chasm, wondering if the tour would really be worth the time and money. She realized she could head over to Lake Placid and spend a day skiing at Whiteface, but again decided against it based on time and money. Nevertheless, she thought, I might need a day away from all this to clear my head. Halia considered the available tourist distractions but decided that being away from her work routine and the conveniences of home, and thus being inconvenienced by constantly having to deal with arranging such necessities as eating, sleeping, and driving were sufficient distractions. With that she limited her multitasking to reading Mapquest directions to Joann's former home as she drove.

Halia slowed to a halt on the quiet side street, and looked at all the houses. It was vintage upstate New York: wooden frame two story houses, many of them front gabled with full front porches. Most of them were white, and most were one hundred years old. Halia thought the appearance of the street was not unlike streets she'd seen from Beacon to Gloversville, Cazenovia to Millerton. She scanned the numbers on the turned porch posts from the driver's seat of her Honda Insight, rolling along slowly until she found the one that had been Joann's.

Halia parked her car and stood on the sidewalk, considering her options for the home visit game plan. She shrugged her shoulders and decided to be blunt and bold. She walked up the porch steps and knocked on the door.

A young latina woman answered her knock. After a few tries in broken English and rudimentary Spanish, the woman indicated that Halia should wait, and returned with a child. The girl looked to be about 7 or 8, and apparently was accustomed to translating for her mom. She listened to Halia's request and relayed it to her mother.

"No, señora," the child waited while her mother continued. "We wanted your aunt to hold the mortgage for us, but she said no. She said no because she said she wasn't going to have an address for a while, and there wouldn't be a place to send the checks."

"Oh, si." Halia nodded to the little girl and her mom. "I understand that a little bit, but I still wonder – where is she? Did she say anything else?"

The girl spoke to her mother, listened to a long reply, opened her mouth to speak to Halia, and then closed it blushing and laughing and looked up at her mother. The woman reminded her where to begin, and the little girl began with renewed confidence. "My mother says that your aunt did say many things to my father and mother. She said that this is a good house and a nice town and that the school here is good. She said that she spent a lot of good years in this house and that it has been a happy place for her, and that she was ready to go. She said she wants us to be happy here." The girl paused, consulted with her mother, and continued. "Mami says maybe your aunt is traveling. She says many old people travel when they stop working." Again, they consulted, this time at the mother's insistence. "Mami says she did say something about finishing something she started a long time ago."

"Can your mom explain that even a little bit more?" Halia nearly begged the little girl.

"Ok," the little girl spoke almost like an adult woman comforting a child. "I ask her." The woman's answer came back via the girl, but losing little in intensity. "Your aunt spoke good Spanish, like a person from Spain. When she talked with Mami, Mami says she understood good what Señora Joann said. And Señora Joann said only what I said before: she is going to finish something she started a long time ago, and she said that she was going someplace that didn't have an address. That was all she said. Mami says it was like she was keeping a secret. When she said those things Mami asked her 'what do you mean?' but Señora Joann just smiled and said 'nada.'" The little girl grinned at Halia. "You know this Spanish word: nada – right?"

"Yes." Halia smiled back at her. "Thank you so much for helping me talk to your mom." Halia lifted her eyes from the child to the woman's face. "Muchas gracias, señora."

"Espera! Wait!" The little girl interrupted, speaking to her mother quickly and passionately. The mother answered and the little girl turned to Halia. "Won't you please join us for lunch? Mami cooked arroz con pollo, and it is rico!"

"Rico?" Halia asked.

"Yummy!" The little girl cried and scampered off. Her mother reached out and grasped Halia's arm firmly.

"You come, eat," she said shyly. "La Señora Joann – good lady. You sad. I help. You eat here, aqui, a la casa di tia Joann. Si?"

Halia felt herself being drawn in – emotionally as well as physically. Being unable to speak freely to this woman suddenly underlined every nuance of non- verbal communication. Halia felt this woman emanate the importance of family, and compassion for someone who appeared to be orphaned and abandoned. Halia couldn't explain her own history, her family, her marriage, her childlessness ... she just knew what she presented at the front door: a woman alone seeking someone who was gone. And she felt a tiny salty lump in her throat at the degree of truth in that.

She was led into the house and rapidly the child reappeared carrying a toddler. "Me llamo Delfina," she spoke slowly and clearly to Halia as if Halia were a young child herself. "Y el nino se llama Fortinbras."

"Si??? Fortinbras?" Halia asked, dubious that she had heard correctly.

"No!" Her mom got involved. "El pero se llama Fortinbras. Mi nino se llama Enrique."

"Como te llama?" Delfina asked Halia.

"Me llamo Halia," Halia said her name as clearly as she could. The children both giggled at her American accent and disappeared.

Lunch was a delicious venture into the home of Delfina, Enrique and their mother, Marisol. Halia felt by the end of the meal as if she had been on vacation, somewhere far from upstate New York, and farther still from being a middle school science teacher seeking her ex-husband's father's cousin. She left Aunt Joann's former home – now the home of a vibrant family - with a feeling of satiety that was body-based but transcended the physical.

She checked her watch, and decided to go back to the motel. It was time, she thought, to sit and sort things out. It was starting to rain, and Halia felt ready to retreat from the world into her snail shell of a motel room and take stock.

Dinner hours came and went without hunger as Marisol's portions had been as generous as they were "rico." Halia spent the entire late afternoon and evening writing notes, making lists, reviewing notes from the conversations she'd had thus far, and planning the next day's itinerary. Drained, she fell asleep early and slept a deep dreamless sleep.

She awoke Wednesday morning thoroughly disoriented. A near panicked look at the clock, and the thought of first period starting 25 minutes ago propelled her to her feet before she recognized the motel room and remembered her situation. A second wave of panic hit as she realized she needed to shower, dress, eat, and prepare to meet with Rachel Zimmerman, LCSW. Halia checked her watch and calmed down. Plenty of time, she told herself. Plenty of time.

She decided to head down to Port Kent, to the ferry dock for breakfast, banking on her assumption that such a place would have a snack bar. It did, and she ate a simple and inexpensive meal, looking through the huge windows at the grey drizzle and steely lake. Once again on this trip, Halia found the dining establishment most definitely Not Upscale, and amused herself imagining Grace's discomfort in such a place. Atmosphere-aholic, she thought affectionately. Grace will cringe just hearing about the cafeteria's fluorescent lighting and anti-décor, which was definitely inspired by American public school circa 1970. Actually, this place was Spartan enough to elicit a comment from even the likes of Lukey Jane. Although not typically a connoisseur of food or décor, Lukey would often surprise the gang by revealing a well-informed and distinguished opinion regarding such things. For Halia, every meal was business, first and foremost. Fill the tank, so to speak. Whether in Rome, Italy or Rome, New York, Halia would be able to ignore her surroundings – grand or otherwise - equally effectively in order to quell a physical need and move on to the task at hand.

She went over her list for the day and her questions for Rachel Zimmerman, before circling back to the two key questions that nagged at her: what was Aunt Joann's secret, and what place has no address? Halia pondered these absently tapping her pen against her open notebook, and allowing her gaze to glaze over into a vacant almost sleepy stare in the direction of Vermont. She had some ideas, nascent and unformed. She jotted two words onto a blank page in her notebook, then suddenly, violently, snapped the book shut, collected her belongings, and strode along the small sandy beach back to her car.

Rachel Zimmerman, LCSW, was older than Halia but younger than Joann. She greeted Halia warmly at the door of her home office on Route 9 just outside downtown Plattsburgh. Halia, as always, noticed everything there was to glean from a visual inspection. She realized than Joann had selected this woman to confide in and learn from, and that now she herself was about to do the same. She remembered how exposed she had felt that night in the graveyard when she spoke to Asha for the first time. She'd prefer to avoid a similar emotional experience, if possible.

All this in mind, Halia stated her case as clearly and concisely as she could. As she finished explaining why she had come to see Ms. Zimmerman, she noticed the therapist's body language change very slightly.

"You've come to see me hoping to discover your relative's secret?" Ms. Zimmerman's warmth dissipated very slightly. "But surely you understand confidentiality? I can't tell you anything about any of my patients, past or present, without their written consent. You must be aware of that."

"Well, yes," Halia felt a touch of temper burn color into her cheeks. "Although I do know about confidentiality, yes, I did hope that perhaps there would be some way we could talk that would be legal and ethical, and yet help me find an address for this woman. I was thinking perhaps we could speak hypothetically…"

"You need an address for this woman because …" Ms. Zimmerman's voice and eyebrows rose in unison.

"I owe her money. I need an address to which I can mail monthly payments."

"You knew I couldn't divulge any information and yet you came to see me anyway." She did a fair job of appearing to muse aloud.

Halia felt her jaw muscles begin to clench involuntarily. "Yes." She considered saying more, but didn't fully trust her ability to be professional and courteous.

Ms. Zimmerman leaned in and sought eye contact with Halia. "I don't buy it. You wouldn't waste your time or mine with something so obviously impossible. You seem far too intelligent for that." She paused, but not long enough for Halia to respond. "And I don't believe this is about money." Again a brief pause. "When you are ready to work, I'll be here, ready to help. But you know the only one we can work with is you." This pause was even shorter. "Oh, I can see you're angry. But are you really angry with me? Or are you angry at the woman who moved, for leaving you?" Rachel Zimmerman was on a roll and gaining momentum. "Your anger is energy – let's use that energy for healing, to move forward. What do you think?" The woman's enthusiasm was palpable and Halia experienced it as an assault.

In response, Halia pressed her lips together and stood up. Her exit was so fast she heard the door bang shut behind her almost before she knew she was leaving. It was distant, as if she had wads of cotton wool in her ears – the sound reached her through the much louder pounding of her own angry pulse. It wasn't until she was behind the wheel of her car that she realized tears were streaming down her face.

"This is Halia. May I speak with Grace, please?" She fought to keep her voice even, to breathe without hiccupping sobs.

"Hali?" Grace sounded concerned. "Are you ok?"

Melting under the warmth of Grace's caring voice, Halia utterly dissolved. She managed to choke out a report of the past twenty-four hours, starting with Jogue's antiques and ending with Rachel Zimmerman's attempt to engage Halia in psychotherapy.

"Oh Hali, you must be so frustrated," Grace said compassionately.

Halia half sobbed, half coughed in reply.

"Hali, did she really invite you to work on your anger issues?" Grace asked gently.

Suddenly Halia saw the past 30 minutes through new eyes. Grace felt the change before Halia even spoke. "Ok, I'm beginning to see the humor in this."

Grace started to laugh. "You need anger management? You?" She laughed harder.

Halia joined in laughing and hiccupping as her sobs dissipated. "Hang on, Grace, I'm a mess. Let me wipe all this snot and spit off the phone."

When Halia returned, Grace said, "Well, that was earthy of you." She paused then continued, her voice once again full of care and concern. "What happens next?"

Halia took a deep breath. She'd been so distracted by her frustration at all the quasi clues and lack of real information, she had allowed her upcoming meeting with Joann's brother to slip her mind. She told Grace about her conversation with Justin Grant and her appointment with him Friday morning.

"That sounds kind of dark, but it also sounds like maybe you will finally find out something."

Halia heard background noise from the animal hospital, and said, "You'd better go, Grace. Tell Louise and Rose that I'll drive home tomorrow."

"Really? Tomorrow?" Grace asked. "Are you sure there isn't anything else you need to do while you're there?"

"Yes. I've pretty well covered these bases. I want some time at home before I have to go back to school." Halia silently ran through the list of tasks that awaited her as a homeowner and middle school teacher, above and beyond the lists searching for Joann created. "I want some time to prepare for the school week." Thinking out loud she said "I'll meet you at The Eft on Friday, as usual, ok? I'll have met with Justin that morning, so I may have something to report."

"Sounds good. I'll see you then," Grace called to someone in the animal hospital "I'll be right there!" before reminding Halia to drive safely and call if she needed anything. Halia agreed and they both hung up, Halia in much better shape than when she had picked up the phone.

Halia did take Joy Barker's advice and went to McLean's Dairy Bar for lunch on her way back to Keeseville. She was pleasantly surprised by the homemade goodness of her chicken pot pie and left the restaurant feeling almost too full. Needing to walk off the stuffed sensation, she spent the afternoon wandering around Ausable Chasm, braving the cold mist and staunchly ignoring the strange lonely feeling that had settled in her core.

The motel room depressed Halia that night to such a large degree that she actually turned on the television and watched mindless tv shows for several hours. Eager to get home, Halia left Keeseville early Thursday morning, aiming for an arrival back in Dover by mid afternoon.

She sorted through the pile of mail Rose left neatly stacked on her kitchen table, tossing junk mail into her recycling bin unopened. After an hour or so of unpacking, tidying, and organizing, Halia used the internet to obtain directions to The Runcible Spoon in Nyack. She indulged in the hope that the coffee would be to her liking. Ready for her meeting with Justin Grant, Halia decided to move around a bit as an antidote for the morning's long car ride.

The weather was acceptable for walking outdoors, so Halia headed for the cemetery. She walked as one hungry for motion, arms swinging, and legs pumping. Seamlessly, she broke into a run at the gates and sprinted the length and breadth of the graveyard in an "L" pattern. Doubling back she slowed to a walk, reading stones and compulsively adding or subtracting to come up with ages or dates. She actually circled the entire graveyard a second time, enjoying her mathematical calisthenics, enjoying the sensation of her body in motion and un-encased by a vehicle, and even (despite resisting this notion intellectually) enjoying being back on familiar turf. "The next thing I know, I'll be calling this place home," she chided herself.

Friday morning Halia woke up to her alarm, and went through the mechanics of morning without thinking or feeling much of anything. Her level of preparedness rendered that possible, even easy. She trained herself to stay in the moment, looking at her toast, tasting her coffee, emptying her consciousness to allow room for the moment in all its fullness to rush in and soak every crevice and chink of awareness. She collected her items neatly laid out for the trip, and headed south.

The car ride was somewhat less zen in nature. Halia let her mind wander, exploring the puzzles Keeseville's conversations left her grappling with. What places have no address? Where can one go, in the 21st century, that has no address? Just how literally was Halia to take those words? And what kind of direction should she go in if a figurative meaning is indicated? The lady holds a secret, has a secret smile, looks to be in love, changed noticeably after last Thanksgiving, and has gone somewhere that has no address. And, Halia thought sardonically, doesn't especially seem to need cash.

Halia was on time, and The Runcible Spoon was bigger and more crowded that she expected. From the sound of Justin's gruff voice and gruffer attitude, Halia expected a place that might have felt less inviting, less youthful and hip, than the Runcible Spoon. She got her coffee at the counter and scanned for a man of Justin Grant's age. Her eyes met the ice blue eyes of a heavy grey-haired man sitting alone in the corner by the front window, the only man of his age in the place. He nodded to her and half stood up. She made her way over to the table and sat down across from him. "Halia?" he asked.

"Mr. Grant," she began, but he cut her off.

"Call me Justin," he interrupted. "We're not going to

bother with being formal." He appraised her critically and stated, "Bones is an idiot. Everyone in the family knows it." He saw her face change and continued, "I just wanted to get that out of the way. We all knew you were too good for him, but you know how that goes." Justin shrugged heavily. "Everybody makes their own mistakes."

"Justin," Halia started again, "you saw Joann last week?"

"Yeah, last week, or the week before ... it wasn't a long time ago, but it might have been as much as two weeks. Something like that."

"Did she say where she was going? After Nyack, I mean. After visiting Jesse's grave."

"No. We didn't talk much. When I tell you about how Jesse died, maybe you'll understand why." He looked hard into Halia's face, his brow creased in concentration or anger – Halia was not certain which. "Jesse and I were twins. Joann is three years older. We grew up in Pottersville, but our parents lived here, in Nyack, as kids. That's why the graves are here, up in Oak Hill Cemetery. Jesse, and my parents are all up there together." He took a sip of coffee and Halia subconsciously mirrored him, tasting hers. It was good.

"Like I said, we grew up in Pottersville and Jesse and I could be a little wild. Nothing really bad, you know, but we drove Joann crazy. Practical jokes, pranks, tricks – there must be a million different ways we cuckolded her right into some type of trap, usually ending up with Jesse jumping out of somewhere yelling 'Boo!' and making Joann scream her head off. He was always coming up with something, and it would start with me begging Joann for help – 'come look for Jesse' or 'come quick, Jesse's hurt' or something like that." Justin had softened somewhat talking about his twin brother. The fond memories seemed to make him almost happy, if such a word could be used. Halia felt herself bracing emotionally for what was coming.

"The summer we were 14, Joann was 17. Our family went camping at North Lake, in the Catskills. Our parents let us go with Joann to the big waterfall over there – Kaaterskill Falls. A whole bunch of kids were going – most of the teenagers in the whole campground. It was a hot day – mid-July – and when we got there, tons of kids were already messing around in the pool at the bottom of the falls. A bunch of us were jumping off rocks, but Joann got too cold pretty quick and left Jesse and I in the pool there while she went to get her towel. I saw her up by the path, wrapped in that towel, trying to make time with some guy. Well, Jesse got the stupid idea to dive in off this one big rock – he had to climb pretty high to get up there. We all thought he was going to jump, but he did this-" Justin's voice began to reveal the emotion just below the surface as he passed his hand over his eyes. "He did this swan dive into the pool. He didn't come up. At first I barely noticed – there was a ton of kids there, and I stopped watching him so closely after he dove. I was just waiting for him to come up next to me and say 'How was that?' – you know?" Halia nodded, feeling tears well up in her own eyes. "It was a couple of minutes before I started looking for him and fretting. I might have been 14, but I was just a scared kid at heart whenever anything went wrong, so I went running off to get my big sister." Justin cleared his throat, a deep rumbling sound that made Halia suspect years of smoking. "Joann wouldn't listen to me. It sounded exactly like the beginning of a dozen other

tricks we played on her, and there were rocks every-
where, perfect for jumping out from behind. But no, she
was too busy trying to flirt with some guy to come help
me." Justin was openly crying now, dabbing at his face
with the restaurant's paper napkins. "She was a better
swimmer than me. Maybe she could have saved him ...
We sent other kids back to get help at the campground
and get our parents. Some kids started looking for
him in the woods, or behind the falls, stuff like that.
They had gotten to know us a little and thought maybe
Jesse was playing a trick on all of us, hiding somewhere
ready to scare us really bad once we gave him up for
dead." Justin blew his nose and struggled to regain his
composure. "It took a little while, but we found him.
Hit his head underwater. Joann blamed herself, but got
mad at me for blaming her. I blamed myself but took it
out on Joann. We just kind of hurried on to being grown
up and away from each other and our parents and our
memories." Again Justin cleared his throat, and Halia
felt a wave of compassion and concern for this coarse
old man wash over her. "I came here, Joann went to
Plattsburgh, and our folks struggled to keep it together
in Pottersville for a few more years, but carrying on really was more than either of them could manage. They
were probably blaming themselves too."

Halia wiped away her own tears. She had origi-
nally thought to take notes, and brought a notebook for
that purpose, but each word of Justin Grant's narrative
burned indelibly into her memory. She whispered hus-
kily, "I'm so sorry. What a terrible loss for all of you."

Justin nodded and looked away. "So now you want
to find Joann, and I didn't even know she was missing.
Is that what you'd call ironic?"

"Perhaps."

"What are you going to do next?" There was both concern and distrust in his voice.

"I have a clue, sort of … maybe one or two leads to follow." Halia summarized for Justin her findings while in Keeseville.

"Well, I'm sure I can't help you with figuring out her secrets," Justin responded. "We haven't really talked about anything in 50 years."

"How about her going someplace that has no address? Any ideas about that?"

"No. I don't even know if she's playing games with those words. It almost sounds like a riddle – an old fashioned riddle."

"Yeah," Halia agreed, "and I haven't come up with a solution yet. Is there anything else you can think of that might help? Anything she said to you, even if it's not about where she is or where she's going, that might lead us somewhere?"

"No," Justin had fully returned to his pre-story crankiness. "And don't say 'us.' Don't drag me into this. I'm not looking for her – you are."

"I'm sorry," Halia said automatically. "I didn't mean to speak for you. I'm sorry …" She retreated into silence, vicariously experiencing the pain of losing Jesse, and 50 years of guilt, sadness, and anger. She felt old beyond her own 37 years. Old, tired, and raw, and she knew she was feeling all that Justin had been unable to put into words. She raised her eyes from her lap to look into his and held his gaze. They sat in silence, wordlessly crossing the gulf that lay between them, each absorbing the truth of the other's existence, measured breath by breath. It was the old man who spoke first.

"You go. That's all I had to say to you." His voice and his eyes were gentle now, his words blunt but without malice. "Go on. Go find her. And when you do, call me. I'll be wanting to hear that she's ok."

Halia left him sitting at the table in the window, looking out at Broadway on a Friday morning, on a warm spring day. As she got in her car, she noticed the old silver-blue sedan with the Bud's Taxi magnetic sign on the door, parked across the street.

Halia drove north on Broadway to the park on the banks of the Hudson. She left the car under the sycamores, and walked beyond the picnic area, to the small beach. She sat down on the sand and drew her fingers through it, making patterns, ignoring the chill and dampness. A family strolled by: mother, father and two daughters. The children burst onto the beach with unbridled exuberance – the father, a dark-skinned short man with a huge smile began playing a silly game with them that involved screaming, running, and giggling. The mother, a redhead with an hourglass figure and a British accent, called to all of them to be careful several times before giving up and joining the game. After several minutes they moved on, heading back up the hill towards Broadway. Halia thought they probably hadn't noticed her tears.

Chapter 5

Inertia – inert - that sense of death and stillness. Stripped of its association with apathy, inertia sounds innocent – just keep going until something (or someone?) pushes or pulls you in a new direction. The notion of a body continuing to do what it was doing until someone or something interferes with it – now that sounds like my ex-husband. In relationships inertia makes one think of long afternoons spent wallowing in angst, feeling sorry for oneself and all the richness one could be enjoying if that dud of a partner would just step up to the plate. Life could be a jewelry commercial, complete with cozy fireplaces, playful roughhousing, and an emotionally tweaking soundtrack. Life could be the fantasy you had when you were 7 years old and you thought to yourself, each time your parents fought, or yelled at you, "I'll do it right when I'm grown up." Life could be satisfying, without the loneliness, the dull hollow feeling when you tell people you're "fine," the ache. And yet you don't leave. You stay, inert.

*When the end came for me, after years of idiotic hopeful-
ness that his inertia would magically disappear one day if I
was patient enough or enthusiastic enough or sexy enough,
ad nauseum, it packed a wallop beyond anything I could have
imagined. Remembering makes me slightly dizzy; my eyes go
blurry, not with tears but with the confusion of unanticipated
impact. Whiplash. The image of him with her – that stunned
moment of unveiling, not only all that he was, but just as im-
portantly all that we were not and never had been – assaulted
me. It swims before my eyes as if I had been struck – in the
head, in the heart, in the pit of the stomach... all, simultaneously. The result was definitely diagnosable post traumatic
stress disorder – the dreams, the intrusive images, the ambiva-
lent avoidance and the secret longing to return to that spot,
and to all the spots where we had been. Never before had I understood the twisted mind of the stalker so well – the desire to
just drive past his house – for what? To worry at the inflamed
wound a little more by seeing her car there? To nurse insane
self-negating false hope that I could go back in time to when he
loved me (a fiction) – that she was a blip (also a fiction), and
that we really could reconcile (a self destructive fiction), that I
could forgive (What if I do? What if I can't?) ...*

*Halia never forgave Bones, and if the past is any predic-
tor of the future at all, never will. And Halia, ruling queen of
the exception, does not remain connected to Bones through her
refusal to forgive. She has cut him out, opted for the psychic
surgery approach, and removed him like a tumor. Nothing –
pure absence – is an improvement over the presence of Bones
in her psyche.*

Halia chose the Bear Mountain Bridge as her Hudson River crossing. She knew it was not necessarily faster, more direct, or easier in any way than taking the Thruway up to Newburgh, but it was her choice nevertheless. There was something about the Bear Mountain Bridge's toll plaza – it reminded Halia of a fairy tale castle. After paying the toll, crossing the high narrow bridge gave rise to the feeling of crossing a moat. The naked face of Anthony's Nose loomed over her, and Halia indulged herself in an aesthetic and visceral rather than intellectual experience of it. She chose not to think, but to feel. She did not think about history and the American Revolution and Benedict Arnold's flight, or the chains across the Hudson. She did not think about native tribes using the river, knowing its tides, and all they must have seen – the seals, the eagles, the sturgeon and stripers and shad. She did not think about the unit on the earth's crust she was soon to begin with her seventh graders, and the process of formation of the huge rocky outcroppings of both Anthony's Nose and Breakneck.

She wallowed instead in immediate emotional experience, and let the enormous rock and the deep narrows of World's End dwarf her. It had been an emotional morning – a fitting culmination of an emotional week, and Halia felt as though the morning left a stain, an indelible residue on her very skin. Letting in the pain and the knowledge of Justin's story had changed Halia forever and she knew it. She knew she would drive back to Dover and return to her middle school classroom on Monday and go right back into being Ms. Frank, but she also knew that a subtle but profound shift had occurred and that she would never look at the world in quite the same way again.

"Goddamn, I want to know where Joann is." Halia allowed herself to murmur the words she had been keeping at bay for several weeks now. Her brow furrowed, her knuckles white, the miles of pale green early spring rolled by as Halia made her way north and east across Putnam and Dutchess counties.

In Hopewell Junction, she noticed the marquee in front of the hardware store on route 82. Halia's eyes took in the words and she responded before her brain caught the full meaning. "FLY SPRAY GAL," she read. "Fly spray gal," she repeated to herself slowly and thick with confusion. She pictured a young woman – the Fly Spray Gal – wearing a plaid button down shirt and a ten gallon hat. And she smiled. For the first time in what felt like months, if not years, Halia grinned spontaneously out of pure amusement. The picture of the Fly Spray Gal, coupled with the sudden dawning upon Halia of the sale on insecticide, hit her hard in the funny bone and Halia did not even attempt to restrain the laughter that threatened to erupt. The glow of the private joke, albeit at her own expense, stayed with her all the way home, and throughout the evening.

It was last Tuesday at lunchtime that Asha had entered The Blue Eft, striding in with more resolve than was her norm. She approached the bar as a woman with something on her mind. It wasn't until Louise informed her that Halia was away for a few days that Asha's awkwardness and hesitation returned. She was silent and for a moment Louise thought she looked poised on the verge of tears.

"What's wrong, Asha?" Louise, nearly ten years Asha's junior, adopted a motherly tone.

"I had to run in to work, down at the elementary," Asha jerked her thumb southward to indicate which school. "I couldn't find what I was looking for in my office – a parent's phone number – so I went to the main office to ask the secretary. She wasn't at her desk, but I couldn't help but notice my name on her computer screen." Asha took a shaky breath. "She was typing a memo about me." Asha sighed, elbows on the bar, and jammed her knuckles into her eye sockets. They came away wet. "It was pretty bad. The gist of it was enough for me to understand that people have been complaining to the principal about me, and that my caseload, among other things, is under scrutiny."

"What a way to find out," Louise said, handing Asha a soft blue bandanna for her tears.

Asha nodded, accepting the cloth, and using it on her cheeks while swallowing hard. "I knew something was going on – I could feel it. You know that nervous feeling in the pit of your stomach that you can't quite connect to any one thing?" Asha's eyelashes held sparkling tears. Louise nodded. "I had been feeling that for a while – just the shadow of weirdness... ugliness... that wasn't ever really identifiable. I'd get terse notes in my mailbox, but then everything would seem alright for a day or two... and I couldn't ever find anything to fix upon, to say there it is, that's what I'm doing wrong." Asha's eyes remained glued to the bar under her elbows. "So I guess it's good to finally know something concrete. I just have a bad feeling that this is the beginning." Asha looked older and more tired than Louise had ever seen her as the impact of her words drained her face of color.

Her voice dropped to a hoarse whisper. "My gut feeling is that this is the beginning of the end."

"Are you sure you're not just being paranoid?" Louise spoke with too much emphasis, and then realized how she must sound and hurried on, not meaning to accuse Asha, nor meaning to cast doubt upon her ability to read the situation. "I mean, you have tenure, don't you? And why would anyone want you to leave? I've heard about your work from some of the regulars in here. Well, yeah, I guess if your work is known to the regulars in a local bar maybe that's not great," Louise tried humor, to no avail. "But these folks said you really helped them out. Why would teachers or anyone for that matter want you to go?"

Asha looked miserable. "I've asked myself that question over and over again. One thing I think might have influenced people is the way I was hired." Louise raised one eyebrow. "I suspect that maybe at budget time the year before I was hired there was one of those polls or something like that where teachers indicate which new positions they believe the building needs. What if social worker won out over something a bunch of teachers really wanted – a math specialist or a librarian or something – and what if the administration weighed in on the decision in some way? There would be resentment before I ever walked in the door, which is kind of what I felt that first year." Asha looked up at Louise, searching her face. Louise nodded encouragement to explain further. "I didn't understand it and I don't think I handled it well at all. I kind of blundered into a political trap the principal set that first year, and I remember clearly being told, in not so many words, 'stay out of our classrooms and don't interfere unless we tell you what to do.' I thought I could do my job and stay out of their way, but I was wrong. I really should have interfered a lot more, and just pushed for open conflict, and should have kept at it until there was a more healthy resolution, but I didn't." Asha paused, and took a sip of the water Louise had placed in front of her. "I was too afraid, too intimidated, to stake out my territory and insist I had a right to be there and 'bother' them. Besides, I had absolutely no mentor, no supervisor, no leadership, and no support – I should never have thought that was an ok work environment, but I was desperate. And you know what else? Way back in social work school, I swore I'd never be a school social worker – I just thought I wouldn't like the work or the population enough to put up with the school setting." Asha sighed again, wiping at her cheeks again with the bandanna.

"I think maybe this is the result – the seeds were sown back that far – and all the years of teachers not referring kids to me, and me pounding my head against the walls trying to figure out why, can really be explained pretty simply: they set out to make me look bad from the beginning and they had the power to do that. They succeeded." With that melodramatic finish, Asha lowered her head and stopped fighting back the tears.

Louise laid a hand on Asha's forearm, and for a moment felt tears well up in her own eyes, fed by memories from her own collection of unpleasant work experiences. She suspected, hoped, that Asha really was just being paranoid, but not knowing the inner working of the school system, she gave Asha's explanation fair consideration while she said, "Go ahead and fall apart if you need to. Don't bother with being brave – it's overrated. But once you're done beating yourself up or freaking out, then take a step back and get some perspective. Yeah, that was rotten, but now you know more about who you are dealing with. You learned something important about complainers and how the administration deals with them. Information can be really valuable. Take stock of the whole situation, and remember to keep your perspective." Asha looked like she was beginning to endure rather than benefit from this Louise's attempts at comfort and support. She changed tacks. "Besides, you know you're going to bury them." Asha's eyes widened; she looked almost nervous. "It's an expression," Louise hurried to explain. "You'll outlast them – they'll retire before you leave, that's all." Asha relaxed visibly.

Asha heaved a heavy sigh and repeated numbly, "I just needed a phone number. There is a family I made arrangements to check in with later this week."

"Y'think I might have the number here?" Louise wasn't sure if Asha was asking her for help or just spinning her wheels.

"I can't ask you for anyone's phone number. Confidentiality. That's the last thing I need – to actually give them a reason to fire me." Asha visibly tensed.

"Ok. But Larry and I, tending bar, might be able to find an opening in the conversations that spring up around here, where maybe we could get someone to call you?"

"You can send people to me the way you guys always do. If someone needs help, it's fine to tell them to call me. I'll be picking up messages from my voicemail this week at least a couple of times." Asha, elbows still on the bar, rested her forehead on her open palms, her fingers in her hair. "This is going to be hard."

"Do you have any other plans for the rest of the week?" Louise tried changing the subject, hoping to distract Asha a little.

"Well," Asha colored deeply. "Rob and I are trying to spend some time together, maybe Thursday afternoon. He said something about taking me to see incredible wildflowers in Pawling, but he's been really busy with landscaping and gardening jobs up on Quaker Hill. And I do have Pearl for half the vacation." Asha brightened considerably as she reviewed her plans for the week. Louise listened as Asha talked about hiking with Brulee and her daughter in the Catskills, going for extra long runs on the Appalachian Trail, sheetrocking the kitchen ceiling, and so on. Louise could see that Asha thrived on keeping busy and working hard.

"I think most people wouldn't accomplish in a year what you set out to do in a week!"

Asha shrugged. "My mama didn't raise no slouch." She wasn't smiling.

"Well if things ever get really bad, you can always work here. I have a feeling you'd work hard enough for me." Louise half joked.

"Thanks a lot." Asha quipped, her voice tight with sarcasm.

Asha left, and Louise changed places, from tending the bar to seated at it. After several minutes of collecting the necessities for her next task, the bar in front of her held an unconventional still life: a half-full glass of seltzer, with a quarter of a lime squashed against the side of the glass by the back of a spoon, a yellow legal pad, a green-inked gel pen, a 40 mm swarovski crystal with a red ribbon for hanging, and Louise's favorite rose quartz bracelet, all scattered where she had abandoned them. Louise saw none of it, her gaze unfocused, allowing her vision of The Blue Eft several months down the road with her calendar of events in full swing to develop. The Beckerman and Levine show had been a real lesson to her – Louise needed to do a much better job of getting the word out. Yes, it had been Good Friday, but Louise felt that the sparse crowd had been a wake up call. It was time to do a calendar of events and promote the hell out of it.

So far, Louise had compiled a list of possible but unconfirmed events. A poetry reading by Venus Vison, the black and blue ice cream party, a performance by Asha's Shakespeare Club, and an encore concert by Beckerman and Levine took Louise's calendar of events into early fall. Louise felt that the fall holidays – Halloween and Thanksgiving, anyway, should be allowed to inspire but not necessarily dictate the events that take place at that time.

Her next list was of community events. Louise wanted to dovetail with the town as much as possible – thus Venus' poetry reading was scheduled for the evening of the bicentennial celebration. That way, Louise reasoned, Venus would finish in time for the crowd to walk across the street to watch the fireworks from the park. The ice cream party made sense scheduled on the afternoon of the town-wide tag sale day, and Asha's kids could perform after the picnic lunch on the elementary school's field day. Beckerman and Levine would draw a crowd, Louise decided, even if they weren't piggy-backed on another event, as long as Louise got the word out.

The third piece of paper lying on the bar covered in Louise's chicken scratch was a list of advertising options and opportunities. Louise had generated a healthy list of community calendars, both in print and online, as well as a collection of local radio stations to whom she would mail press releases.

She was sitting at the bar, oblivious to her lovely mess, wracking her brains for the missing ingredient – the single additional icing on the cake thing that would help her feel complete and confident. She wrestled with the nagging sense of Almost – and felt like she was spinning her wheels.

Larry approached hesitantly, seeing the look on her face. "Working on your 'Currant Events'?" he joked.

Louise's face cleared. "That's it!" she shrieked, and leapt to her feet. "You're a genius!" She shouted, grabbing Larry's head between her palms and planting an enthusiastic if not sisterly kiss on his forehead. She swept the bar clear of her junk, deftly sorting work items from personal ones and dumping the bracelet and crystal into a jacket pocket while she slid the lists into the back of the pad. Louise tossed her braid across her throat and over one shoulder in a playfully dramatic gesture, and waltzed across the room, headed for the tiny office next to the kitchen where all her technology was housed. For Louise, the next few hours involved telephones, fax machines, emails, graphic design for her flyer, and printing. Larry knew not to expect to see Louise again until she was finished. His original reason for seeking her out in the first place would just have to wait.

The Wednesday after Easter dawned clear, warm and beckoning, promising to be one of the year's ten best days. The sun offered real warmth, not just an early spring tease. Spring fever spread like wildfire throughout the Hudson Valley, inspiring phones to ring at workplaces from Ellenville to Boston Corners with every manner of excuse. If the sweetness of the sun failed to wreak havoc with a work ethic on that glorious April morning, nothing would.

Luckily, Grace had planned this day off weeks in advance, coordinating schedules with Eddie so that they had Andrew's school vacation adequately covered. This Wednesday, the vacation midpoint, Grace and Eddie indulged in a combined day off – an eagerly anticipated treat in their world of tag team parenting.

Grace woke up early, and, as usual, was the first one downstairs. She pulled a grubby sweatshirt and battered pair of Wellingtons on over her pajamas and headed for the barn. That first breath of warm air, and the first palpable touch of spring sunshine left no doubt in her mind – today was the day to return to Columbia County. She trudged across the yard, planning in her mind a day that would engage and delight all three of them. The excitement of a quest put a spring in her step and a twinkle in her eye. As she fed the horses she thought to herself, "I seek the Philmontian coati. How silly is that?"

By Friday evening, The Eft fairly buzzed with anticipation. Grace arrived first, her last patient of the day, a terrier with anal gland issues, having cancelled and rescheduled. Grace was not especially disappointed; emptying anal glands was one of her least favorite veterinary procedures. Catheterizing cats was up there on the least favorite list too.

Grace was almost fidgety waiting for Halia. They had spoken only briefly on the phone a few times during the week, and Grace felt as though she was reading a cliffhanger without owning her own copy. She was anxious to hear the play by play firsthand and to lend her friend the support she deserved. She was also anxious to share her tale of adventure in Philmont, but concerned that perhaps Halia would not be capable of enjoying the story as she might be justifiably preoccupied with Joann's disappearance. Grace told herself, for the seventeenth time in half as many minutes that she would just feel it out and see what kind of mood Halia was in. Grace sipped her alizarin smoke and waited.

Halia and Asha entered the bar together, having bumped into each other on the front doorstep. Grace noticed immediately that both women looked worn and somber. Grace also noticed for the first time that Halia and Asha looked somewhat alike, and could actually pass as sisters. This evening, the "sisters" looked as if they could use a long talk with close friends.

They approached Grace together, and sat down without speaking to each other or Grace. Grace hesitated, looking from one to the other. At the same time, Halia and Asha took note of each other and Grace, and all three of them spoke the same words at once: "What's wrong?"

Amid the ensuing laughter, Asha spoke up first. "Rob and I had our first fight. Well, just a tiff, really, just a misunderstanding, but it's like the icing on the cake. It's been a tough week." Grace and Halia both encouraged the young woman to continue, each of them feeling relieved that nothing more serious had happened to Asha. She told her tale of woe – Rob had surprised her by taking her to the recently opened Malinois Museum in lower Manhattan. While Asha had been charmed by the building – an old warehouse on Peck Slip – she had taken issue with some of the exhibits, arguing with Rob over the appropriateness of some of the displays. Asha felt Rob had been dismissive and arrogant in pressing his point in defense of the curator, and Asha had gotten angry and emotional. It had been a long cold drive back to Dutchess County in stony silence. Now Asha wasn't sure whether to apologize and try to patch things up or wait for Rob to contact her.

"And on top of all this, I have weird crap going on at work, and I'm absolutely dreading going back there on Monday." Halia and Grace exchanged amused glances at the phrase "weird crap." As Asha explained about the discovery that she was the subject of a memo – and that her performance, case load and level of service to teachers were all under a microscope – Halia spoke up.

"This happens. I was warned by the chair of the science department when I was being mentored. Who was your mentor?"

"I didn't have one."

"Well, who's the head of your department?"

"There isn't a department. I'm the only district-hired social worker in the whole district."

"Oh…" Halia realized how alone Asha must feel, and responded with compassion. "You know how to deal with this, don't you?" Halia sought Asha's eyes and held her gaze. "You know how to be careful? How to watch your back?" Asha nodded. "Pretend it's your first week at work. Forget any history you have with any of these people, and just pretend it's all brand new to you. Don't waste any energy being hurt. Just be wise, professional, and careful. And keep focused on what's really important – the kids, and your own life: Pearl, your house, Brulee, running, Rob ..." Halia succeeded in making Asha smile.

Grace chimed in. "Things will work out with Rob. Don't fret over that either. I'll bet you another alizarin smoke that you and Rob leave this bar together this evening."

Asha brightened up considerably and went to the bar to get drinks for the three of them. Halia waited until she returned to begin recounting of her week's events.

Halia was a patient and detailed storyteller, and she began with the strange episode at the bric-a-brac store south of Keeseville. As she finished describing the Buffalo china, Asha suddenly interrupted.

"Hey, wait a minute!" Both Grace and Halia looked at her expectantly. "I think I know something about Aunt Joann." Halia's eyebrows sailed northward behind her bangs. Asha took that as her cue to continue. "There was a night I came in here to meet Joe – that actor Louise knows? – about the Shakespeare Club. I was waiting for him at the bar, and I couldn't help overhearing some guy with a nasal voice and a Yonkers accent talk about getting all kinds of stuff for free."

"Freecycle Sam," Halia and Grace said in unison.

"Yeah, I think he said the word 'Freecycle.' Anyway he talked about driving way upstate to get a whole bunch of stuff from a retired older woman who was moving. I'm sure I heard him say Keeseville because I pictured K-E-Y-S ville, like lock and key, when he said it, and I'm sure he said he got Buffalo china from her. Maybe he chatted with her and found out where she moved to?" Asha's story ended with a crescendo of hope.

"Grace, what is Freecycle Sam's real name?" Halia used the tone of voice normally reserved for errant seventh graders.

"Oh no," Grace groaned. "I have no idea. His first name begins with a J – I'm sure of that – but I don't think I ever heard his last name. Louise might know."

"Or Rob," Asha added. "I think Rob knows him from the plant business."

Halia was nodding and hurrying over to the bar before Asha was even finished. She returned looking tense. "Louise isn't here. Larry didn't know his name." She pulled out a pen and a list from her Santa-sack-sized purse. "A lead to add to the list…"

She resumed telling about her foray into Joann's former surroundings. She described Joy Barker and Silas Nase, and shrugged her shoulders as she told of Dr. Nase's belief that Joann had fallen in love. Asha and Grace considered this, Grace offered the comment: "A woman in love is capable of extraordinary and unpredictable things." Asha looked at Grace as if she wasn't sure whether to agree with her or take offense at her words.

"Is that original?" she asked.

"I can't remember," Grace responded. Halia frowned a tiny impatient frown. Both women returned their attention to her.

She described the bilingual interview at Joann's former home, and the disappointing meeting with Rachel Zimmerman. She sighed over the latter and shook her head. "Was I naïve to think this woman might find a way to dance around her confidentiality laws and actually help me?"

"Yes." Asha answered as kindly and unequivocally as she could.

Halia considered what came next. Telling Asha and Grace about meeting Justin Grant, and learning of Jesse's death would take a lot out of her. She took stock of her energy reserves and sized up her friends. Asha, Halia could see, was distracted by thoughts of Rob: their 'tiff', his ability to be helpful with Freecycle Sam's real name, her hope that he would show up at The Eft tonight. Halia could see that, despite a sweet effort, Asha's eyes darted to the door each time it opened. Halia found herself hoping Rob would wander in soon, for Asha's sake.

Grace, on the other hand, was a different audience. Halia could read her friend well enough to see that Grace had news of her own. She could also see that it was not pressing, as Grace was not struggling with being patient, and that her interest in Halia's week was not only genuine but passionate. Halia weighed her options – tell now, tell later – when Grace spoke up.

"You have more to tell. What happened with Justin today?"

"Let's get refills." Halia stalled, still deciding. Grace got up and carried the empty glasses back to the bar. She returned with virgin lizards for Halia and herself, and a concussed dog for Asha. "It's the kind of week you've had," Grace explained. The women always alternated virgin drinks with their 'smokes' if it promised to be a multi-drink evening. Tonight, Halia suspected, they might be there a while.

Grace and Asha sensed Halia's indecision and responded intuitively by focusing their attention on her. Asha stopped checking every movement near the bar's entryway, and allowed her body to settle into, rather than perch upon, her chair. Halia, still concerned that the story may have a depressing effect on all three of them, but satisfied that at least they were receptive to listening, dove in.

She described the phone call she received while in Keeseville, and Justin's abrupt, cranky manner. She described his face, his clothes, and the taxi he drove. She paused, realized that she was avoiding almost as much as she was saying, and repeated Justin's story very nearly word for word.

"I'm so sorry." Afterward Asha broke the silence first. "What a difficult thing to hear."

Grace laid a hand on Halia's arm and said nothing. The three of them absorbed the story and considered its impact separately for several more minutes before Halia said, "I need to make the connections if they exist. Knowing this chapter of Joann's past …is it going to help me find her now, or is it unrelated? I'm just not sure how to use this piece of her past - where it fits."

"And this idea of going somewhere that has no address," Grace reminded them. "She said that to a few different people. Whatever it meant, she sure seems to have enjoyed tantalizing people with it."

"Yes. I can only guess that she liked the impact that phrase had on people." Halia frowned in concentration, remembering. 'Discover the meaning of the place that has no address' Halia wrote on her list in her notebook.

"Make sure you add Freecycle Sam to that list," Asha suggested.

"Got it." Halia spoke briskly, her manner business-like. Almost secretively, she wrote several more items on her list, all referencing the campground at North Lake and the events that took place 50 years ago, then snapped the notebook shut and unceremoniously dumped it back into the abyss. She looked up at Grace, and studied her closely. "You also have news, and you've been waiting." Halia smiled fondly at Grace. "Thank you for listening to all that." She looked at Asha and nodded to indicate that she was equally grateful to her as well. "I think I may have generated some ideas, just by repeating the story out loud. I really appreciate being able to monopolize the conversation like that."

Asha waved the comments away, mumbling something about thanks being unnecessary. Grace, eyes twinkling, said, "Of course you knew I had something to tell you. But do you already know what it is?"

Halia, enjoying the challenge, studied Grace head to toe. "No fair," she announced at the end of her examination. "Your adventure was days ago, in different clothes, and at least two showers have removed nearly every observable trace of where you've been and what you've done. And you're wearing different shoes." Halia affected irritation. "That said, you've been to Columbia County, and you've been crawling around on the shoulder of Route 217." Halia paused, cocked her head thoughtfully and added, "The north side of 217."

Asha looked perfectly bewildered. She was about to ask one of them to explain when Rob appeared behind her. He laid a hand on her shoulder; she jumped, genuinely startled. "Peel me off the ceiling," she joked, looking up at him.

"Are you ok?" Rob read the residue of the evening's conversation on Asha's face.

"Currently confused, recently saddened, but over-all, yeah, I'm OK." Asha stood up and hugged him. "I'm glad to see you. Join us."

Rob pulled up a chair and slung his jacket over the back of it. He ambled over to the bar, looking as dishev-eled and off center as ever. Asha's cheeks colored but the tension between the couple was palpable despite Asha's efforts to hide it. She frowned a little and looked from Halia to Grace and back. "What was that all about?"

"Just a game," Halia replied.

"Ask Lukey Jane about Halia's special abilities," Grace suggested. Asha still looked confused, but shrugged, ac-cepting for the moment this lack of explanation.

Rob returned with drinks and sat down. "Carry on," he attempted a British accent. The three women good naturedly ignored his effort.

"It was that animal – the escaped South American thing, right?" Halia asked, intentionally lightening the mood by teasing Grace.

"The Philmontian coati," Grace informed them, "and yes, that is where I was and what I was doing. Well, sort of…"

"Is there really an escaped coati in Philmont?" Rob asked, interested.

"Well, that's what I'm trying to find out," Grace admitted. "There's a bit of an urban legend in zoology circles that sprung up after a collector lost an animal a couple of years ago."

"Did you see it?" Rob sounded excited.

"No. The experience got kind of surreal, I guess." Grace explained about Andrew's drawing, and how that prompted a second visit to Philmont. She described find-ing the spot, and parking the car on the side of the road, as she, Andrew and Eddie got out to explore. "We found chuck holes and scat, and all three of us were lying flat on the ground, looking at a footprint, when a trooper pulled up." Grace giggled. "We were pretty dirty, and I was holding a Ziploc bag with scat in it. Eddie had the camera out with the macro lens, and Andrew was sketching the site and measuring with a piece of string and a plastic ruler from school. I had my surgical gloves on ... we looked totally bizarre." Grace shook her head, remembering. "Anyway, apparently if you park your car on the side of a state highway, you're just asking for attention from the state police. Who knew?"

Asha and Halia chuckled, picturing the scene.

"What comes next?" Rob wanted to know.

"What would you have done next, Halia?" Grace challenged her friend again.

"Take the baggie to the Millbrook Zoo for a comparative study."

"That's exactly what I did!" Grace's voice rose with excitement. "The results, however, were unclear. Visual comparison is very unreliable because food and water intake can change the appearance of scat so dramatically, especially in an herbivore." There was no apparent dimming of Grace's smile, despite the lack of conclusive results. "Everything we found in that spot could have been from a groundhog. But," Grace shrugged her shoulders and spread her palms wide, delight evident despite her lack of certainty, "maybe not."

"So you're going back again?" Rob asked. His level of interest had reached the point where Asha looked at him strangely. "I know someone who would be really interested in this," he explained. "Someone you don't know," he added hastily in response to her expectant look.

"Yes. I think the next trip will be just me, at dusk, with borrowed binoculars."

"What happened with the trooper?" Asha asked.

"Nothing really. I didn't say much. Eddie and Andrew handled it. They showed him Andrew's drawing and told him the story and Andrew got all excited about Mommy discovering something 'zoologically important' … I think he just told Eddie to park the car somewhere else and walk back next time." Grace took a sip of her drink before adding, "I guess he could tell there was going to be a next time. And he did mention being careful not to trespass anywhere posted."

That last comment elicited a funny story from Asha about appearing before Dover's Town Judge for trespassing at the quarry in Wingdale. As the laughter died down, Asha remembered that Rob might be helpful to Halia. "Rob – what's that guy's name?" she asked suddenly. Rob looked at her intently, as if he really wanted to know what on earth she was talking about. Asha's cheeks colored, and her hands flew to her mouth in a gesture of embarrassment. "Sorry," she grinned appealingly. "Non sequitur. My bad. Umm – some guy Halia and Grace call Freecycle Sam. What's his real name? Do you know?"

"Oh. Uummm… I think I know. Is it Chuck? Chip? Something like that?"

"We thought it began with a J." Grace informed him.

"No, I don't know his name. I think I'd know him if I saw him, though." Rob emanated the desire to be helpful, but all three women looked a bit crestfallen. Asha offered to fill him in on their way home. Rob and Asha excused themselves and went outside.

Grace said to Halia, "They have their disagreement to work out."

Halia nodded, avoiding feeling anything. Relationships, and their natural ups and downs, were more unpleasant to Halia than a pile of poorly written essays. Worse, she thought, than a calculus lesson badly prepared, and presented to a disinterested class of 27 seniors. On the day before a week long school vacation, last period of the day, she added to herself.

Grace and Halia spent the rest of the evening at The Eft chatting about nothing, just enjoying being out together. Each woman, having shared her story, retreated into the comfort of their friendship, allowing the conversation to be laced with silence. They both let their eyes wander around the room, people-watching, as the evening crowd came and went. The familiarity of both place and company let Halia relax for the first time all week. Despite the news the day brought, and the riddles that remained regarding Joann, Halia chose to sink into the comfort of a Friday evening at The Blue Eft with Grace. It was powerfully good medicine. Finally, as if in response to an unseen cue, both women rose to leave.

currant events

Tuesday June 15, 1:00 pm:
Dover Elementary School's Shakespeare Club presents
Swords and Words: Creative Conflict, Elizabethan Style
At The Blue Eft

Tuesday July 13, 11am – 3pm:
Garden Tours and Skateboarding Demonstrations
At the Dover Plains Community Garden and Skate Park

Saturday August 14, 8am – 5pm:
World Premiere: The Blue Eft introduces
Black and Blue Ice Cream
Fuel your day of treasure hunting with our frozen treats

Friday September 17, 8 pm:
Back to school with jazz and blues
Beckerman and Levine return to The Blue Eft

the blue eft
nellie hill road   dover plains, ny

Chapter 6

Over the next few weeks, Halia lived in the dynamic tension of having learned much but discovered little in terms of locating Joann Grant. The school days flew by consumed by the mad rush to complete all the forms and administrative mandates before year's end. The field trip to Rosendale glittered like a Herkimer diamond on the bottom of the West Canada Creek – an eagerly anticipated bright spot in an otherwise rushing tumult. Halia's emotions were back in check, supported by work, being busy and familiar surroundings; the breakdown incited by Rachel Zimmerman, LCSW, was but a dim memory. Finding Joann Grant was now officially a project of Halia's – the effort had reached that level of recognition. As such, there were times when it was relegated to the back burner, and Halia lived in her day-to-day middle school science teacher life, simply without time to pursue her next steps.

Without Freecycle Sam's name, it was well nigh impossible to track him down. Of course Larry and Louise had been alerted to the situation, but so far "Sam" had not visited The Eft since Asha mentioned him several weeks prior.

Joann's secret... Halia had not really made any headway there either. Joann made no secret of leaving, very publicly pairing down possessions and putting her house on the market. No secrets there. Her new location was a secret but Halia suspected that it was not The Secret she had been hearing about from Keesvillians. Calling her destination "a place without an address" gave rise to several possible theories. It had crossed Halia's mind way back in Keeseville that one "place" that has no address is being in transit. As Marisol, the new owner of Joann's home pointed out, retirees often do travel. Perhaps Joann was seeing the world, as a tourist this time, instead of as an archeologist. That was a distinct possibility, Halia admitted, but with a rather fatal flaw: why all the secrecy? Why on earth would Joann tell no one, leave no forwarding address, keep contact with no one via emails, and make no attempt to maintain a steady source of income? This hypothesis, while technically possible, really failed Halia's "why" test. Possible, but it made no sense.

Halia also considered and ultimately rejected suicide as a possible, albeit bleak, explanation. Yes, it would explain the riddle as far as a place with no address is concerned, and it would also adequately explain the secrecy surrounding her departure, and her apparent lack of concern about money. In fact, it was the number of details suicide explained that made Halia honestly confront such a solemn and morbid possibility. But, Halia reminded herself, no one identified Joann as having been unhappy prior to her move. On the contrary, person after person, from strangers to colleagues indicated just the opposite: "she had trouble closing her mouth over her big smile." Dr. Nase had thought she was in love – surely week after week, month after month, a mistake or a façade of that magnitude could not be believed. If she had been planning to kill herself, there would most likely have been some sign somewhere that she was something other than happy, excited about something, harboring a delicious secret … no, the details may be accounted for in some ways, but ultimately this hypothesis just didn't fit.

Unless something really dramatic and unforeseen happened during or late in the preparations to move, and totally changed Joann's plans at the last moment. What if, Halia considered, Joann had her delicious secret plan for retirement, and began the process – selling and giving away possessions, putting her house on the market, tying up loose ends in Nyack – only to discover something along the way that changed everything? Could a major financial change – or perhaps a sudden health problem – have plunged Joann into an acute depression during which she suicided? Almost too far fetched to even consider, but Halia knew that financial ruin could lead people to commit suicide; it has happened many times. What if Joann had big and wonderful plans, and then experienced some kind of catastrophic loss (maybe a stock became worthless overnight? Halia wasn't even sure whether or not such a thing could happen.)? What if, at her last medical check up before intending to go off to darkest Peru, she was diagnosed with cancer? Halia had spoken with several colleagues over the years, and was fairly well acquainted with what they referred to as the shock and denial phase of grief when confronted with the diagnosis of a terminal illness. During that period of time, Halia knew erratic or impulsive behavior was at least possible, even if not very probable. Nevertheless, after thinking it through, both as a planned act, and as an impulsive reaction to some devastating discovery, Halia rejected suicide as a possibility. That too did not fit Joann – or rather it still was not a good enough fit to account for all the pieces of information Halia had collected.

What, then, was to be made of the visit to Nyack, after selling her home and moving? And the comment to Marisol about finishing something she started long ago? What was the connection from the past, and just how far back should Halia search? A sixty-eight year old woman – Halia checked her calendar and realized Joann was soon to be sixty-nine – had multiple decades worth of past to explore. Halia wasn't sure which one held that clue, and even then if such a clue would un-ravel the whole story or just another small piece. In terms of timing, only Dr. Nase had identified a change in Joann dating back to the previous Thanksgiving.

"Maybe she won the lottery," Louise offered one evening. "That would explain the secret, and her ability to not worry about money. It would also explain why she seemed pleased as punch about her situation – so much so that her colleague thought she was in love."

Halia had considered a sudden coming into money as an explanation, too. One afternoon, Grace dropped Bezef off with Halia while the Taresius family rode the rail trail. Bezef slept at Halia's feet while Halia endured a soporifically boring search through lottery winners' names', starting with last Thanksgiving and running through March. They should have a search function, Halia muttered through gritted teeth, scrolling and scanning through list after list. Finally Halia was ready to say she had checked thoroughly – no support for the lottery winner theory.

Inheritance was another way for Joann to have come into money. Halia had no idea about Grant family fortunes, and felt she had no palatable way to find this out. Calling Bones, or Justin Grant for that matter, was just out of the question. For the time being, Halia felt she would have to keep that possibility alive without any way to gauge its likeliness.

While quickly dismissed as unlikely, Halia also toyed with the notion of Joann being in trouble with the law, or perhaps even having stolen money and being on the run. Equally romantic, and equally easily dismissed, was Halia's consideration of the idea that Joann had run away with a long lost lover.

"The world needs more romance," Asha had said on that Saturday afternoon in May when she and Halia and Pearl had walked Brulee in the graveyard. "Look," Asha pointed across the field to the blue backhoe parked near the edge of the old section. "The graves are dug with that machine." She sounded sad and looked disgusted. "That lacks romance." Halia did not reply, abstaining from all comment on the subject of romance. Pearl rolled her eyes at her mother's comment, preteen allergies to parental contact budding in her nearly 12 year-old psyche. "I vote for the romantic explanation," Asha continued. "I hope what she's done is brave and dashing and risky and bold. I hope she placed all her chips on the most romantic number on the table."

Halia had grinned in surprise at the passionate outburst, and at Asha's use of the gambling metaphor. But then again, Halia thought to herself, of course Asha voted for romance – she was still in the throes of being freshly pierced by Cupid's arrow. As to whether or not Joann would steal, run from the law, or run away with her high school sweetheart, Halia sorely doubted it. Romance, she thought, held a certain allure precisely because normal people under normal circumstances don't behave in ways that earn the epithet "romantic." From everything Halia knew about Joann, dating back to the discussions of lending Halia the money in the first place, Joann was eminently sensible. In fact, she and Halia had seemed to be "two peas in a pod" – scientific personalities, more rational than emotional and content that way.

"Then again," Grace had reminded Halia over the phone, as Halia verbally eliminated the dashing, the daring, and the risky hypotheses, "sometimes the most even keel, sensible of women venture into the white water of romance."

Halia had been silent in response. The chord had been struck. Then suddenly she blurted out, "Grace, can you come over? Now?"

Grace pulled into Halia's driveway on that chilly Sunday afternoon in May, a touch concerned about the condition in which she might find Halia. It was an understatement to describe Halia's sudden demand for Grace's company as unusual. As Grace stepped from her car, Halia banged the front door shut behind her, exiting onto the porch.

"Come, walk in the graveyard with me."

Grace complied, pocketing her keys and falling

in step with Halia. They used the road instead of the path behind Halia's house, as Halia wanted to linger on the little bridge, looking at the stream, for a moment. A few of Halia's students riding bicycles passed the two women, nodding to Halia in greeting. She inclined her head slightly in return.

Halia and Grace walked on in silence, Grace aware of Halia's mood above all else. Halia's knitted brow and set mouth spoke volumes. Grace allowed Halia to guide once they passed between the stone columns and iron gates. Halia led them through the usual tour of the oldest graves first, appearing to look at them without taking anything in. Through that section, and on to the newer section west of the Valley View gates, and back again they walked in silence. Suddenly at a cluster of graves all from a single family, they stopped. A small stone with a birthdate and a date of death only one day apart had caught Halia's notice. She stayed there, reading the stone for several minutes, her eyes cloudy and her face drawn. Then she reached for Grace's hand, squeezed and released it. She looked into Grace's face and her eyes cleared. "Think of all the lives that were forever changed by that one day. All the people that were touched by that one life... the entry and the departure..." Halia fell silent again, and they walked back to her house enveloped in the mood evoked by her words.

They sat, shoulder to shoulder, on the front porch steps. Grace waited for Halia to speak, patient, concerned and quiet. Eventually, Halia's mood shifted, and as suddenly as her urgently voiced request for company had been issued, the tense silence she had drawn Grace into was broken by passionate outburst.

"She can't be gone without a trace. That's just not possible. There must be clues. There must be a trail." Her voice changed from angry to plaintive. "Why can't I find it?"

At the Widow Jane Mine, Halia and a docent held flashlights. At one point, to appreciate the natural play of light and darkness, they both turned the flashlights off. Amid the giggling, hushed whispers, and a scuffling of feet, Halia distinctly heard one student ask of another "Do ants float?" Halia made a mental note to write that down as it struck an odd, yet profound chord within her.

The students were more impressed with the document storage and "city underground" uses of the caves than with the mushroom cultivation, although several of the girls planned a Campbell's soup night to commemorate the field trip. They ate their lunch on a grassy field above the Widow Jane Mine. Halia chatted with the students and their parents (the chaperones) about the pickle festival, the street fairs, and the music recorded in the mine. Several boys braved the poison ivy to explore an overgrown graveyard nearby. Halia watched them as she continued her conversation, ready to intervene if safety or propriety became an issue. Several moments later, they summoned her with a shout.

"Ms. Frank, come look!" It was Dillon calling her. "The name on this grave – it's so cool."

Halia picked her way carefully to where Dillon stood pointing. Margaret Morningstar, she read. She looked questioningly at Dillon.

"Morningstar," he read out loud. "Morning star." He looked up into Halia's dark eyes, shaded by her thick fringe of bangs. His face was a picture of innocence and earnestness. "Do you think that's an Indian name?"

Halia read the entire stone – a child, born and died in the late 1800's. "No, I don't think so," she told him gently, anticipating his disappointment. "I think Morningstar is a beautiful name, but I have a feeling these people were not Native Americans." Mourning star might be a more appropriate name for this family, Halia thought.

"Yeah, think about it," one of Dillon's buddies reminded him. "The Indians didn't use stones like this to mark their graves."

"Oh yeah," Dillon said sheepishly. The boys wandered off. Halia looked at the grave with the beautiful name for a few long moments before turning to go. I seem to have an even greater than usual affinity for graveyards lately, she realized.

That evening Halia discovered a note from Grace in her mailbox and Bezef in her kitchen – Grace was taking Andrew away for the weekend and Eddie wouldn't be back until quite late. Halia was impressed into puppy-sitting service. After dinner, Halia sank into her couch, reviewing the day and scratching behind the puppy's floppy ears. Bezef responded to the attention by melting to the floor and rolling onto her back playfully. Halia rubbed her rose colored belly with one foot and mentally listed the triumphs of the day.

- No one got sick on the bus or anywhere else
- Everyone, adults included, kept their behavior within acceptable limits all day

- Approximately 60% (Halia estimated) actually paid attention and made connections between classroom content and the field trip site
- Closer to 90% enjoyed the field trip in some way
- No unforeseen disasters – no one fell in the underground lake, no bus breakdowns, no natural disasters, payment issues or traffic jams.

"Overall, a great field trip, right, Bezef?" Halia spoke in a sing song inviting voice. The puppy wagged her tail and let her tongue hang out in an expression of unadulterated canine goofiness. Halia enjoyed her evening with Bezef, her spirits lifted somewhat by the simple satisfaction of a field trip without problems. No mess to clean up tomorrow at work – that should make administrators happy, Halia thought. Close on the heels of that thought, Halia considered Asha's situation. Word had made it to the middle school that something was amiss with Asha and the elementary principal, and talk had sprung up in the faculty room. That was bad. Since Halia avoided the faculty room and spoke very little with most of her colleagues, it was a bad sign that even she had picked up on something. It meant that Asha's privacy and dignity were now casualties of whatever it was that was happening. Halia worried about her friend, but knew there was little she could do.

The humbling and frustrating impact of meeting with dead end after dead end in terms of locating Joann Grant had also begun to weigh down Halia's mood. The beautiful spring weather, Bezef's company, and small successes like today's field trip counteracted the heaviness somewhat, but Halia was aware that she was reaching a dangerous level of obsession with the search for Joann. Halia was like a dog with a bone, and school was becoming an irritating disruption of the search.

I need to branch out a little, at least mentally, she thought. She smiled wryly at herself. Yeah. Right.

Sitting on the couch, rubbing Bezef's belly, Halia resolved that at least her evenings at The Blue Eft could no longer contain updates on her progress or lack thereof. We all need a break from this story, she thought.

Chapter 7

"Gorgo?" Grace asked.

"Yeah, Gorgo. It's a movie. I guess it was the British response to Godzilla," Asha explained. "Rob loves it. It's very cheesy and unintentionally hilarious in parts."

The Blue Eft was crowded with a joyous bunch of revelers, inspired by the combination of the advent of a long weekend and a warm and clear evening. Inhabitants of Dover were out of doors, on front porches, taking walks, and seeking food and drink. It was the kind of night where all roads lead to The Eft.

"Gorgo?" Grace asked again, loudly.

"Yes, Gorgo." Asha felt like she was shouting to be heard. "It's a big lizard-like dinosaur thing. Sort of like a giant T-Rex with an attitude. I don't want to say too much - that'll end up giving away the ending."

Grace's eyebrows knitted together, and she looked as though she might repeat the name of the movie again, but held back. Halia watched both women pensively, playing more with the straw in her alizarin smoke than drinking it. Grace glanced at Halia, and failing to catch her eye, asked Asha, "This is Rob's idea?"

"Yes. Rob thinks I need to see this movie because he says Brulee looks kind of like the monster." Asha looked torn between taking Rob seriously and presenting his suggestion respectfully, versus allowing her own amusement to show through.

"Rob thinks your dog looks like a giant reptile?" Grace was feigning astonishment.

"Yes." Asha was laughing out loud. "Rob thinks Brulee looks like Gorgo."

Grace, punchy after a grueling work week rendered more so by her partner's vacation, repeated "Gorgo?" one last time. Even Halia laughed.

"Gorgo?" An unfamiliar male voice caused all three heads to turn. "Did I hear someone say Gorgo? The British answer to Godzilla – that Gorgo?" It was the man they called Freecycle Sam, standing over their table with a hungry look in his eye. "Does one of you have Gorgo memorabilia?"

"No." Asha, not realizing to whom she spoke, answered the man while still laughing at Grace. "I have a friend who says my dog looks like Gorgo." While Asha and Grace dissolved in helpless giggles and the effort to stifle them, Halia snapped into business mode. "Sam" had turned to go, but Halia called him back, her teacher voice rising above the conversational din.

"Wait," she barked.

He stopped and turned around, hope lighting up his face.

"I need to ask you about something you found on

Freecycle a few months ago."

Sam's face fell but he obeyed and made to pull up a chair. "Let's step outside," Halia suggested. "There aren't any empty chairs and we'll have to shout to make ourselves heard." With that Halia stood up, pulled her notebook and pen from the suitcase-sized sack next to her chair and headed for the door. Asha and Grace realized what was going on and crossed their fingers that Halia would learn something significant. Sam followed Halia to the door.

In Halia's absence, Grace informed Asha of her new and improved names for the phases of the moon. "Fingernail moon, Slice-o-melon moon, Pierogi moon, and Apple pie moon," she recited.

"What do you call the new moon?" was the question Halia returned in time to hear.

She sat down and unceremoniously deposited pen and notebook in the sack. "No news," she reported, her face unreadable. "Just one more lead to cross off the list."

Grace, aware of Halia's determination not to let evenings at The Eft turn into brainstorming sessions, asked Asha about the upcoming Shakespeare Club performance.

"I'm so grateful to Louise," Asha replied. "Her 'Currant Events' calendar is totally exciting for the kids and their families. They are working so hard, putting their hearts and souls into this."

"Are you guys doing a play?" Halia asked.

"No, just scenes," Asha explained. "This being our first year, I didn't want to be overly ambitious. They chose a selection of scenes for a bunch of different reasons and we found ways to string them together so that the overall performance has a flow and a feeling of completeness. The kids themselves have written bridges or connectors to link the different scenes. Some of the bridges are an attempt to use Shakespearean language." Asha grinned. "Someone discovered the Shakespearean insulter on the web and wrote an introduction to the fight scene that is just hilarious."

"Fight scene?" Halia asked.

"Yeah. We're doing some really athletic sword play scenes. They've been a fun challenge to choreograph."

"Are you guys ready to perform?" Grace wanted to know.

"Well no," Asha admitted. "We definitely are going to need the next two weeks to tighten things up. But I have confidence in those kids – I'm sure we'll be ready by field day. Will you come?"

"Eddie and I are taking the day off. Was piggybacking on field day your idea or Louise's?"

"We kind of came up with it together."

"Well, it's a great idea. I think you'll have a big crowd. We will definitely be there, all three of us. Andrew is kicking himself for not joining Shakespeare Club."

"He can join next year – we'll need 5th grade boys. We're losing some of our best actors." Asha looked both serious and intense, and truly happy as she talked about her students and the club. Happier, perhaps, than Grace or Halia had seen her in months, if not ever. Halia remarked upon this.

"There's nothing like a job well done to put a smile on your face," Asha responded.

"Things are better than a few weeks ago?"

"I think the damage is done. There's a certain loss of naiveté that has hardened me. But it is so much better to know where you stand, even when you're standing nostril-deep in shark-infested waters."

"Well put," Halia said, her own nose wrinkling involuntarily.

"Nice image," Grace laughed.

"But where do you stand?" Halia's question was more serious than the mood in the bar could tolerate, and Asha just shrugged her off.

"I'm looking around and considering my options. Why work your ass off to stay somewhere you're not wanted?" Halia gave no indication of pursuing the topic and Grace took her cue to change the subject.

"Have you and Rob straightened things out?"

"Yeah, although I think we're both a little stressed out lately, and it seems to make both of us kind of touchy. I seem to be either snapping at him or apologizing all the time these days."

Grace was about to reply when Anne Marie and Lukey Jane entered the bar. They had passed Halia talking to Freecycle Sam on the way in. They made their way over to Grace, Asha and Halia's table, and Anne Marie greeted the women quietly.

"Hey Halia!" Lukey's voice carried over the ambient din. "Hi Asha. Hi Grace." Anne Marie snagged a chair from a neighboring table; Lukey Jane sat on her heels in between Halia and Grace.

"How's everything?" Grace asked.

"Y'all are not going to believe this!" Lukey Jane's level of enthusiasm was called into question by Anne Marie's rolling eyes. Halia caught enough nuance of the gesture to understand that Anne Marie was not truly annoyed with Lukey Jane, and that Lukey Jane was fully expecting the mock annoyance. It was a vaudeville routine they had been unintentionally honing over the past few days.

"What?" Asha and Grace asked in unison. Halia, privy to more details regarding recent events at the garden, wondered if the meeting she had suggested had taken place.

"We got on the list of Currant Events!" Lukey Jane gloated. "We're gonna have a garden tour and skate-boarding demonstration in July."

Grace snorted with laughter. Anne Marie looked from Grace to Lukey Jane and back again, before she too began to chuckle. Asha looked as if she wasn't sure what the joke was, and Halia sipped her drink serenely.

"It's like the perfect combination," Lukey Jane explained. Grace took a deep breath, seeking control. "Teenagers can spend the afternoon with their parents. Something for everyone."

Grace rubbed her cheeks and squeaked in a little girl voice, "My cheeks are starting to hurt from all this laughing."

That seemed to hit Asha and Lukey Jane just right, and another round of laughter erupted. Anne Marie leaned over to Halia and spoke near her ear to be heard. "Is she drunk?" she jerked her head in Grace's direction.

"No, exhausted," Halia replied honestly. "How did the addition to the calendar come about?"

As Anne Marie explained to Halia about the meeting of the gardeners, the skateboarders, and employees of the park, the hilarity subsided. Lukey Jane took over, explaining how the skateboarders had immediately offered to set up a clinic for those gardeners interested in learning to skate safely and look cool doing it. The maintenance crew had suggested buying and storing some equipment on site so that helmets and pads could be available for spontaneous skating. The boarders came up with the idea of a "cage" where they'd sell drinks and snacks and rent the equipment, and recycle the profits back into the park. They even set up a schedule for volunteering at the cage so that Lukey didn't need to hire anyone to run it.

"They're doing everything cooperatively at this point. It's pretty amazing how responsible they're being. Thirteen year olds are showing up for their shifts early, and really enjoying their role as teacher." Anne Marie, whose fifteen year old son was one of the core members of the skate crew, flushed with pride. "They run the clinic for free Saturday mornings, and I've seen them out there teaching little kids or older women – you name it!"

"Yeah, like women your age," Lukey Jane teased.

Anne Marie ignored her, the others offering only a perfunctory grin. "When the kids saw the Calendar of Currant Events posted all around town -"

"And, of course, on our own bulletin board at the cage," Lukey Jane interrupted. Anne Marie acquiesced and Lukey Jane continued. "When the kids saw that, they started talking and I guess they got the gardeners all interested too. Anyway, a bunch of them marched over here last Monday when Louise was here and pitched their idea. The way I heard it, Louise laughed her head off too, and said it was a great idea."

"We talked about making it the same day as the ice cream party but the gardeners pointed out that a July date would show off the gardens better. Better variety of bloom at that time is what they said. And then, we didn't want to compete with the tag sale – I think most of our gardeners are pretty devoted to tag sale-ing too."

"The boarders are going to do a skate equipment tag sale of their own that day, and have the cage going in full swing, so they said no to that day too." Anne Marie put in.

"So we got our own day – the third Saturday in July. Y'all better show up!" Lukey Jane straightened up and headed toward the bar, calling back over her shoulder, "anybody want anything from Larry?"

She returned several moments later, empty-handed. No one was surprised when she explained, "Larry wouldn't let me carry the tray." She gestured back toward the bar. "Five drinks, crowded room … he'll be right over." She looked around and spotted a chair. Retrieving it involved terrifying the uninitiated, as Lukey grabbed and lifted the chair powerfully over two tables and many people's heads. Anne Marie breathed a small sigh of relief once Lukey was comfortably seated and Larry served the drinks. "Hey Halia," Lukey Jane turned to her. "Any news about the lady who moved?"

Only Grace noticed Halia's hesitation, knowing, in fact anticipating, her aversion to taking the conversation down that path. Grace wracked her brain for a polite quip to get Halia off the hook, but her wit wasn't sharp enough and Halia answered first.

"I haven't found her yet," Halia said, "but I'm not giving up. Maybe you can help?" Halia adopted a tone that belied the weight this problem laid upon her shoulders. "Tell me," she looked engagingly from Lukey Jane to Anne Marie, "what place has no address?"

Lukey Jane and Anne Marie exchanged glances. "I know – on a boat!" Lukey Jane looked like she had just won the fifth grade spelling bee.

"Sorry, honey," Anne Marie was not being sarcastic. "Nowadays, between email, satellite connections, ship to shore phone lines and GPS ... I think even boats have addresses." Anne Marie scratched her head. "In fact, take it from me – if it's someplace on this planet – it has an address. Being in the travel business for all these years, that's something I can tell you with great certainty." Halia wore an entranced expression, clearly riveted but already far off on a tangent, stimulated by something one of them had said. Anne Marie continued, "Now, twenty years ago, when I first started, it could have been said that there were places that had no address." Halia's raised eyebrows asked the question for her. "Like remote places – deep forests, mountain tops, hey even parts of the Adirondacks, accessible only by hiking without maintained trails – if you eliminate GPS coordinates, I guess there are places that would qualify as having no address. They can be named or described, but I guess it's really the truth that they don't have an address."

"Yeah, like on a boat," Lukey Jane insisted. "Like a yacht sailing around the Caribbean – tiny unnamed islands to moor off ..."

"Since when do you know so much about sailing yachts around the Caribbean?" Anne Marie teased.

"I know, I know." Lukey Jane tossed her hair defiantly. "Y'all think I'm just a hick from Oklahoma." Heads nodded around the table, winks and grins added to assure good will. "Well I'm a whole heckuva lot more worldly than y'all might think. And yes, Miss Travel Agent, I've sailed around the Caribbean in a private yacht." Lukey Jane waited for that to sink in before continuing. "It was a long time ago – the summer after graduating from high school. Friends of my friend's parents – something like that. My best friend and I helped crew for about ten days. It was real fun. And I think we really did have no address for those ten days."

Halia looked lost in thought, clearly working something out. Asha looked at her watch and excused herself.

"Is this Gorgo thing tonight?" Halia asked.

Before Asha could answer, Grace, Lukey Jane, and Anne Marie all repeated "Gorgo?" and Grace's laughter drowned out all other sounds in the room for a full minute or two. Asha looked a little embarrassed, but mostly delighted. "Yes, tonight is Gorgo night for Rob and me. What junk food do you serve with a movie like Gorgo?"

"English junk food," Anne Marie surprised them with her apparent voice of authority on the subject. "Chocolate covered digestive biscuits, or maybe a packet of crisps."

"Quit showing off," Luke Jane joked. "Have fun, Asha. Gorgo's great." Lukey Jane cocked her head and said thoughtfully, "Y'know, your dog looks kinda like Gorgo."

That was the end of self control for Grace. The self-perpetuating, slightly frenetic laughter of the utterly exhausted woman switched from being infectious to being uncomfortable. Asha left amid Grace's guffaws.

Halia left soon after and Grace decided to walk her home. "I have Bezef in the truck. Let's take her for a walk – it's such a beautiful night," Grace suggested.

Grace had left her truck in Halia's driveway (well hidden among the waist-high weeds) so they returned to Halia's house to collect Bezef. The women walked the puppy back towards The Eft under the railway over-pass and into the community garden. It was not yet fully dark, the sky an unearthly shade of blue and the hills to the east tinted a deep peach-pink by the sun's dying rays. Both Halia and Grace thought about Asha, so pleased with her new relationship, so tickled by dis-covering Rob's quirks, and so dangerously blind to his flaws. Both women remembered their own moments of falling in love, each cognizant that the other's experi-ence was very different from her own.

"I'm still in love with Eddie," Grace said quietly. "I still feel that nervous excited feeling when I hear his car in the driveway, or his footsteps on the gravel. I didn't know how lucky I was when I first fell for him – how lucky I was going to feel 15 years later."

Halia nodded, appreciating Grace's words. Halia also appreciated how pleasant it was to spend time around someone who was happy and fulfilled. The memories of her own experience being romantically involved with Bones made her cringe, but reaching deeper into her past, Halia could recover dim memories of awkward hopeful passion, and even a high school version of falling in love, that evoked a self-conscious smile.

They sat on a bench in the garden, petting Bezef and enjoying the night. Halia's thoughts turned to Lukey Jane's and Anne Marie's answers to her query. She replayed the entire conversation in her head several times in her head, hitting her internal stop, rewind and play buttons several times each, considering the pos-sibilities.

Suddenly Grace spoke. "Do you think it's stupid of me to try to find the Philmontian coati?"

Halia, wrenched from her own internal musings, looked like she just woke up. A touch bleary, she answered, "No. Definitely not. Are you doubting yourself?"

"Well, yeah." Grace looked sheepish. "It's not as splashy as Bigfoot or the Loch Ness monster, but it may be as far-fetched. Maybe I should spend my precious free time on something a little less bizarre and silly."

"I don't know that you should compare this to Bigfoot or Nessie." Halia thought this was probably the first time she had ever mentioned either creature in a serious conversation. "There definitely was an escaped coati. A real animal and a documented escape. So it's not all that crazy to try to figure out what happened to it."

Grace looked both pleased and doubtful.

"Do you have a good reason to pursue this?" Halia challenged Grace to consider her motives.

"Well, it would definitely be important in the world of zoology," Grace's confidence returned with this thought. "And if it has mated with local animals that could be pretty important. I mean, if one individual animal swam across the Hudson and survived Columbia County winters, whether or not it has mated this would all be pretty relevant to the study of these animals more generally."

"And?" Halia pushed Grace to continue.

"I don't know…" Grace shrugged evasively. Halia waited. "You mean why me? Why now?" Halia nodded. "I guess it has something to do with role modeling for Andrew." Grace said thoughtfully. "I feel like the person he's known all his life is only one part of me. I've been so wrapped up in all the responsibilities of my practice and the farm and parenting, I haven't really expressed the curious, adventurous, spontaneous parts of me. I guess most parents don't get a chance to do that most of the time, but here it is. This opportunity landed in my lap. I mean, Philmont is less than an hour away. It's so easy ... I guess I feel like I owe it to myself to pursue an adventure, but now I'm having second thoughts."

"I think second thoughts are part of the process. They make the results that much sweeter." Halia listened to her own words and frowned inadvertently. For once she was glad Grace was not looking at her, and was relieved that she didn't have to explain her expression. The truth was that her own lack of progress and acknowledgement of near obsession with The Search for Joann had led to pretty serious second thoughts and self doubt, and part of the process or not, these feelings angered her.

They continued to talk about self doubt and commitment, about role modeling and being true to oneself, while darkness fell. It was Bezef, desiring movement, that roused them from their bench and interrupted the conversation. They strolled back to Halia's together, Grace having requested a cup of tea before driving home.

"Eddie and Andrew went to catch a movie tonight after baseball practice. I think I might still beat them home." Grace spoke as she fixed the tea herself.

Halia took Bezef's leash off and ran her hands over the puppy, checking for ticks. "She is such a unique looking dog," Halia mused aloud. "I just can't get over your ears," she gently tousled the puppy's head, and Bezef melted to the floor, tongue hanging out, tail wagging with a rhythmic thump on the floor.

"At least she doesn't look like Gorgo," Grace said over her shoulder as she busied herself in the kitchen. She didn't laugh this time, but allowed the ghost of a smile to flit across her lips. Halia didn't have to look up from the dog to catch her expression.

Another school week came and went, the hectic pace of end of the school year CSE meetings and 504 plan update meetings exacerbated by the avalanche of administrative directives landing in Halia's mailbox on a daily basis. Grumblings about administrators finally getting around to cleaning off their desks were common at the copier machine, in the faculty room, and wherever else teachers congregated. Halia tried not to listen, knowing she needed to simply plow through the work, rather than complain. She also chose to learn from Asha's experience – which seemed to refuse to go away. Halia heard that the Board of Education had discussed Asha's future behind closed doors. That was never good. Halia knew that Asha was actively looking for a job at this point, which seemed to be the wisest move, but it had all meant all kinds of stress and challenges for Asha, not the least of which was Pearl's father and Pearl's school being right here in Dover. Halia also knew that Asha and Rob were talking about moving in together, and that seemed dangerously premature to Halia. Halia had only known Asha as more than an acquaintance for a few months, and while Asha and Rob certainly spent a whole lot more time together than Halia and she ever did, they got together after she and Halia met that night in the graveyard. Deciding to move in together after only two or three months just seemed ill-advised to Halia. It was way too soon to take such a huge step, especially since Pearl was involved.

Halia knew that Asha was scared. Actions arising from fear never seem to pan out – Halia had had that lesson pounded into her head by her long and arduous process of merging and then untangling her future with someone she should never have even held hands with. Halia knew, both at the time and forever after, that she should not have trusted Bones. She was trying to be someone she was not – she had been acting a part for which she was poorly suited. Fear had been part of that role – dependence and then fear. No one, Halia thought, should ever need another person to survive – once fledged, it seemed a grave error to recreate that vulnerability and dependence. Perhaps romantic love is good (for other people, Halia was willing to consider this possibility), but financial interdependence is very tricky and should not be all mixed up with emotions. Of that Halia was quite certain.

Halia found herself thinking good thoughts for Asha while at work – performing an action that others might call offering up a prayer, except Halia would eschew the religious implications of such a label. But engaging in the action was about all Halia could do for Asha at this point – Asha was not able to hear Halia's and Grace's admonitions to be careful about taking major relationship steps out of fear, and neither woman could offer anything more solidly comforting. Asha's dependence upon her income was a different story – she was having trouble finding options in the job market that would pay her mortgage and leave her any time at all for parenting.

Asha's stress also hit Halia hard as an exhortation to pay closer attention to her own behavior at work. She had always kept to herself somewhat and placed discretion and tact high on her list of qualities to cultivate. Asha's experience strengthened Halia's resolve to refrain from complaining about anyone, at all, ever. Although Halia generally did not think in terms of shibboleths, in this case she kept the saying "Before you criticize your brother, walk a mile in his moccasins" top of mind. Perhaps there was some accurate and well deserved criticism being served up regarding lazy colleagues or disorganized administrators, but Halia decided it was unproductive and inefficient to spend time walking in those shoes. The truth was that none of the forms to fill out or other things she had been asked to do were really all that onerous. It took less time to comply than to complain.

As Asha's Shakespeare Club performance approached, Halia noticed that she saw quite a bit less of Asha, and that even Asha's and Brulee's running schedule seemed adversely affected. Halia offered to take Brulee with her when she exercised Bezef for Grace. Asha had gratefully accepted.

"Between Rob's help and the high school kids putting in community service hours, I think I have the sets done," Asha's hands were in her hair when Halia stopped by to pick up Brulee. Halia hadn't asked her how things were shaping up, and it wasn't completely clear whether Asha was talking to Halia or just thinking out loud. "Sophia Steers has the costumes all sewn up." Asha went on, failing to notice the pun. Halia left with the dog, Asha still talking after the car door shut.

On the day of the performance, the timing was very tight, but due to several small logistical miracles Halia was able to slide into a seat in the back just moments before the "curtain" rose. Louise's Eft had been cleared of tables and transformed into a miniature auditorium. The stage had been enlarged thanks to Rob and Larry's ingenuity, and a veritable army of assistants had done the rest: parents corralling performers into the backstage area and wrestling excited 8 year olds into costumes, applying stage makeup, keeping props safe and organized, setting up chairs out front, and passing around Louise's complimentary desserts. Pitchers of iced black currant tea and blueberry lemonade were filled and refilled over and over by Larry, Asha, Rob or Louise – whoever noticed them empty. The whole place hummed with frenetic nervous excited energy. Halia took it all in at a glance.

The performance itself could not have gone better. Even the mistakes and forgotten lines added charm. Halia knew there was not much more beautiful and more moving than to see a community gather to celebrate its children. Halia felt a new sense of admiration for Asha, as she saw the performance as an incredibly rich, detailed, multifaceted gift that Asha had given these families. Halia watched the dads with camcorders, knowing that in years to come they would show the videos, proudly proclaiming "the camera shook here because I was laughing so hard."

After the performance the children glowed with pride. They also began to wilt, what with field day, a picnic, a performance, and now a "reception" for cast and crew. Gradually families collected up their children and strolled back to the school parking lot. Snatches of dialog echoed in the quiet Dover street, fourth graders lobbing 14th century insults at each other and singing "I'll tell thee a tale..." Many seemed loathe to leave, Halia noticed, unwilling to break the spell that the performance had woven around all of them. Halia felt honored to have been a part of it.

She walked home, having helped Louise and Larry with returning the "auditorium" to its pre-performance state. The street, now quiet and empty, and the prospect of the evening's worth of grading sobered her. Left alone with her thoughts, Halia mentally groped for the next lead. Freecycle Sam's lack of information had been a frustrating but not unexpected turn of events.

Halia reconsidered the conversation with Lukey Jane and Anne Marie. Yes, she thought, the gap between reality and perception might be at play here. What if Joann meant for her addresslessness to be taken literally, when in fact she simply did not know about GPS systems and the unromantic truth about location.

Joann was an archeologist, Halia reminded herself. There's no way she's ignorant about GPS. But what if her comments were meant not literally in terms of mapability, but literally in terms of post offices and mail delivery? One can spend time in a location that has an "address" in the sense of an identifiable position, but still be unreachable by most reasonable means. That made the most sense to Halia – that the place without an address was meant to indicate a lack of mail delivery, rather than a true lack of address.

But how much does that help, really? Halia wondered where would sixty-eight year old Joann Grant, the former archeology professor, go without telling anyone? Why would it involve retiring from her job and selling her house? Halia sat at her kitchen table while the dusk deepened to twilight, and East Mountain glowed as if a rose-orange spotlight were trained on it. The sky was indecent blue, and the hillside just a couple of miles away was awash with pale green flecked with white from the shad's bloom. Halia missed all of it, sitting inside, her head propped up by her hand on her forehead, her Joann file open and the list of hypotheses on top of the pile.

She started a new list on a fresh piece of paper. Places that have no address, she wrote across the top in stout capital letters. Travel, and then the subcategories began to fill the page: car/road trip, air/overseas travel, hiking/camping/backwoods, cruise, trains, boats (added with a grin at remembering Lukey Jane's insistence) … Halia paused, allowing a question to take shape – how will I be able to follow up on all these? Halia shrugged it off and continued brainstorming, the list lengthening and the dinner hour long gone by the time she laid down her pen.

Halia scrounged around her kitchen for something to eat. She settled on whole wheat fig bars from the oriental market in Hopewell (a gift from Rob and Asha for helping with Brulee while Asha had been so busy with rehearsals), and smeared them with peanut butter. Something about the appearance of the brown rectangles she was consuming made Halia think of camping and the food she'd eaten when backpacking many years prior. Suddenly Halia crammed the remains of the cookie into her mouth, grabbed a pen and her list and began scribbling. Then she reached for the phone, checking her watch to make sure it wasn't too late to make phone calls.

"Hello?" Eddie answered the phone.

"Hi, it's Halia, can I talk to Grace?" Halia managed to mumble through peanut butter and fig bar.

"Yeah, I'll get her for you – are you ok, Hali?"

"Yes, I'm fine," Halia, having swallowed, sounded more like herself. "I just have an idea that I wanted to check out with Grace."

"She's in the barn," Eddie explained. "Want me to go get her?"

"No, you might know this." Halia realized Eddie might have the information she sought. "Did you ever hike the Appalachian Trail?"

"Parts of it, sure. We go pretty often on some part of it – either in Connecticut, New York, or Massachusetts. Why?"

"No, I mean a through hike, or a big section. Weeks or months on the trail. Did Grace ever do that?" Halia realized this was something she didn't know about her friend.

"I don't think so," Halia could see Eddie's thoughtful expression in her mind's eye. "I'm pretty sure she never did. Why?"

Halia explained her sudden interest in through hiking the AT. "Joann talked about not having an address. I suddenly put it together that being in transit, and being in a remote location or in wilderness could add up to being on the AT. And I think for many people it beckons, like the Catskill 35 or Mount Marcy."

Eddie grunted the verbal equivalent of nodding.

"I'm just trying to figure out if being on the trail could be what Joann meant about being somewhere that has no address. I don't know much about through hiking, but I know that frequently hikers are in populated places, and can get to phones and post offices. I don't really know if visiting civilization for supplies on a semi regular basis would qualify in Joann's mind as being somewhere that has no address..." Halia trailed off. "I don't know Joann all that well, but I thought she might be the kind of person who would want to hike the AT. The more I think about it, though, the more I doubt it."

"Would you recognize her handwriting?"

"I have old Christmas cards," Halia replied, her mind stretching to grasp Eddie's unspoken idea.

"Maybe you can get to look at a section of log books from a couple of shelters – say from mid-March through mid-April or so. You could probably get a good sense of whether or not she passed through. I look at log books when I take Andrew out by Bull's Bridge, or along the Housatonic. It sure seems like everyone who passes through writes in those books."

Halia had enough information, and a sufficient idea of how to proceed to thank Eddie and hang up. Thus began the search for Joann in the log books of the Appalachian Trail.

It was an odyssey of emails and phone calls before the packages arrived: three in all – from Springer Mountain in Georgia, Hawk Mountain in Pennsylvania, and Katahdin in Maine. Halia spent hours pouring over photocopied handwritten journal entries, by people with trail names that would impress even the most adept instant messengers. She searched for an entry that matched Joann's handwriting, or a mention of someone who fit Joann's description. Although the log book entries were touching and precious to Halia, so full of hope and excitement and wit and humor, after scouring the third and last set of photocopies, Halia admitted defeat. She could find no mention of a grey-haired lady, traveling alone or in a group, and no entry in a hand that came close to Joann's. She could have started later, or from another part of the trail, but Halia knew that finding Joann on the AT now, in mid-June, without knowing where or when or if she started, was awfully close to looking for the proverbial needle in a haystack. At Grace and Eddie's urging, Halia hiked out to the Ten Mile River shelter (Bezef borrowed for the occasion) and wrote her own entry in the log book there, asking for help in locating Joann. In the weeks that followed Halia heard nothing and added the hypothesis that Joann's lack of an address was actually a way of saying she was hiking the Appalachian Trail to the collection of ideas that didn't pan out.

The school year ended, anticlimactically as usual. Searching the log books of the AT overlapped with the last two weeks of school. The intensity of each project somehow took the edge off the other. The last day came as a relief – the culmination of a week of cleaning and packing each day after school and burying herself in the log books each evening.

Summer. Without school to absorb and structure her time, Halia eyed the two months time warily as it stretched out before her. The risk of continuing this obsession, coupled with the very real possibility of total frustration, loomed large. Halia gritted her teeth and girded her loins in response. This is a task that can be done, she told herself, and I have enough time now to do it. End of story.

Chapter 8

What I do know is that when it happens, everyone knows immediately. More than immediately – simultaneously. When you are lying in bed next to her, and the final last straw – that last shred of resolve – breaks, and the decision is made, she knows. She might not want to, she might pretend she doesn't, she might even pretend so thoroughly and skillfully that she believes it herself, but she knows. Whether the decision is to leave or to cheat, or to ask her to marry you, it doesn't matter. The point is the same – when one strikes out with an independent thought that forever changes the course of the relationship, the other knows instantaneously. The vibrational shift, the subtle change in vocal timbre, the pheromone difference… I don't know what it is that gets communicated nor how it happens, but I do know that the other always knows. When the betrayal is finally revealed, swimming among the sick feelings in the pit of the stomach is foreknowledge unheeded. The clues were there, I saw them, I chose not to look at them, I chose not to see them. I have myself to blame.

You don't even have to be there, in the room. Geographic proximity is not required for the communication to come in loud and clear. It must be evidence of Bell's theorem – a nonlocal phenomenon. You can be across town or across the globe – there is that moment when it hits and you know and everything is different. You wish you didn't, and you might pretend you don't, but you do feel it and you do know. Your stomach does that flip flop and the jolt of adrenaline shoots through you like a car crash. The bravest among us just face it and await the inevitable phone call-email-instant message-whatever, knowing that something irrevocable has occurred. Tolerating the knowing is a different issue but that we know when we do is undeniable.

No, I don't think the prescience is false - a struggle to regain control when feeling out of control. As in, if I knew about this and failed to act, then somehow it was my fault, which then translates (in the desperate throes of post-dumped destitution) into I did this, so I can undo it. Maybe for most of us it's not even that clear, and rarely is it that fully thought out. And, no, I don't think knowing about it and failing to act makes it our own fault. I'm not letting the cheaters (or leavers or you name it – fill-in-the-blank) off the hook. Knowledge denied and intentional blindness is a forgivable offense – stupid and lame, but free from ill intent. Even repeat offenders need help, not blame. Taking responsibility for one's own ostrich behavior is a growth-promoting and necessary step, but it isn't the same as turning it into your own fault. There will be no blaming the victim.

Let the anger be righteous. Let the truth be revealed, dry-eyed and point blank.

"I lost my job." The torn open envelope was still in her hand, the typed letter lay on her kitchen table. Asha clutched the phone to her ear, her breath giving way to silent sobs. "I need to deal with this – to come up with a plan – before Pearl comes home."

"I am so sorry, honey," Rob's voice was broken by the static of a bad cell phone connection. "I'll be there as soon as I can."

"Ok." Asha hung up and immediately dialed another number.

The letter may as well have been bloodstained, for its effect on Asha. She swallowed hard and folded it up, rendered nauseous by the sight of the black marks on the white paper and the huge amounts of adrenaline being released into her bloodstream. She spoke to Pearl's father, fighting for control of her voice, struggling word by word to stay focused. Carl agreed to keep Pearl for the evening and overnight, agreeing that Asha was in no condition to present this information to a twelve-year-old. Asha called her mother, and wept freely, blurting out all her fears – losing the house, losing custody of Pearl, losing her sense of competence as a parent and an adult... Asha spiraled downward into despair and panic, while her mother listened and waited.

"How did it happen?" Her mother wanted to know.

"The administration decided the school has a greater need for psychology services, and just eliminated my position. They used my low caseload to justify that decision."

"Tenure doesn't matter?"

"No."

Asha's mother paused, but Asha did not elaborate. "I'm here, Asha," she offered.

"I know, mom."

"You'll get through this, Asha. I know you will."

"I know, mom."

"Whatever you need, honey. You know I'm here for you."

"I know. Thanks, mom."

Asha hung up, her hands still trembling, the metallic taste of sheer panic lingering in her mouth. Brulee had come to sit beside her, and Asha stroked the soft black fur on her face. Brulee leaned in and Asha petted her rhythmically, mechanically, using the simple motion as a meditation. Exhaustion slowly replaced the adrenaline rush, and Asha made her way, drunkenly, to the living room and the tattered thrift store couch. She sank down, and covered herself with a blanket, despite the summer heat. Brulee sat next to the couch, offering protection and support. Unable to relax, Asha lay there, fists balled up under Pearl's favorite fleece blanket (the one with the horses on it), her mind racing. Rob found her there several hours later.

The heatwave caught the Hudson Valley rather off guard. Although residents could boast familiarity with nearly every type of severe weather event, from tornadoes (we all remember Millbrook in '91) to hurricanes, drought, flooding, ice storms, blizzards, wind shears, etc., as temperatures soared into triple digits for the fourth day in a row, over and over again in the Freshtown supermarket, the movie theatre, Cousin's deli, and all the other places Doverites rubbed elbows, the complaint was repeated: "I'm just not ready for this. It's not even July yet."

Grace took Andrew and Bezef to the AT trailhead in Kent, out by St. John's Ledges, to let them swim in the Housatonic every afternoon while heatwave lasted. Grace waded, splashed, and threw sticks for Bezef, who seemed to think nothing of diving underwater in search of items to chew. She seemed almost surprised by the fact that she couldn't breathe the water and entertained Grace and Andrew with her attempts.

School being out for the summer meant Halia had time to travel again, if need be, to once again look for clues as to where Joann might have gone. Frustrated, Halia admitted to herself that she didn't know where to go or what to pursue next. Three full months had passed since Joann had sold her home. Three and a half months, Halia corrected herself, as she remembered the March 15 date. Three and a half months is a long time, Halia decided. Long enough so that wherever one is, and whatever one is doing, after 14 or so weeks, it is no longer new. Halia felt this and knew that wherever Joann was at that moment, she felt it too.

Would there be regrets? Halia wondered. Was Joann contemplating coming home? Where would home be, now that the Keeseville house was sold? Was she considering making a change or having second thoughts? Halia worked hard at turning her intiuitive feelings into rational conclusions, her hunches into hypotheses. She knew the truth; it was inescapable: Halia felt in her gut that something was happening with Joann. A border had been crossed, or a point of no return reached, or some other shift had occurred. Seeking Joann had connected Halia to her, and one result of this connection was that somewhere unidentifiable, deep within, Halia could just sense things that were happening to Joann. Later, when it was all over, she would tell her friends that she believed she had known all along that Joann was alright. She never trusted those feelings the way she relied upon her intellect, but she was unable to discount them either. The heat made her languid and slow and thoughtful and these were the thoughts that filled those hot days.

Finally, on July 3rd, the heat wave broke with a dramatic and cleansing thunderstorm. Halia and Asha watched the lightning from Asha's back porch while Bezef and Brulee were beside themselves indoors.

"Will you be at the poetry reading tomorrow?" Halia asked Asha.

"Yes. I don't know much about the poet, but I'm very curious. He sounds like a real performer." Asha was still sweating despite the 20 degree reduction in temperature. She looked a trifle thin and exhausted, her exercise regime having changed very little, despite the heat and her impressive stress level. Halia considered sharing her observations, then, instead, silently fetched Asha and herself another glass of water. "Rob will meet me there, I think. He mentioned something about needing to work on his kitchen ceiling." The women exchanged a knowing look, like sisters in a family with an eccentric brother.

"On July 4th, on Dover's bicentennial celebration day, on the day of Venus Vison's poetry reading, Rob has decided to become Mr. Handyman?" Halia joked, her words softened by her affectionate tone.

"I know, I know," Asha shrugged. "But remember, he was amazing about my Shakespeare club extravaganza. He really saved the day many times over."

Halia didn't respond aloud right away, but appraised Asha thoughtfully for a moment first. "And since then?"

"You know we're planning to move in together. We're talking about moving to Orange County, or maybe Sullivan… We're trying to find a place where we can afford the land he needs to grow the currants." Asha met Halia's eyes and admitted wordlessly that she wasn't answering Halia's question. Her eyes dropped to her lap. "He is in the role of rescuer… it isn't good. I need to pull myself together and get out of this mess by myself, but …" Asha looked in danger of breaking down. She chewed her lower lip for a moment, then choked out, "I do need his help."

Halia nodded.

"It is putting pressure on the relationship. I'm a mess, and Pearl is just being amazing, but she needs more from me - more time, more support, more comfort … and suddenly instead of being in a fun new falling-in-love relationship, Rob's thrust into rescue mode. He isn't saying he minds, but I can see it. He just wants things to be the way they were, and so do I, but that's gone. I don't know if I can ever get back to that…"

Asha looked so profoundly sad, Halia was worried. "What do you mean?"

"You know I traveled around India about 15 years ago?" Halia shook her head. "Well, yeah, I went to India back before I married Pearl's dad. It started out as a project – I was taking photographs." Halia's eyes were continuing to widen as Asha revealed the details. Asha saw this and brightened up. "The photo career didn't work out, and my camera got stolen... it's a long story. Actually, I guess it's a few different long stories," she said, watching the beads of water running down the outside of her water glass. "When I was in India, it was so intense sometimes – the constant fighting and struggling to try to protect yourself and your stuff. You had to constantly try to make sure that you don't get ripped off, that people charge you the right price for everything... there was so much that you needed to know, to be able to play the game of traveling without getting into dangerous situations, or getting permanently separated from your belongings." Asha continued to fix her gaze upon the glass, speaking slowly, as if she was giving the memories time to reach the surface. "Sometimes I'd be somewhere safe – a restaurant, or a café, a hotel room – and then I'd remember that I had to go back 'out there' into the fight. And my heart would sink, and I'd feel all the fear and exhaustion rush back into me – like an injection, it felt like it was just flowing through my veins, all of a sudden. The one thought, and BAM – I was depressed, anxious... tense." Asha paused. "These days it's kind of similar – every time I relax and enjoy myself, and feel safe for a few minutes, it creeps back up on me. Something reminds me, or whatever it is that we're doing comes to an end... and I'm tensed again, ready to start trying to think my way out of this again." Asha raised her eyes to search Halia's face for understanding. "Like, we watch a movie together, and I can forget what's going on and get lost in the movie, but the minute it's over, I'm just wired again." Asha sighed. "I know Pearl feels it, no matter how hard I try to be cheery around her. She's perceptive and way too savvy for her age. She is letting me act ok around her, but I have a feeling she's complaining mightily to her dad." Asha's lip quivered involuntarily. "And Rob... he didn't sign up for this. He is stepping up to the plate and all, but I just feel guilty. I feel like I let him down. Like I'm letting everyone down."

Halia frowned hard. Her voice was low and thick with anger. "You are not letting anyone down. That's ridiculous. When you and Rob chose to be involved with each other, of course you both hoped for the fairy tale romance. But love," Halia was too angry to recognize the absurd irony in her playing the role of expert on matters of the heart, "shouldn't – can't – be a fair weather proposition. That's not love." Halia paused, then added with quiet intensity, "That's something else. Something cheap and unworthy of you and Pearl."

Asha didn't answer right away. She looked at Halia, and her face flashed understanding so briefly Halia almost missed it. Then Asha resumed her tense, stonily stoic expression of poorly masked worry.

"I don't know what I'll do – the job situation so far hasn't been great – a couple of interviews here and there, but nothing that feels good. I can only imagine the energy I bring to a job interview – I'm desperate, hurt, angry, terrified... I think even with a flawless resume and my dress-for-success suit, I still just have this vibe of misery and disaster." Asha shrugged. "I am busting my ass trying to get this place ready to put on the market – that's been a good way for me to focus my energy."

Halia pressed her lips together. Asha's house was so quintessentially Asha, Halia disliked the idea that she would sell. It felt wrong. Asha felt Halia's disapproval and went inside to busy herself with filling Brulee's water bowl.

The storm had subsided, the rumblings distant and the flashes just reflections of faraway bolts. It was early evening and the day seemed to be dawning rather than ending, climbing out from under the oppressive heaviness of the heat and storm. The conversation lightened up as well.

"You know my 20 year high school reunion is scheduled for this week." Asha announced.

Halia nodded.

"Usually the reunions are scheduled for Thanksgiving weekend – I guess the people organizing it think that's when everyone goes 'home.' This year they changed it to July 4th and planned a picnic and softball game. I guess at 20 years past high school, everyone figures we're traveling with spouse and kids. It's a much more family-oriented event this year."

"Where did you go to high school?"

"Nyack, in Rockland County. Do you know where that is?"

Halia nodded again, her gaze thoughtful. "Asha? Could I have a piece of paper and a pencil?"

Writing implements provided, Halia jotted down a few notes.

"Everything ok? Was it something I said?" Asha half joked.

"Just a thought I want to follow up on later."

"About Joann?"

"Yes, about Joann." Halia refrained from saying more and Asha didn't press. High school reunions… she would have to check Joann's age again to be sure. And go over her notes from her interview with Silas

Nase. A few moments later Halia's cell phone rang. "Excuse me," she murmured to Asha and answered the phone. She walked out into Asha's yard admiring the perennial border as she spoke. Halia called out to Asha, "Grace is on the phone – she wants to know what we're doing."

"Invite her to join us. And tell her Bezef did just fine during the storm." Asha let the dogs out, and returned to her kitchen to make Grace a drink.

Grace was calling from the animal hospital only half a mile away, and was seated on Asha's back porch, a cold drink in her hand and canine muzzles in her lap before Halia had returned to her former seat on the pleasantly crowded porch.

Grace lifted her grapefruit juice and tonic water in a "cheers" gesture and looked at Halia. Halia examined Grace from head to toe in a sweeping glance and beamed a huge smile. "You found evidence up in Philmont!"

Grace looked herself over, peering at the undersides of her shoes and checking under her fingernails. "What gave it away?" she demanded, laughing delightedly.

"Who cares?" Halia referred to her talent dismissively, waving her hand as if to shoo away the question and refocus on Grace's discovery. "Tell us – what did you find?"

Grace told the story of her most recent visit to Philmont with great drama and obvious pleasure at being able to relive the adventure in its telling. She stressed the heat and dust as if she'd been stranded on the Gangetic Plain in an exceptionally hot dry season, and Halia and Asha made appropriately sympathetic or impressed noises as the occasions arose. She had gone up to Philmont in the afternoon and set up a stakeout through the evening hours. Her efforts had been rewarded with an uncanny sight: Grace produced photographs of a small band of creatures, adorable yet bizarre in appearance. Their long pointy faces on woodchuck-like bodies with long striped tails added up to such an incongruous picture both Asha and Halia blurted out the same response.

"They look like a photoshop joke – like a jacka-lope!"

All three women laughed, although Grace feigned hurt feelings and pouted. "Forget it then, I won't show you their scat."

"Do you have some with you?" Asha wasn't sure if Grace was joking or not.

"Uhh, I'm proud of this discovery," Grace stated thrusting her chest and chin outward and looking down her nose at her friends, "but not that proud." She grinned and added, "Besides, it doesn't look like much. I left it at the animal hospital – I figure we can run all our in-house lab work on it – parasites, stuff like that – and see if anything would indicate that these are not just Philmontian woodchucks - " a giggle escaped from behind Asha's hand covering her mouth " - but something a little more exotic."

"Grace, all joking aside, no one would think these are woodchucks." Halia studied the photos intently. "I count four in this shot, but look," she pointed to a shadowy corner of a different photograph. "Here are these four and then here in this corner, I think I see a fifth snout. See that?"

Grace took the photograph and studied it too. Asha turned the porch light on over their heads and squinted at the photo as well. "Yes, I do see it. Well, well …"

Grace trailed off and met Halia's eyes. "Sure looks like Momma, doesn't it?"

"That's what I was thinking. Look at that snout. It's really different from the others. It's much longer and narrower." Halia shrugged and encouraged Grace, "I guess you need to go back to Philmont again to look for your source of these half-breeds."

"Yup," Grace agreed. "I have a feeling the locals are getting used to seeing me there." She checked her watch and collected the photos, placing them back in their paperboard envelope. "I need to go," she explained. "Eddie and I joined the town's co-ed softball team and we have a game tonight. I'm meeting Eddie and Andrew in Wingdale for pizza before the game."

Asha's eyes lit up. "Softball? Really?"

Halia suppressed a smile. It seemed that Asha hadn't met a sport she didn't like. Halia didn't get it.

Later that evening Halia had time to follow up on the lead Asha had inadvertently given her. So Thanksgiving weekend was when high school reunions were typically held… Halia hadn't known that, oblivious as she was to her own reunions. It took several phone calls to Pottersville before Halia found someone who was both knowledgeable and willing to talk, but finally she did. Although Halia took precise notes throughout the conversation, she managed to extract a promise from the alumnae association president of North Warren High School that photocopies of the materials Halia was interested in would also be mailed to her, if last year's materials were still available. Satisfied, Halia

slept peacefully, the gurgling of the swollen creek murmuring answers to the questions her conscious mind
had not yet posed.

Halia had been helping Louise all afternoon, setting up chairs, cleaning, tidying, and arranging, getting ready for Venus's poetry reading. A celebrity and a
local legend, Louise was anticipating that Venus would
draw a large crowd, especially considering that the park
across the street was just about the best spot in town to
watch the fireworks.

They were taking a break and Louise was fixing
virgin lizards for both of them when Venus strolled in
with a skinny dark-haired youth.

"Hi! You're early!" Louise hurriedly finished making the drinks and flew out from behind the bar into
Venus's outstretched arms. Loud smacking kisses were
planted on both her cheeks, and he playfully tugged at
her braid.

"How are you, Weezy?" he greeted her affectionately, and snaking an arm around her waist, introduced
his companion. "Louise, I'd like you to meet Kennedy
Edmonds. He's a folk singer – you know, like Rufus
Wainwright."

Louise looked inquiringly from Venus to Kennedy.

"Yeah. I'm a lot like Rufus Wainwright, only I don't
have famous parents." He seemed sweet, direct and
honest. Louise liked his face.

"This is Halia Frank." Louise introduced her
friend.

"How do you do?" Halia heard herself utter the

outdated phrase, and surprised herself by deciding that those were precisely the right words.

Venus, a fifty-ish man – tall, thin and reminiscent of David Bowie circa Ziggy Stardust – was wearing purple and pink eye shadow and heaps of black eye liner and mascara. He had done a good job with it, and his face had an overall air brushed look. It was hard to picture this man as a seventh grader in her science class, but Halia reminded herself that Venus had indeed gone through the public schools in town. Although he no longer lived in Dover full time, he divided his time between an apartment in Manhattan (the west village, of course) and the cabin out in the farm field on Plymouth Hill. Halia already knew this about Venus, and in meeting him took in these apparent contradictions. Venus gave every outward appearance of a man who would not enjoy a hermit's lifestyle.

Halia turned her observing eye to Kennedy Edmonds. Glossy black hair hung in untidy waves around his Ivory Boy face. He looked young, trying to look older by working on appearing laid back and unconcerned. Black eyes, black t-shirt, black hair, and black boots failed to darken his appearance. Halia could see eagerness leaking around every edge of his façade, and there was something so engaging, so innocently charming about his efforts that Halia found herself feeling almost motherly towards him.

"If it's ok with you," Venus spoke to Louise, "I'd like to share the bill with Ken tonight. Sort of a 'special guest' thing. Is that kosher?"

"That sounds great." Louise shrugged happily. "What a treat. Can you use the same stage and equipment and all that?" Louise gestured to the area behind them, where she and Halia had arranged the chairs and created the stage.

"Oh that's fine for me," Ken investigated briefly and struggled to look low key about it. "I don't need much. I'm doing an all acoustic set anyway."

"I want a wireless head set," Venus whined. "I'll settle for nothing less."

Louise rolled her eyes. "You can have whatever you want when you're headlining at the Garden," she quipped in return. Then, in mock horror, she added, "You haven't added singing to your repertoire?"

"Touché." Venus also looked over the stage set up and complimented Louise and Halia on their efforts. "We'll be back later," he called over his shoulder. "Toodles!"

"Don't be late for dinner," Louise's voice carried across the room as Venus and Ken headed for the door. Halia saw Kennedy's eyes flick to Venus to determine how to respond.

"We wouldn't miss it for the world, darling!" Venus called airily over his shoulder, his silk poet's shirt rippling with the movement. Halia heard him explaining to Ken that performers receive a complimentary meal at Louise's. As they disappeared out of earshot, Halia could have sworn she heard Ken say "Really? Free?" and she began to feel curious about Ken's songwriting. What would this little boy who played at being a worldly man have to say?

"What a character," Louise summarized the brief interaction.

"Both of them," Halia agreed. "How do you know Venus?"

"When I was in college, up in Northhampton,"

Louise began, sliding Halia her drink and clambering onto a barstool, "he did a reading. I went. He read 'The Bob-Haired Bandit of Brooklyn' – it's a lyrical poem about a female Robin Hood from Brooklyn in the 1920's. As I listened to the poem, I realized he was describing my grandmother." A laugh escaped from Halia. She smothered it quickly, eager for Louise to go on. "She was a flapper and she led a crazy life style – she was married with children but did these burglaries in wealthy neighborhoods, but never for her own gain. She did go to jail, several times, I think. She's one of the more colorful characters on my mom's side of the family.

Anyway, after the performance I went to find Venus backstage and tell him that he's written a poem about my grandmother. We talked for a while that night – he told me about reading her story in a history of Brooklyn, and also about his cabin here in Dover, up on Plymouth Hill. You know, he stays up there for days on end when he's writing." Halia nodded, impressed but not surprised. "Well, we kind of struck up a friendship, I guess. After college, you know I owned The Braid and Bonnet for a while. Venus did readings for me there." Louise smiled fondly, remembering. "He is really such a showman, such a performer. He has a charisma on stage the likes of which is rare." Louise had been gazing into space, picturing her memories. She now looked at Halia and adopted a more conversational tone. "You know the talents of writing poetry and performing poetry are really different. I think he has both."

Halia had been entertained by Venus already. "I'm really looking forward to the show," she told Louise. "Do you know anything about young Kennedy Edmonds?"

"Not a thing," admitted Louise, "but I trust Venus.

He knows the Dover audience pretty well, between growing up here and performing at the college, and around. If he thinks Ken will be right for this event, I'm satisfied." Louise paused, then continued, "how old do you think Ken is?"

"Mid twenties, I'd guess."

"He's pretty cute, don't you think?"

Halia found Ken cute the way one might find an eight year old boy cute, but she chose an only slightly more tactful response. "Louise, he seems so innocent and naïve, like a sweet little boy! He makes me feel motherly!" Halia exaggerated the word with such drama both women burst out laughing.

Halia finished her drink and went home to change out of her furniture moving outfit. She also felt the need to pay some attention to Bezef, since Grace parked her at Halia's for the afternoon.

"Fireworks tonight," she told the long-limbed canine. "How are you going to react?"

Bezef barked at Halia's tone. Halia shook her head, never failing to be impressed with Bezef's sensitivity. She could tell by the tone of Halia's voice or the angle of incline of Halia's head whether or not to bark. She seemed to learn routines before Halia had even realized those activities had become routinized, and she seemed to know that if she hammed up the goofy act, Halia would laugh. In fact, Bezef seemed truly motivated to make Halia laugh; Halia was sure she saw Bezef "experimenting" with behaviors, repeating the ones that elicited laughter. Sometimes Halia thought she was less dog-like than most dogs – more like half cat, half monkey.

"You are the smartest nit wit I ever met," Halia

rubbed her forehead. Bezef wagged her whole body, and Halia added, "and the sweetest."

Halia was ready to head back to The Eft with plenty of time to find a good seat and maybe find Eddie and Grace or Lukey Jane or Asha and Rob to sit with. She knew pretty much everyone would be at The Eft tonight, and she was glad she'd helped Louise get set up.

Almost as an afterthought, Halia grabbed her mail from the mailbox and headed towards the house, intending to drop off the pile just inside the front door and continue to Louise's. Her cursory glance through the envelopes, though, stopped her in her tracks. Her eyes fell upon the postcard – a lovely Gauguin of Tahitian women. Turning it over, she recognized the handwriting from years of Christmas cards.

"Well it might not be Tahiti but I'm having a grand time. Hope all is well with you. Best, Joann Grant."

Chapter 9

Are There Wolves in Your Garden?

Restless dogtrotting in repetitive circles
sniffing hanging baskets, noses lifted
as if in mid howl
crushing the begonias as they sprawl for an afternoon nap
Waking in the evening
to the scent of jasmine
pale white trumpet shaped blooms
amplifying their early evening calls
Many moons caught and reflected
in the white flowers
the heavy sweet scent
and the cool humid night air
Stretching luxuriously, long claws rake soft earthen beds
like the tines of your hand held cultivator
as you weed

and groom
and tidy up
each morning.
Howl.
Nose pressed against thick panes of antique glass
holding you in as your breath streams out.
Howl.

Venus finished and after the hushed moment, applause erupted. With dramatic flair, he relinquished the stage, and young Kennedy Edmonds stepped up, front and center, to the microphone.

A sweet song of love and longing provided the perfect counterpoint to Venus's more abstract poetry. Ken had dedicated the song to "Leah" and Halia felt Louise scowl from across the room. Venus and Ken traded off songs and poems several more times, each somehow setting up the next piece just so. Each individual song or poem stood on its own merit, but by the end of Venus's last word, the lasting impression was of an overall whole – one event, one song, one poem, one show. Venus and Ken touched nerves, but they did so gently and subtly. Audience members headed across the street smiling, the evening lingering pleasantly upon their senses. Fireworks seemed almost garish in comparison.

Halia's head was spinning for the first few minutes of the show, but true to form, she reasoned that there was no decisive action she could take at that moment, and simply chose to absorb the latest Joann Grant development later. For this evening, Halia willed herself to be present, focused on the activity at hand.

She was rewarded by enjoying the show thoroughly. Grace, Eddie and Andrew sat on her left, Asha alone up front (Rob having begged off with a headache), and Louise even found a few minutes to slide into the seat beside her. Halia caught sight of Anne Marie and Lukey Jane, both elegantly attired and as Lukey Jane would say, all gussied up. Halia smiled at the sight of Lukey Jane, her hair smoothed, her clothes full of drape and shimmer, with Anne Marie standing guard over her to prevent any close calls. Halia also noticed several photographers, one of whom she recognized from various special events at school. Halia felt pleased for Louise – this evening could not have gone over better.

Fireworks. Halia stood just a little apart from the crowd, noticing a chill in the air. Couples fended off the cool dampness by leaning against each other, braiding arms into arms and becoming one unit. Halia experienced the night without romance, taking it all on its own terms, unmediated by a sense of 'us.' She slipped away without making perfunctory goodbyes, and walked home without watching the sky, feeling the finale rather than seeing it.

Deep in thought, Halia reached her front porch and was badly startled by young Kennedy Edmonds, seated on the top step. Before she recovered, he began speaking.

"Halia, I wanted to … oh, I'm sorry, I guess this is weird. I asked Larry about you … I'm not stalking you or anything like that, I just …" He trailed off, stood up and looked into her eyes. "I just … uuhhh… I thought maybe I could, like, get to know you. Maybe we could talk?" His hands were shoved deep into his pockets and he looked brave and terrified all at once. "I, ummm, oh shit," Ken had been shifting his weight from foot to foot as he spoke, and he managed to stumble off the step, catching himself before he crashed into Halia. She backed up a couple of steps and waited for him to regain his balance and his train of thought. "Is this ok?" he asked.

"Me?" Halia asked, her incredulous tone making her opinion apparent. "You want to be alone with me? Like that?"

"Yes," Ken answered, a little miserably.

"No," Halia stated firmly, if not emphatically.

The hurt in Ken's face chiseled at her resolve. Her hesitation was dangerously close to being misinterpreted, and she hastened to correct this. "Ken, no. Absolutely not. No way." She tried to speak firmly, giving no chink to stick a wedge into, while also sounding kind.

"Oh," Ken's chin drooped and his shiny hair hid his face. "Well, that makes this just a little awkward..." Ken trailed off. He wrestled with a number of other things to say – how he felt something really strong and serene from her. That her eyes drew him in and made him want to know what she was thinking. That her air of independence and self sufficiency was really sexy to him. He was tempted to beg: "Just let me get to know you a little. It doesn't have to mean... anything." He stood there, an arm's length away from her in the darkness, and said nothing.

Halia did not break his silence, as she was reeling from the surprise of finding him here. Even more surprising to her was his reason for seeking her out. Me??? Attractive to him? Halia was floored. It had been years since she had been confronted with a suitor. Ken seemed like a sweet, kind, and slightly crazy young man, to Halia, but even crazier was that catch in her throat and the curiosity she recognized in the strange sensation in her chest. On the one hand, she wanted – felt compelled - to deliver the speech: "I am not available now, not for the immeasureable future. I am not open to getting to know anyone, and I can't let anyone get to know me. In the five minutes total that I've known you so far, I have gotten the impression that you are a nice person, and you deserve a wonderful woman who can make you feel special. I am not that." And on the other hand, she felt that tiny curious twinge of openness – the temptation to invite Ken to sit down on the front steps. She said nothing and waited for both urges diminish.

Halia sat down somewhat heavily on the porch step, not trusting herself to speak. Ken sat down on her right, the presence of her right thigh and shoulder dominating his awareness. After several silent minutes, Ken cleared his throat softly and began again.

"I'm sorry, Halia. I guess this doesn't make any sense."

Halia nodded slowly, keeping her eyes averted. She didn't answer. Kennedy got up and walked away, having decided not to wait for Venus after all. Halia sat still and silent on the porch steps for a long time before finally going inside.

The postmark was from the MidHudson Post Office, in Poughkeepsie, dated July 1st. The card was from the Museum of Modern Art. Halia was stumped. And Joann was having a Grand Time.

Halia had set herself up to be able to become immersed in The Joann Project. Now that it was summer and Halia wasn't working, while Grace's hours were as long as ever, Bezef spent increasing amounts of time at Halia's house. She had been walked, fed, played with, and given a bone (the canine equivalent to being sat in front of a television set, Halia thought); in this manner, Halia thought she had probably purchased at least an hour or two of uninterrupted pondering. Her notes covered the kitchen table – notes from the Silas Nase interview and from the recent conversation at Asha's house on top of neat stacks of paper scraps, backs of envelopes, and small spiral notebooks. Halia doodled, scribbled, and wrote lists and questions as she became more and more deeply consumed with The Problem. Finally, hours after sitting down, her left elbow propped on the table, her left hand holding her neglectedly long bangs out of her eyes, Halia laid down her pen.

Something added up. It worked forward, backward and sideways as an explanation. Farfetched, Halia admitted, but airtight as far as she could tell. No clue was ignored, and basic questions regarding motive, means and timing were satisfactorily answered. Halia felt ready to tie this hypothesis in with her intuitions of a few weeks ago, and she could make that fit too. And, while there was nothing left for her to do but wait, because if she had truly figured this out correctly, Joann would reappear just as Joy Barker had said she would - popping back up as if her absence had been unremarkable – Halia was left with two fairly major unanswered questions. She still didn't know where Joann was. Knowing what Joann had done didn't include knowing where she had actually gone. Nor did Halia know who she was with, although she was certain Joann was not alone. Halia had to admit that as much as she knew for sure, she still needed a few details to consider her search truly completed. And, she also felt frustratingly forced to admit, her conclusions at this point stalled further searching. She did not know where to look next to come up with those last two pieces of information.

For a moment, Halia was tempted to review it all again, just to double check her calculations, but she resisted, knowing that would be compulsive. She was also tempted to parade her findings down to The Eft, call all her friends, and publicly declare herself triumphant, but that urge was even more easily resisted. Although the challenge had absorbed her for months and there was a tremendous sense of relief in finally reaching a palatable conclusion, the feeling was not exactly one of triumph. She felt relieved that, if she was indeed proved correct, Joann was safe and happy. She felt the weight the problem bore somewhat lightened, but still very much present upon her shoulders. She couldn't quite resist eagerly anticipating the opportunity to ask Joann a few questions, to clear up those last few details that remained obscure.

Summer in the Harlem Valley meant Grace battled fleas at work and flies at home, while Asha had the summer off. With Asha's time was increasingly absorbed by planning her move, and Grace's free time was constrained by the demands of work and family, Halia was left to her own devices more often than not, and felt herself to be at loose ends. With neither work to structure her time, nor companions to share in her leisure, Halia lavished attention on Bezef. They walked together, played together, and since Grace had informed Halia regarding all the best swimming spots, they splashed together too. As the summer wore on, Halia reaped the benefits of regular exercise. Between the sun, the exercise, and the easing of her mind regarding Joann's whereabouts, the glow noticed by her colleagues last spring blossomed into radiance.

Halia bumped into Venus Vison at the post office a few weeks after the reading at The Eft, and true to form Venus was over the top, complete with noisy air kisses hello. "If Ken could see you now," Venus stage whispered, "you look positively gorgeous. Whatever - or whoever – you're doing, keep it up. It works for you."

Halia was both embarrassed and flattered. Venus was a strange but genuine man. Looking good was an irrelevant and slightly uncomfortable addition to Halia's self image. She knew herself fairly well, she thought, but ever since Joann had moved leaving no forwarding address, she suspected a difference. She remembered being cajoled by Louise about taking one of the stray kittens the Benson brothers had found outside behind The Eft. And then she remembered meeting Asha in the graveyard the night Halia had telephoned Bones. That was before Joann's departure had taken on the status of a project, but Halia was already undergoing some form of transformation. Aspects of her self previously unknown were coming to the fore. Indeed, Halia realized, even taking an interest in Grace's puppy was a symptom of a change rather than its herald.

The change began that weekend last spring when her basement flooded and she learned of Joann's departure. Observation is my forte, Halia thought somewhat ruefully, not analysis. I see the change, but I don't know if I can break it down and capture its meaning. That would require a different set of skills; a shift of emphasis from the rational to the emotional. It was a leap Halia lacked the skills to make.

Being summer, Andrew attended day camp while Grace and Eddie worked – there was little time leftover for coati hunting and no more than the usual amount of Friday-evening-at-The-Eft times for Halia and Grace to touch base. Halia chose to be close-mouthed about her latest hypothesis, and Grace, still thinking it was related to the aftermath of her trip to Keeseville, helped to steer the conversation in other directions.

"How are the plans for the ice cream party coming along?" Grace knew Halia was on Louise's planning committee.

"Louise and I have come up with a menu so far. It really showcases the whole black currant and blueberry theme. If there was anyone left in the Hudson Valley that didn't know about The Blue Eft's commitment to all things blue and currant, they definitely will after this." Halia looked at her alizarin smoke critically before continuing. "We're hoping for a good day weather-wise because we kind of want a garden party feel, with outdoor seating and maybe even a serving area across the street in the garden as well as over here."

"Have you worked out all the bugs for the recipes?"

"Well," Halia hedged, "every blueberry ice cream attempt has come out a grey color that Louise finds unappealing. We're trying to come up with a cassis sauce – you know, to make a sundae kind of thing – and so far all our test batches have been too sweet and not strongly black currant flavored enough. I think Louise wants to make an authentic English style trifle starring blueberries and black currants too – the Benson brothers have been working with her on that." Halia shrugged. "I guess it will all come together in time." She paused long enough to allow the change of topics to take place. "What's up in Philmont? Have you heard back from the DEC yet?"

Grace had emailed her photographs to the local DEC Wildlife biologist over in New Paltz to see what they thought about the animals in the pictures. "No, I haven't heard back from them yet. I plan to go back with Eddie and Andrew this weekend, though, because there are fireworks in Hudson tomorrow night. It's part of their concert in the park series or some such thing. Anyway, I've heard that the fireworks in Hudson are the best in the whole valley! I think we can have an early dinner, do a little twilight coati watching, and make it to Hudson for the fireworks. Want to join us?"

Halia laughed. "Sure. I feel like I already know this animal – it will be fun to finally see her in the … fur?"

Grace laughed too.

The coati-hunting, fireworks-in-Hudson adventure ended up being more taxing than fun for all of them. It was hot and dusty on the side of Route 217 and Andrew got antsy. Then the coatis failed to show up and Andrew got bored, while Grace got disappointed and Eddie got irritated. There were no fresh tracks, and no scat, so the Taresius family, in their disgruntled state, and Halia, moved on to Hudson somewhat earlier than planned.

The concert in the park down by the river, Grace had neglected to mention, featured singer-songwriter Kennedy Edmonds. Halia wondered idly if every time she had the opportunity to watch fireworks, from now on Ken would somehow be involved. She knew it was pointless to hope their paths wouldn't cross – there were hundreds of people at the concert and more were arriving in teeming throngs for the fireworks, but Halia knew enough about fate and luck to know that she and Ken would come face to face again.

"What does he see in me?" Halia wondered. "What could he possibly be imagining that has fooled him into seeing me with such starry eyes?" Halia spent no time scanning the crowd – increasingly impossible in the gathering darkness anyway. She could feel that Kennedy would find her without even looking.

When he did arrive at her side, moments after the fireworks started, Halia did not indulge her vanity in even a split second of celebration of her psychic abilities. She also decided not to be disappointed that her experience of fireworks was now going to include interacting with Ken. The first few explosions did seem better than average; Grace had not been misinformed as to the quality of the Hudson show. Ken stood quietly next to Halia, and watched the fireworks. His presence was distracting but not unpleasant, and Halia chose to watch the fireworks and wait him out, rather than divide her attention.

After the show, Ken turned to Halia. "Fireworks again," he began. "Did you catch any of my set?"

"Just the last two songs. You sounded great."

"I'm sorry if I wierded you out that night at your house."

"It's ok."

"I'm staying at Venus's place on Plymouth Hill for the rest of the summer."

"Yeah?" Halia wasn't sure what to make of this.

"Venus is staying in the city." Ken offered that aspect of the explanation. Halia's eyebrows failed to fall, so Ken continued to explain. "I want to do some writing and just take some time up here... get into some solitude, y'know?"

"Yeah."

"I, um, I'd like to spend some time with you at some point, if you change your mind about us getting to know each other." Ken fought the stammer by speeding through the suggestion. Once finished, he tightened his jaw, and peeked through his hair at Halia.

"I'll be in touch if I change my mind."

Ken hesitated for a moment, and then reached for Halia. Startled, she returned the chest-only hug, wondering what, if anything, to say.

"Ok, well, good night," Ken excused himself and stalked off into the dispersing crowd. Halia watched him go, and smiled to herself. She turned to Grace, and was confronted by three wide-eyed and open mouthed stares.

"That was Kennedy Edmonds," Eddie stated.

"That was the guy on the stage," Andrew added for emphasis.

Grace didn't need to speak.

Grace recovered her composure first and herded Halia toward the car, the movement breaking the spell Eddie and Andrew seemed to be under. All the way home, all three of them stole curious, impressed glances at Halia, until Andrew fell asleep, Grace returned her attention to the coati hunt, and Eddie kept his eyes on the road. Halia looked out the window at the blackened landscapes and wondered why Kennedy Edmonds found her compelling enough to pursue.

Yes, Ken was attractive, in his "I'm unconcerned about my looks" way. His face did make Halia stop and think about what it had been like to have intimacy in her life. She remembered what it was like to know the texture of another person's lips, to recognize their scent on the sheets, to feel her pulse quicken at the crunch of the gravel under their tires, knowing the beloved is back home. Long before Bones had left such a bad taste in her mouth, Halia had tried relationships. She had dabbled – experimented – with intimacy. She knew that many people would tell her to give it another try – to get back on that horse, so to speak. Ken's attention and that small flicker of interest she knew she felt forced the issue to the forefront of her consciousness – was she ready to consider a partner, on any level?

Love can heal, Halia admitted to herself, and wallowing in self pity and mistrust would be a real memorial to the marriage and Bones. But, she told herself, I know that whatever healing I might need to do, I can do it alone. I know that I have to. No one else should come along for this ride. I've been working this out for years now and I am finally getting close to being where I want to be. But it's my process – my journey – whatever you want to call it. Halia realized she wasn't sure who she was addressing so vehemently, as she noticed her thoughts sounded rather like one side of an argument. She continued, reserving a small part of her awareness for self-observation, awaiting the revelation as to why she was defending her position. Getting over a bad marriage doesn't necessarily mean being ready for another relationship. It might mean that for some people, but not for me. Some people are different – I'm different. That doctor's suggestion to my parents was that they needed to leave me alone and expect me to act detached or aloof. Some people don't want or need anyone close to them. Some people really are happiest all by themselves.

In fact, Halia realized, I probably married Bones partly because he was such an asshole. I knew he wouldn't be faithful to me – shit, everyone and their brother told me what kind of guy he was. But I was so taken with the idea of being "normal" and of what that would mean for my mom and dad... what that would mean for me, if I could fake it well enough to actually believe it. Bones would never push me into any real intimacy – he kept a getaway car running out back, always had one foot out the door, emotionally speaking. If I am brutally honest with myself, Halia thought as they reached the Route 44 exit on the Taconic State Parkway, I chose Bones as much because I wouldn't ever really risk anything with him, as he chose me because I would never really want true intimacy from him. It was a meeting of the pathologies. Halia smiled a small tight smile that didn't reach her eyes.

Being totally, ruthlessly honest about who I am seems to be the only chance I have at real happiness, Halia decided. I honestly don't want to be with anyone. I don't want that thing that everyone else seems to want so much. I don't want to share my life with anyone. I'm not lonely or morose or antisocial. I'm just ...neutral.

At that point Andrew's sleepiness became contagious. The recipient of this internal tirade, Halia realized, was herself. She was combating that slippery slide down the slope of not resisting Ken. It would be too easy to let something happen between them, and that, Halia realized, was not what she wanted. Acknowledging the temptation and thinking it through – that was the point of this little chat she just had with herself. Halia let her eyes fall closed and dozed the rest of the way home.

Perhaps it came to her in a dream, because Halia woke several mornings later to certainty. She knew what to do next to work on determining Joann's current location, and hopefully, to gain a positive identification for her companion. Unfortunately for Halia, this awakening of knowledge occurred at 6:45 a.m., and the necessary phone calls would have to wait until after nine. Halia showered, dressed, and ate breakfast, then scowled at the clock: 7:40 a.m.

"Road trip it is," she told Bezef, weighing the risks involved. "If I strike out completely, I will still have seen a good bit of New York's finest scenery." Halia tossed a change of clothes into her day pack, and grabbed Cliff bars and bottled water from the kitchen. With her trusty map of New York State open on the front seat and Bezef curled up and wagging in the back seat, Halia was ready to roll.

Route 22 north was as breathtaking as ever; this time Halia chose to notice. Amenia's four corners, the muddy cows just south of Millerton, the views of the Taconics all the way to Hillsdale... Halia made the choice to pay attention to what she saw, her mind drifting very little. Turning west onto Route 23, and passing the folk festival site, Halia remained connected to her surroundings, drinking in the uniquely upstate New York flavor of all she saw. Despite the number of years she had lived in New York, she still saw it with an outsider's eye. Part of Halia's character, it seemed, was to be an outsider, no matter where she was. She was always a half step apart – separate and a little different. Even in her classroom, her incredible facility with the subject matter somehow made her seem less at home – more like a guest lecturer than a classroom teacher – and her respectful manner around all the lab equipment almost made her students think she was borrowing someone else's stuff. Halia rolled west across Columbia county, heading for the Rip Van Winkle bridge, dimly aware of the fact that, once again, she was playing the role of a resident tourist.

Navigating downtown Catskill involved several twists and turns. The road to North Lake campground – Route 23A – was more dramatic and quite a bit more challenging than the open farmland from across the river. Halia concentrated on the road, forgetting about Bezef in the back seat. She found herself murmuring aloud in response to the Catskill scenery – no more bucolic pastures, nor quaint towns, but cliffs, ravines, rapids and oncoming traffic. Focused on the task at hand, Halia found herself unable to mentally rehearse the upcoming conversations until the campground gates were upon her.

The teenager at the kiosk listened patiently to Halia's question, collected her day use fee, and directed her to the campground office. Halia pulled up to the dark brown log structure and drew in a long slow breath.

The uniformed clerk behind the counter was probably ten years younger than Halia, and but his receding hairline and pot belly made him look years older. Halia explained briefly about Joann's disappearance, and her reasons for seeking information from the campground. She ended with her request. "Do you have records of who stayed here going back to the 1950's?"

The young man's expansive forehead wrinkled. "I don't think so," he sounded impressed with the whole situation, inadvertently romanticizing Halia's search for Joann. "If we do, I have no idea where ..." he trailed off, thinking. "Let me see if someone else knows." He gestured for Halia to wait, and disappeared into an office. He returned a moment later with a woman, also clad in park ranger greens, who could have been a cosmic twin to Louise, only 40 years her senior. A waist length grey braid hung down her back, like a rope.

"Come on in," the woman invited Halia to join them, lifting the hinged counter. Halia entered the small, spartan office. "Have a seat if you want. Coffee?" She jerked her chin towards the coffee maker sitting atop the filing cabinet. The smell of freshly brewed coffee was surprisingly fabulous to Halia, and she helped herself. Her host stood, her back to Halia, deftly fingering through files in one of the four drawer filing cabinets behind her desk while Halia sat, politely silent and patient, on the only spare chair in the office. Each slight movement of the ranger's squirrel-like pawing sent gentle shivers down her braid. Halia watched, sipped her coffee, and indulged her taste buds in their little victory dance – she was sure it was Trader Joe's Bay blend. She waited. "1956?" The woman asked.

"Yes, I believe so." Halia said. "If you have '55 and '57 I could look at them too."

"1956," the woman announced, turning around. Halia read the name on her green and white plastic name tag: R. Chrisjohn. "We had to keep it, y'know." She handed a heavy ledger book, filled with line after line of handwritten entries, across the desk. Halia set the coffee cup down hurriedly. "Who're you looking for?"

Halia explained about Joann Grant's disappearance. She hesitated, then continued, describing her interview with Joann's brother. She ended by telling Ms. Chrisjohn her theory, and how the remaining questions of current location and companion were the last pieces of the puzzle that Halia sought.

Halia scanned the list of names, starting with arrivals in June. She realized that she didn't know when the Grant family arrived, but she hoped they would be the only Grant's from Pottersville. Deep into her task, Halia took only the most cursory note of Ms. Chrisjohn's exit.

The Grant family, party of five, arrived July 17, 1956. Halia counted other arrivals that day, and then expanded forwards and backwards by two days. A total of seven other families from Pottersville checked in during those three days. Halia was writing down names when Ms. Chrisjohn reappeared, a file folder in her hand.

"It's kind of sad, but I thought you might want to see it anyway." With that, she opened the file and laid it upon her desk. Halia stood up and looked at the yellowed newspaper clipping from above.

The headline read "Tragedy at Kaaterskill Falls – Teen Drowns, Family Devastated." There was a brief article that echoed what Justin Grant had already told Halia, and a photograph.

Halia sank back into her seat, and took the fragile clipping by the edges. She studied it, her concentration complete. It was a vintage Halia moment: her face expressionless as she read every nuance of body language and expression on each person in the photo. Joann, Justin, and their parents stood in a tight knot, while other unidentified people clustered around them looking tearful and offering sympathy. Halia devoured the photo, taking longer than usual to complete her examination. Finally she looked up and met Ms. Chrisjohn's gaze. "Could I get a photocopy of this?" she handed the ranger the clipping.

"Already done. Knew you'd want one." R. Chrisjohn handed Halia the sheet of paper, the image made even more stark by being devoid of greys.

"Thank you." Halia looked over the photocopy, and then slipped it into her notebook. She took another sip of her coffee and added "Thank you for this coffee too. It's very good."

"It's not coffee unless it smells like burnt tires and tastes like jet fuel," Ms. Chrisjohn answered in her clipped way.

Halia grinned, and considered responding with an appreciative quip of her own, but R. Chrisjohn was very busy with the filing cabinet, her back to Halia. Halia lingered for a moment longer, loathe to throw away the remains of her beverage, but unable to gulp it down.

"You can leave the cup – I'll get to it later."

Halia understood that she was being dismissed. She set the cup down with a gentle clunk, after consuming as much as she could. Thanking the pleasant young man at the counter on her way out, Halia strode to her car feeling equipped for the next challenge.

In order to continue her road trip, though, Halia needed to let Bezef get some exercise and water. No better place, Halia thought, than Kaaterskill Falls – the trail was just the right length for the amount of time Halia was willing to spend on the endeavor. And after looking at the newspaper clipping, Halia also felt the need to visit the location where it happened. It was a strange, almost macabre need to put herself through that emotional experience, but somehow it felt important. A necessary part of the day, she realized – it was inevitable that once here at North Lake she would visit the falls. Halia accepted this type of inevitability with patience and grace.

Bezef terrified Halia with her antics as they walked along Route 23A from the parking area to the trail. Thankfully very few cars passed along that narrow stretch as they walked, Bezef playing with the leash and leaping away from Halia's attempts to corral her onto the side of the road. It was still early, and relatively few people would be at the falls, judging by the number of cars in the parking lot. Good, Halia thought – she wasn't sure how she'd feel once she arrived, and didn't especially want an audience.

The Kaaterskill Creek roared over boulders as Halia and Bezef turned onto the well worn track. Bezef was not allowed off the leash; between the cliffs, the potential for other hikers and dogs, and the swift current, not to mention Halia's awareness of the danger the water posed, her freedom seemed like a small price to pay for safety.

Several adults and half a dozen children were loosely gathered at the base of the falls; children splashing and playing in the red mud, adults talking and supervising the kids way too casually, Halia thought. Halia allowed Bezef to greet the children that were interested, and then made her way toward the second level of the falls.

She found a spot to sit, her back to the cliffs, her face misted by the spray. Halia sat and allowed her mind to wander, noticing the scene, imagining the similarities and differences between what she observed and what she knew occurred in 1956. She couldn't really hear the shouts and laughter from below – the falls blotted out all other sounds. Halia was lulled by the white noise into a deep and private space within herself, and for the second time since learning of Jesse's death, she wept.

For the second time in her life, and the second time that year, Halia headed north on the Northway. And for the second time on the Northway, Halia fought the monotony with music. The Gil Knight Trio 1956 sessions blared from the car speakers as Halia time-traveled to a smoky jazz club in the Village half a century ago. Beckerman as a young man ... Halia wondered what he would have been like. His advanced age seemed to be such a defining characteristic. Halia allowed herself to get lost in the music and her imaginings, and found herself approaching Pottersville feeling as if she had just left the Catskills.

The reference shelves at the Chestertown Public Library held the volume that Halia was counting on – the 1956 Warren Central High yearbook. Equipped with her list of names and her photocopied newspaper clipping, Halia sat down at a table and got to work. She looked up each of the seven family names from the campground ledger, and examined each face carefully. The first two were sophomore girls, with no indication of older brothers. The next was a junior girl. The fourth family was the DeRuyters – an old Pottersville family, Halia surmised, judging from the number of times she had seen the name on various businesses along Route 9. There was a son, Henry, who was a junior in 1956. Entries number 5 and 6 either had young children or no children at all. Number 7 was Joseph Mott, also a junior in 1956.

Halia studied the faces, comparing yearbook photos to the grainy images of teenagers in the background of the newspaper clipping, for some time. She compared Joann and Justin's faces, too, and found herself drawn to Jesse's yearbook picture. Jesse, a slightly thinner version of Justin, with plainly mischievous eyes, gazed back at her. Halia felt the powerful pang of loss again. Seated in the library in Jesse's hometown, she felt the trembling aftershocks of his death. With no frame of reference as a mother, nor as a sister, Halia felt the loss not so much with her heart but with her soul. The pain was deep, silent and profound. Halia gazed into Jesse's eyes. Time passed.

And then the moment was over, and Halia simply circled Henry DeRuyter and Joseph Mott on her list.

Chapter 10

Heisenberg had it all wrong. When it comes to relationships, he didn't go far enough. Uncertainty, he said, meant that you could know about position or momentum but not both. Choose one and you can get a measurement – get a beat on it. But the mere act of choosing eliminates the ability to pin down the other. I disagree - not in relationships. No matter how little you might know about where you are as a couple, you never can determine your momentum. Not with any certainty at all. You've heard that saying "Want to make God laugh? Make plans." Determining momentum would involve knowing your future direction. Ha ha. Halia would have argued that if you have a partner like Bones, you can't even know your present position (regardless of how little you may know about where you are headed) because all data is suspect.

The problem with a liar – particularly a good liar – is that they weave in just enough truth to maintain plausible deniability. They keep you guessing, and they keep you hooked. You begin to believe that the uncertainty you feel is your own flaw, your own issues, your own baggage. You grope around in the smokescreen they create, searching for something solid to hang onto, and then they manage to help you feel guilty because you didn't trust the smoke. Living with a partner like that is a lesson in uncertainty beyond the likes of which Heisenberg could ever have imagined – the off balance, profound anxiety of loving unsafely, and the ache – day in and day out – of longing. The longing is not necessarily a longing to be loved – there is love requited in fits and starts – just enough to keep you hooked. The longing is for safety, for rest, for trust that makes sense.

Uncertainty, yes. But total uncertainty. None of this: "If I know this, I can't know that." In relationships, neither position nor momentum can be measured or known with any accuracy at all. If you disagree and provide evidence, I'll say that's just plain luck and hindsight. You can't know – you can only choose to believe. All of it is uncertain. There is only the choice to have faith, to trust, to let your own "momentum" – that catapulting headlong, wind screaming in your ears (deafening you to sensible cautions), descent down the slippery slope of falling in love – guide you.

Months later, if Halia was asked "What was noteworthy about life in Dutchess County last August?" her most likely response would have been a shrug, a reflection of the question, or, just maybe, she might reply "Uuhh, was that the month of the ice cream party?" The truth was that while the rest of the population of Dutchess County suffered and complained about the hottest and driest August since 1986, Halia barely noticed the weather. It simply made no impression upon her.

Halia's August days were dominated anew by The Search For Joann, although they were rather liberally peppered with the normal assortment of mundane tasks. Halia put most of these off until further procrastination would have resulted in utter disaster. Her kitchen table was no longer an option for eating meals –after her trip to North Lake and Pottersville it had been taken over, spread with notes from interviews, transcripts of conversations, maps, scraps of papers, backs of envelopes, lists – in short every item that could earn entry into the search for Joann scrap book was there.

Halia was there too, even when she was not. The two remaining questions so absorbed her, she found herself picturing that tabletop and mentally leafing through the papers once again, while she mowed the lawn or ventured out to get the mail. The heat and drought actually were her allies, as they meant she needed to mow less often. Interrupted from her study of clues only by necessity, the ice cream party at Louise's held an almost surreal appeal for Halia as it stood in such stark contrast to her daily life.

The Townwide Tag Sale and Louise's summer bash (as Louise had informally dubbed it) were scheduled for Saturday, August 17th. On that day, Halia was awakened by the sound of cars rolling down her normally quiet street at 8 a.m. Halia's first sleepy thought was that there was a funeral, as so many cars passed by, heading over the bridge and toward the graveyard. As Halia watched out the window, noticing an absence of sad faces and black clothing, and a large number of passenger seat navigators holding photocopied maps, it dawned on her: Tag Sales. There was the skate park tag sale to the north, and a number of families had set up on the "front lawn" of Valley View cemetery. The day had begun early and enthusiastically, by the looks of it.

Louise, ever the opportunistic entrepreneur, was ready at The Eft to provide early bird breakfasts. Coffee and blackcurrant buns were available in the park at a small stall next to the skater's deluxe used equipment spread. Halia wandered over to help out, and found herself selling liters of Poland Spring hand over fist. Louise, Lukey Jane, and the Benson brothers kept the stall stocked, taking turns crossing the park and piazza to get to The Eft. By 11 a.m., Halia was sure the cash box contained an unsafe amount of bills, and sent the first of many fistfuls back with Louise to Larry at the register.

Virgin lizards, mango-ginger slushies, and cassis snowcones were the sweetened alternatives to bottled water, and between 11 a.m. and noon, Halia marveled at how her hands could be freezing from so much contact with ice, while the rest of her sweltered in the heat. The skaters had rearranged their shop to take advantage of the shade, and from time to time pairs of them would slip over to the potting shed to spray each other with the hose. The heat, Halia thought, seemed to have a suppressing effect on behavior – the teenagers she knew from school to be cut ups were lounging quietly, saving up energy for selling to younger kids, their parents, and the other bargain hunters out despite the heat.

Lukey Jane joined Halia at the drink booth, helped herself to a snowcone, and consumed it at the speed of light.

"It's great that y'all help out like this," Lukey slung an arm around Halia's shoulders and Halia staggered under the impact. "Ain't seen much a you lately – you still tryin' to track down that aunt of yours?"

Lukey Jane, reigning queen of tact, was lucky that Halia was neither emotional nor sensitive about such comments.

"Yes." Halia's response was matter of fact.

"Well, y'all better hurry up. Summer'll be over 'fore ya know it, and then it's back to work. If ya want to sew this thing up nice and neat, you should do it now while y'all got the time."

The phrase "No shit, Sherlock" seemed to fit, but Halia resisted the temptation to utter it. "Yes, that had occurred to me, but I don't exactly have the ability to hurry. I only have one speed when it comes to dealing with this sort of thing." Come to think of it, Halia thought, I don't have any prior experience dealing with this sort of thing. Maybe, she added to herself wryly, I could increase the speed with which I locate missing relatives with practice.

"Well, y'all just let me know if there's anything I can do to help, especially once you're back at school. I really appreciate you giving up a day like this to come out here and sweat with us. I owe you one." Lukey Jane gave Halia's shoulders a grateful squeeze and Halia nearly crumbled to her knees. "Hey, you tried using the internet to look for her? Maybe she's listed on Classmates.com."

"Well, yes, I started back in April with internet searches, but the only address I ever came up with was the one I already had." Halia considered Lukey Jane's suggestion a bit further. "I think you may have just paid your debt," she said slowly. "I did check Classmates.com for Joann's address…" Halia trailed off and grabbed the closest thing to write on – a paper napkin – with red, icy fingers. "Got a pen?" she asked Lukey Jane, but as fast as Lukey produced one, Halia changed her mind.

Lukey Jane looked confused, uncertain as to how she had been helpful. She held out the pen tentatively and managed to form the question "What did I do?"

"Tell you later. Can you take over here for a while? I need to run home for a minute." With that Halia took off, hightailing it out of the park, under the railroad bridge, and back home at a speed that was both noteworthy and unhealthy in the heat. She took the stairs two at a time, and threw herself into the chair at her computer, restraining herself from hitting the power button with all of the momentum gained since her first step away from Lukey Jane.

Normally patient, Halia tapped her fingers and wiggled in her chair, waiting for the computer to boot up. She keyed in the desired website address and then raced down the stairs to the kitchen. Pawing through the papers littering the kitchen table, she found the one she needed and sprinted back to the computer.

Once again seated, she read the error message on her screen with a mixture of anger, disbelief, and ironic amusement. Why now, she fumed, of all times, is a server down? She tried all the tricks she knew, from refreshing the screen to rebooting the computer, but was foiled at all turns. Some problem with the Classmates. com server, she decided. Just my luck.

Halia shut down the computer and took note of her situation: she was sticky with sweat and sweets, and could use a little freshening up. After a shower and clean clothes, Halia braved the blinding sun and baking temperature, and returned, this time slowly, to the park.

Louise and Lukey Jane had created an oasis under the borrowed tent and were still arranging tables and chairs when Halia arrived. Anne Marie's son and another boy helped make cut flower centerpieces for the tables while Larry hauled ice. Halia had the fleeting impression of a wedding.

After consulting briefly with Louise, Halia stationed herself as a server. There were three ice cream choices: studded vanilla – vanilla ice cream with whole black currants and high bush blueberries, kir royale swirl – a delicate champagne flavored ice swirled with a black currant ribbon, and a decadent dark chocolate, served with a black currant syrup and whipped cream. The crowd was light for the first 40 minutes or so, and Halia's attention was definitely not under the tent. Nor was it even in Dutchess County. Her latest possibility, and her failure to eliminate it from her list, siphoned off a large measure of her attention. As nothing compelling tethered her to the present, she let herself go, reviewing, reconsidering, and planning the next step.

By the time the five gallon tubs were empty, Halia's white tee shirt looked rather studded and swirled. The last few customers were still enjoying their rapidly melting treats when Louise arrived at Halia's serving station and pressed a tumbler of iced coffee into her hand.

"Thanks," Halia accepted it gratefully. The unsweetened cold beverage felt like fuel entering Halia's veins.

"Come," Louise invited, "let's just sit and relax for a few minutes before I have to retool for the evening." Louise flopped heavily into a chair and admired the flowers.

Halia sat down more delicately, and savored her drink. "How did you do today?" she asked.

"Very well." Louise looked tired but happy. "This was a good idea. I needed to cover my expenses, and I did by quite a bit between breakfast, the drinks cart, and the ice cream. I think the guys did pretty well too." Louise gestured and Halia looked over at the skater boys' spread. Compared to when Halia had last looked, it was picked clean. It was at that moment that Halia realized two of the boys were making their way over to her table, carrying bundles.

"Uh, Ms. Frank, your t-shirt is kind of a mess." The taller boy who Halia recognized from hall duty spoke first.

"Yeah," the shorter, dark-haired boy was not familiar to Halia. Perhaps a sixth grader, she thought, or maybe new to the district. "You need a clean t-shirt, don't you know?" The boy's Midwestern accent made Halia smile. The two boys exchanged a glance and in tandem they unfurled two blue-black tee shirts with sophisticated grey lettering. "Currant Events 2007" read the front of the shirt, and the back contained the actual schedule, with the skate park events highlighted.

"These are for you," the tall boy laid the shirts on the table in front of the two women. "Wear them in good health." The dark haired boy looked rather embarrassed by his friend's theatrical flourish and incongruously formal words.

Louise and Halia thanked them and admired the design. The boys ate up the praise hungrily, then departed. Lukey Jane had also departed some time earlier, and Anne Marie had already collected her son and gone home for the day, both of them promising to return the following morning to complete the clean up.

Halia and Louise enjoyed sharing the end of the day, and sat reviewing the highlights for several minutes. From seemingly opposite directions, Grace, Asha and Rob all converged upon Halia and Louise simultaneously. In nearly the same breath, all three of them asked "How'd today go?"

"Judging by the condition of your clothes, I'd say you were pretty busy," Grace observed, glancing at the formerly white shirt her friend wore.

They all talked for a few more minutes while Halia finished her iced coffee. The conversation rapidly spun off in different directions after Asha and Rob began naming their prized finds of the day at different tag sales. Asha's attitude toward selling her home and moving across the river with Rob vacillated between hope and grief, but this full day with him, treasure hunting, seemed to lift her spirits. Rob was also in a buoyant mood, the worried crease in his brow smoothed. Grace, fresh from rounds at the air conditioned animal hospital, also walked with a spring in her step and an easy smile. She had done some tagsale-ing before going in to work at noon, and proudly rattled off all the toys and clothes she had found for Andrew. Louise feigned jealousy that her friends were all out shopping while she worked, so Halia made a great show of bringing her the cashbox. As the sun ended its descent behind Chestnut Ridge, the entire group moved into The Blue Eft.

Larry mixed alizarin smokes at a breakneck pace, the bar already bustling and the restaurant nearly full of families unwilling to heat up their kitchens at home. Grace led the way to a table in the corner.

Once settled, Halia excused herself and changed into her new shirt in the ladies room. She returned and was showered with compliments. As she slid into her chair next to Grace, she murmured, "Talk to the collector – the women who lost the coati in the first place. Let her help you trap it."

"Omigod, Halia, if you weren't so helpful you'd be infuriating! How did you know that I was going to ask you about getting someone to help me with the traps?"

Halia flicked her eyes over Grace in an exaggerated gesture and shrugged. She might have launched into an explanation, but Asha interrupted them.

"Would you guys like to go to the drive-in tonight? Rob and I are thinking of going."

A brief discussion ensued, resulting in Grace calling Andrew and Eddie on her cell phone, and Halia politely begging off. "I hate getting all damp and cold from the dew," she explained. Within minutes the party had broken up and Halia was heading home. Although her physical form walked down Nellie Hill Road in the present tense, her mind was lost somewhere in North Lake campground, in the summer of 1956. "What have I missed?" she asked herself. "What have I overlooked?"

Too early for bed, Halia dove into the organized chaos of the kitchen table. The photocopy of the newspaper photo lay atop everything else, and Halia took it in hand first. She had studied the faces until she knew them inside out. "There must be something else here…" she grunted through gritted teeth. Halia fetched a magnifying glass and methodically examined the photo as if divided into a grid. In square M7, Halia saw it. Stopped dead in her tracks, she smiled slowly to herself, and mouthed the words, "ah-ha."

There, on Joann's finger, was a boy's class ring. While the stone's color was indistinguishable, the image of a winged shoe was clear.

Taking the stairs two at a time, Halia sailed up to the computer, feeling a thrill of anticipation. "I hope that goddamned server is back up," she muttered, as she waited for the screen to appear.

Although it seemed like Joseph Mott didn't have an entry of his own, the search for him indicated participation in winter track freshman year. Ok, Halia thought. That's a definite maybe.

Henry DeRuyter's entry was the eureka Halia had hoped for: winter track freshman year, cross country sophomore and junior years, and spring track all three years. Halia had found her man. Or, more to the point, Halia had found Joann's man.

Chapter 11

Driving south on Route 22 to the high school-middle school complex, Halia smiled ruefully – she had turned on the heater in her car, and used the windshield wipers to combat the mist. It must really be fall, Halia thought. She remembered her first year teaching in the Dover school district, when she was still married to Bones and commuting from Staatsburg. She remembered driving across Dutchess County in glorious sunshine, the air clear and crisp, a welcome relief after summer's hazy humidity. Light and color always seemed to intensify in September and Halia would drink in the visual evidence of the season's change with thirsty eyes. The view across the Harlem Valley from the top of Plymouth Hill had startled her that first time: a blanket of mist lay across the entire valley, like a white down comforter. As she descended into it, she experienced the fog in layers: as a seventh grade science teacher understanding the fog, and as a woman who needed to leave her husband, feeling the fog swallow her. Halia recalled coastal California, and the daily rolling in and out of the fog; it might burn off early, late, or not at all, but each morning it was there, like clockwork. Halia had never expected to find something similar in upstate New York. She remembered how September 11th had been a similar day, and her first horrified and incredulous response to the news had been to ask "Was there fog?"

In subsequent years, Halia had found a friend in the fog. Fall in the Hudson Valley heralded by these chilly misty mornings had come to be Halia's favorite time of year. Unfortunately, the first few days of September, often some of the ten best days of the year, were also the first few days of school. This year, Halia experienced a powerful riptide of regret coming back to school. Summer had been such a rollercoaster of hope and disappointment, red herrings and dead ends. Halia was relieved, at one level, that the end of available time meant she could place Joann's disappearance on the bottom of her "to do" list, but she was deeply disappointed with the continued lack of tangible results. The notion of failure lurked at the edges of her thoughts, threatening to drag her into its quicksand. Halia avoided such a demise by getting angry, but the anger had no role in her classroom. It was an internal dance, nursing the anger to avoid despair, but holding onto enough optimism and confidence to be able to face her students daily.

"Ms. Frank? Can we learn about sleep this semester?"

Halia thought approximately 5 thoughts simultaneously while checking the clock and measuring the amount of time it would take to answer versus putting off the question. She opened the sleep file in her brain, scanned its contents, and translated its condensed code into seventh grade lesson plans. Halia decided that, being the first day of school, her plan to cover logistics and "housekeeping" details could be dramatically shortened, and the sleep question could be addressed then. All this took approximately three seconds, while the students waited for her answer.

"I will answer that question in about seven minutes." Halia was not trying to be cute or funny by being so precise, but several girls in the front row giggled. Halia noticed and chose to ignore the response. "First I need to go over other details. Please pay attention, as I will be moving through this quickly." With that, Halia swept through the materials needed, fire drills, and academic expectations. She handed out an outline for the semester that had "How To Get An A" clearly detailed on the back.

It was exactly seven minutes later when Halia stopped and made eye contact with the student who asked about sleep.

"Ok, Neil," Halia was constantly amazing her students on the first day of class with her ability to use their names before she had been introduced. She was legendary for this "trick" which of course was nothing more than observation. Neil's name was written on his notebook under his chair. "Can you re-ask your question?"

"Well, I want to ask about this cool thing that happens to me sometimes."

Halia smiled at Neil's openness. She nodded for him to continue.

Neil took the class on a tour of the process of losing oneself in deep sleep, and waking to the wondrous moment of selflessness. Halia played the role of moderator for the forum that ensued, shepherding the students' responses on the subject and helping several students less articulate than Neil describe their experiences of sleep and waking. While Halia waited for all the students who wished to be heard to have their opportunity, she planned where to steer the discussion. Neil's next question caught her somewhat off guard.

"Ms. Frank – what about you? Does this happen to you too?"

Halia hesitated for a split second, recalling all she knew about divulging personal information. Satisfied that she could respond appropriately, she began. "Yes. I think that throughout my life I've had this experience from time to time. I never talked about it as a kid, but yes, I did feel it." Halia watched the students carefully, ready to switch gears if she saw them glaze over. She still had them, however, so she continued. "As an adult, I find that sometimes I wake up and I am simply awake." She hesitated again, having stressed the word awake dramatically.

"What do you mean?" This time it was Joe who spoke up.

"Well, the first thing, when I wake up, that I realize, or my first conscious thought is just plain 'I am awake.'" Halia watched Joe and the others nod. "After that, sometimes, my very next thought is an awareness that my awareness is so limited. It is a sensation of being empty; being here, alive, conscious, but not Me." Halia grinned and wrote Me on the board and underlined the capital M. The students smiled.

"Then slowly, whether I want to or not, I become Me. I think the first thing that happens is I recognize myself by recognizing the 'sound' of the voice in my head. You know, the internal narrator? That voice that thinks your thoughts in words? I recognize that voice, and then it's almost like getting dressed. I put on the parts of my identity like putting clothes on – in layers." Many students nodded their heads but some looked confused.

"For example, Neil might put his identity together by realizing male, middle school student, Janine's boyfriend." The gasps and giggles helped Halia know she had hit the mark. She continued to tick off identity components on her fingers, watching her students' expressions clear and the non-nodders began to unfurrow their brows. Keeping an eye on the time, Halia then asked the class, "When else do you have the experience of losing your Self?"

After a moment, several hands shot into the air.

"Sometimes when I run," Neil offered.

"When I do artwork," Edgardo called out.

"When I ride my horse," Jackie added.

"Yes!" Halia felt pleased. This discussion had developed into an opportunity for Halia to circle back to her original plan for the day – introducing goals and expectations for the year. Halia enjoyed it when discussion could have symmetry – especially when seizing and manipulating a spontaneous question wove together the students' interests with her own purpose. "Ok, my goal for this year is that each and every one of you has this experience – of being so absorbed in what we are doing that you feel almost as is you are waking up, or coming back to yourself when the bell rings – at least once. Once a month would be great. And," Halia grinned playfully, having gotten caught up in the pleasure of a connected discussion, "I plan to present each lesson with ample opportunities for you to do so."

The bell rang and the students left, but each of them felt the positive charge in the room. Whatever else happens today, Halia thought, I have one class that is set up for a magical experience. Halia felt the smile leave her face and settle in the center of her being.

That first full week of school ended with Halia and Grace's Friday evening ritual of smokes at The Eft. Grace was waiting at a table near the open garage door when Halia unceremoniously collapsed into the empty chair. She gratefully accepted the drink Grace pushed across the table.

"Have you been here long?" Halia asked. Grace opened her mouth to answer, then stopped, realizing Halia had already answered with her own observations. "Sorry," Halia grinned. "Bad habit, this asking the obvious. Let me start over. How are you? How was your day?"

"Unexpectedly shortened. Last appointment of the day cancelled, on a Friday! Yahoo! Andrew is with Eddie, playing softball this evening, but I'm gonna go meet them in a little while." Grace shifted in her chair, and reached for her drink. "So yes, I've been here for a little while, and it has been great. Louise started telling me about menu changes for fall, and this season's series of currant events, Asha ran by and said something about stopping in after her run, and it is just a totally gorgeous evening. Life is good." Grace shifted in her seat and attempted to study Halia the way Halia so often studied others. "How about you? How is it being back this year?"

"Ok. There are some great kids and I'm excited about some changes to the curriculum. The committee that worked on it over the summer did a really good job with the seventh grade units." Halia looked less than enthusiastic and Grace waited. "It's just so frustrating to have no time. The summer was my window of opportunity and now it's over." Halia pressed her lips together in a gesture that made them all but disappear. Then with a sigh, she relaxed and her expression resumed its neutrality. "I can't find any information about Henry DeRuyter's whereabouts online. Nothing more recent than February of this year. He was in Albany – well, Troy actually – until then, as far as I can tell, but it looks like he sold his house in February and left no forwarding address."

"Another disappearance? This is a little ridiculous! Why would both of them be so secretive?"

"Well, I haven't really dug very deeply into Henry's situation. There may be a whole lot more of a trail than Joann left, but I've only just started my pursuit. I haven't called his old job or anything. That's why I'm frustrated," Halia's circled back to Grace's original question. "It seems to me that in order to find Joann, I'm going to have to find Henry, but I don't really know whether or not he's missing. And I have no time to start all over, driving around upstate New York, making phone calls, and whatever else might be involved..." Halia realized she sounded as if she was complaining and once again composed herself to erase all trace of emotion from her face. "Besides," her neutral tone and demeanor returned, "I'm not sure how I feel about searching for this man. Joann is different – I owe her money. This poor guy is entitled to his privacy."

"Halia," Grace, a commanding tone matching the intensity on her face, leaned forward as she raised her voice. "At the risk of annoying you, there's something

I feel the need to point out." She plowed on without pausing to allow Halia time to react. "Bullshit to this 'I owe her money' nonsense. You are allowed to care. A woman worked her whole life, she helped you at a critical moment in your life, and then she vanished. You are allowed to have feelings about her. You are allowed to try to find her because you need to set your mind at ease. It is natural that you are worried about her and it is normal to care." Grace paused only for breath, and continued. "You know that if you were looking in from the outside, and you heard yourself say it was all about the money, you wouldn't believe yourself for a second. You know that, right?" Grace allowed her voice to rise again, just a bit. "As a motive for the level of effort you've put into finding her, it just doesn't cut it. You're not being honest with yourself. The truth is that you're worried about her and you care about her and you feel connected to her. Maybe even more connected to her now because of all the searching and all you've found out about her, and her family. And," Grace's voice inadvertently softened, "all you found out about Jesse. So stop trying to convince yourself or fool me into thinking that you have pursued this woman for half a year and across New York State and across half a century, all so that you can resume writing your monthly checks. Just give it up because that simply doesn't ring true."

Halia's face remained unchanged during Grace's tirade. She considered responding as Grace had apparently ended her efforts to set Halia straight, but as she internally composed a response, Asha arrived.

"Hi Grace! Hi Hali!" Asha's cheeriness startled both women out of their intense moment. "How was work this week?"

Asha, in the midst of a major life transition, radiated joy, hope, and a certain frenetic chaos. Ever since finding a house in Warwick, over in Orange County, and finalizing plans for the move, it seemed that nearly anything could spill out of Asha's purse or out of her mouth at any time. The stress and the excitement had unhinged her even more than usual, and she was an emotional loose cannon. Her timing, to show up so closely on the heels of Grace's confrontational monolog, was par for Asha's course these days. That she was oblivious to what she was interrupting was only all the more typical of Asha under stress. At the current moment it could have been manners that prevented her from commenting on the obvious tension in the air.

Grace answered first, giving Halia time to absorb her prior words. The rundown of Andrew's new teachers and schedule, and the ups and downs of managing the animal hospital hours, coordinating with Eddie's work schedule, and recreating the logistical masterpiece called life in the suburbs with a child for a new school year led to talk of time to pursue trapping the coati.

"I did get in touch with Loni Greene – the woman who owned Stella." Grace grinned at Asha's repeating the word "Stella" questioningly. "Yes, the coati was – is – named Stella, and Loni Greene and I plan to attempt to lure her out of the woods this weekend with peanut butter. Apparently peanut butter spread on carob rice cakes is the ultimate treat for a coati. We'll try tomorrow. If that doesn't work, we have one more weekend, then Dr. Greene is off to Peru for the rest of the semester – some research project – so the pressure is on."

"Have you seen Stella recently? I mean, are you sure she's still there?" Asha asked.

"Yeah. I was up there two weeks ago in the evening with Eddie. Andrew was visiting Eddie's parents for the weekend, and we went up and met Loni Greene there. We caught sight of Stella and Loni gave the positive ID. This time we have the traps and the proper bait, and we're prepared. Loni Greene wants to trap some of her offspring too." Grace appraised Asha and asked, "What are you doing tomorrow? Do you want to help out?"

Asha begged off, citing the numerous chores related to packing and moving as preventing her participation. Grace nodded and said quietly, "I think the three of us might be the busiest people in this room."

"Well, maybe," Asha laughed, "but the truly busy people aren't here. They can't make time to hang out with friends like this."

"And of course there is more than one type of busy." Halia rejoined the conversation, breaking a silence of several minutes. Asha and Grace turned to her, ready to be entertained by Halia's expounding upon the different ways in which one can be busy. Halia, of course, adopted her teacher voice and presented the lecture as if it were a seventh grade science lesson. Asha and Grace regressed, and acted their parts as middle school students, complete with whispering and giggling.

Over the next half an hour or so, Grace stole cautious glances at Halia, trying to gauge the response to her words. Halia, as always, was unreadable: neutral and composed. Grace decided that all was well, and risked asking a favor. "So tomorrow may end up being kind of a long day," Grace steered the conversation back to tomorrow's events, as she saw that Halia was getting ready to leave. "Would you mind keeping Bezef with you, Hali? I'll drop her off in the morning and pick her up on my way home from the Stella capture." Since the school year had started back up, Grace had reclaimed Bezef during the week, with Halia being back at work. For the most part it was difficult to discern who actually puppy-sat for whom, but neither of them cared much.

Halia agreed to spend her day with Bezef, and left The Eft to walk home while it was still twilight. Asha stayed with Grace, awaiting Rob who had called to say he'd be late. Halia overheard Asha say something about "black currant honey" as she left. Halia allowed her curiosity about its flavor to carry her home.

Chapter 12

Late Saturday afternoon Halia took Bezef for a walk in the Valley View cemetery. She flopped down onto the grass near the gravestone whose inscription she often pondered, not really feeling interested in the aerobic workout a circumnavigation would provide, but happy to sit still and watch Bezef play with her stick. Halia was taking a much needed break from everything. She remembered her grandfather's standard line: "Stop the world, I want to get off." Halia took some respite in those moments, sitting and staring and allowing her "thinking muscles" to relax completely. She allowed herself to get lost in the sensation of the afternoon sun on her skin, the syncopated rhythm of Bezef's chewing siphoning off her conscious attention and the overall result being deep and profound relaxation.

"It's wrong, you know." A voice from behind her made Halia jump involuntarily. Her head spun around, her mind already racing to connect the content of the comment with the voice. Joann Grant stood behind Halia, the afternoon sun illuminating her profile, adding drama to the already adrenaline-filled moment. Before Halia was able to form coherent words, Joann continued. "The battle of Loral Hill was months earlier. In July, not October. This man was killed in a skirmish at Derbytown Road. The date matches, and he's listed in the records as being among the Union soldiers from New York lost in that battle. But that," she shrugged her shoulders and gestured toward the stone, "that inscription is definitely incorrect. Odd, isn't it?"

"Yes." Halia answered, looking at Joann. It was the patented Halia all inclusive once-over, only Halia felt as if it were happening in slow motion.

Joann, unaware of the full meaning behind the look, explained. "Your friend at The Blue Eft – that lovely young woman with the long braid – told me to look for you here."

Halia struggled to recover from her surprise. She was flooded with so many questions, she felt her speech circuits overload and she just couldn't get a single word out. Finally she embraced the older woman warmly. "It's good to see you," were the only words Halia was able to put together at that moment. "Shall we head back to my house?"

"Yes." Joann and Halia started back, Bezef abandoning her stick and joining them. "Your house is positively charming, dear. Did you choose that green color for the trim?"

Halia laughed, and as she did she felt the overwhelming pang of shock begin to subside. "Joann, I've been trying to track you down since last March. Where have you been?" Halia realized that she spoke with a level of passion and emphasis that exposed her concern.

Joann patted her arm and said, "It's a long story, dear. I had no idea you were concerned until I spoke with your friend just a few minutes ago. I did send you a card, over the summer – surely that reached you?"

"Well, yes, it did," Halia admitted, "but there was no return address. I was relieved that you were ok, but I wanted to know where to send the checks." Halia finished lamely, feeling confused, apologetic, and terribly curious.

"I am sorry Halia. I had no idea how much you cared." Joann seemed to allow the words to sink in, both into her own consciousness and into Halia's. "I didn't realize you were trying to find me. I would have let you know where I was but it all happened rather quickly. I can do a better job of explaining back at your house, with a cup of tea, and my ..." Joann blushed prettily and seemed to savor the word: "husband." Ignoring Halia's dropped jaw, Joann continued, "He can help me fill in the blanks."

"You're married?!" Halia had to laugh at herself, knowing she sounded like either a nosy child, or a disapproving parent. She hastened to correct those impressions. "I mean, I know you reconnected with Henry last Thanksgiving -"

"At your house, dear." Joann patted her arm again, unperturbed by Halia's seemingly psychic outburst. Joann knew her well enough to expect no less. "We'll do this nicely, sitting at a table, with tea, and perhaps we'll send Henry out for some biscuits or something. And we'll tell you the whole story. Alright, Halia?"

Halia nodded, and caught her lower lip between

her teeth. They emerged from the graveyard. Halia had a moment of omniscient awareness, the bird's eye view of the two women, a generation apart, and the dog on the leash, walking down the road. She felt that to the eyes of those who knew neither herself nor Joann, the picture would tell a very different story. She wondered if she looked like Joann – if they could be mistaken for mother and daughter. She decided not – that Mediterranean genes dominated her appearance, while Joann's height, straight hair and prominent cheekbones gave an overall impression of being Scandinavian. What then, Halia wondered, would people make up about us? What story would they tell?

They arrived at the stucco and goodness-gracious-green house to find Louise on the front porch with a silver-haired gentleman wearing a barn jacket and jeans.

"I left Larry in charge," Louise explained, "and came right over. I didn't want to leave your husband alone here while you went to find Halia."

"Louise has been very pleasant company," Henry DeRuyter smiled politely in her direction. He continued, his pleasantly deep voice lowered to an intimate tone, "but I still missed you, sweetheart." He stepped to Joann's side and swung an arm around her adoringly. From this position he introduced himself, and shook hands with Halia. They all went inside.

Halia, near desperate to hear Joann's story, bustled about the kitchen, putting the kettle on and gathering mugs and spoons and the milk and sugar. The housekeeping seemed endless, but finally Halia was able to sit down at the table with her guests.

"Ok, I know that you went to high school together,

and were in the same class. I know that you were the young man Joann was talking to at Kaaterskill Falls the day that Jesse died. And I know that you got back in touch a year ago, when your 50th high school reunion was being planned for Thanksgiving weekend." Halia's rapidly delivered accounting elicited a stunned silence from her small audience. She was about to continue when a knock at the door spurred Bezef into action, barking wildly and leaping up and down.

Halia excused herself and returned with Asha, drenched in sweat, dressed in running attire.

"I ran past the graveyard a few minutes ago, and I saw you two, and well... I just thought I'd stop in and ask – is this Joann Grant?" Asha's eyes flicked back and forth from Halia to Joann.

Joann looked pleasantly embarrassed and stood up, extending her hand. "I am she," she said formally.

"Asha Jackson," Asha grasped Joann's hand briefly, then looked around the room. "Please excuse me," she apologized, "I didn't mean to barge in."

"Not at all," Halia answered before Asha could continue. "We were just having some tea. Shall I pour you a cup?" Halia masked her impatience well.

"No... well, sure, but I'll run home and clean up before I come back and drink it, ok?" With that, Asha was gone.

As Halia retrieved an additional cup from the cupboard, Louise spoke up. "Uuh, Halia? Maybe you should get another cup down." Halia turned to face Louise, her eyebrows soaring skyward in a look of near exasperation. "I thought Grace would want to be here. I called her from The Eft. She said she could get away in about," Louise glanced at the clock, "10 minutes."

Louise looked sheepish and her delivery was haltingly apologetic, but Halia knew she was completely delighted. This was the biggest news their circle of friends had enjoyed all year.

"Ok," Halia placed an additional mug next to the others. "Anyone else I should know about?"

"I think Rob might be at Asha's," Louise allowed her mischievous delight to peek around the edges of her voice. "And I'm sure Lukey Jane is at the garden, helping with getting the soaker hoses installed. I think I saw her truck there. Shall I go get her?"

"No need," Lukey Jane bellowed, entering Halia's kitchen with Bezef in her arms. "Asha told me on her way back home." Bezef looked comfortable and relaxed in Lukey Jane's confident grasp. The puppy placed her chin on Lukey's shoulder and watched the front door.

"Is that your dog, dear?" Joann asked Halia. "I didn't think you had any pets at all."

"Actually no, Bezef is mine." Grace squeezed past Lukey Jane into Halia's kitchen, petting Bezef as she did. She caught Halia's eye and added, "Ok, not exclusively mine. Halia and I share her."

"What breed is she?" Henry asked.

Halia realized they would need more chairs, and excused herself to figure out how many more people she would need to seat and how she would manage, as Grace, Lukey Jane, and Henry chatted about dog breeds. She found Asha and Rob on her front porch and ushered them in. "I think I need to move everyone into the living room – we've run out of chairs in the kitchen." Asha and Rob immediately began helping Halia herd people out of the crowded kitchen and carry chairs into the living room.

Finally everyone was seated in the living room, beverage in hand. Everyone, except Lukey Jane, who was sprawled on the floor with Bezef. Mugs and tea cups were carefully placed out of the danger zone. Halia realized that in order to get Joann and Henry to tell their story, she would have to interrupt the conversations that had sprung up on their own. "I'm having a party," Halia thought to herself. "This is a party. Good lord."

It was Lukey Jane, however, who interrupted Joann and Henry's questions to Asha and Rob about the house they were buying on the outskirts of Warwick to call them to task. "Y'all know we're here to find out where in God's creation y'all have been since last spring. Ever since her," Lukey Jane jerked her chin in Halia's direction, "check came back with that 'No Forwarding Address' stamp on it, we've all been on the edge of our seats, wondering where y'all could go like that. What gol dang place has no address?" Lukey Jane's last words tumbled out half plaintive, half challenging. "Tell me you were on a boat!"

"We were on a boat," Joann answered. Henry's arm draped affectionately around her shoulders pulled just a touch tighter in response to Lukey Jane's tone.

"My boat," he added. "We were sailing in the Caribbean and visiting some friends of mine."

"I knew it! I knew it! I said that. I said y'all were on a boat. I told Halia last summer!" Lukey Jane's triumphant shouting excited Bezef, who leapt at Lukey's chin, wagging her tail furiously and barking. Exuberance breeds exuberance, Halia thought. Henry and Joann looked amused; everyone else looked concerned.

"Maybe we could back up. How did you reconnect? Was it before the reunion, or did you meet there?" Halia asked.

"How did you know we were there?" Henry wanted to know.

"Observation and deduction, and nothing weird! I figured things out, but only from what was available for all to see. Please don't misunderstand – I'm a science teacher, not a detective, and I would never cross that line and compromise your privacy." Halia had been addressing Henry, but now she included Joann. "At first I just wanted to find an address so I could continue to pay you. When I found out that you had retired and sold the house, I got … concerned." Everyone in the room looked at Halia and raised their eyebrows. Halia smiled self consciously. "Ok, I got worried, and curious. And after I talked to Justin, and I found out about Jesse, something happened." Halia swallowed and dropped her gaze to the floor, suddenly interested in the large collection of feet within her field of vision. "I felt like I stumbled into someone's life uninvited and now I was … in. Connected. The only thing to do was to find you… to make sure you were ok." Grace nodded at Halia and smiled: so she was listening that night at The Eft. "After I received your postcard, I knew that you were ok, but I didn't know where you were. I admit it – at that point, I wanted to find you partly out of sheer ego. But there was something else too. By the time I'd gotten that postcard, it was like we were … family, I guess, for lack of a better word. I'd gotten to know you, in a way, and I needed to find you … maybe so that I could tell you all that." Even Lukey Jane sat still and silent, absorbing Halia's words. "But at the very last moment, it was you that found me." Halia smiled broadly. "Well done."

It was Grace who rescued Halia from the spotlight, turning the beam back on Joann and Henry. "Your story must be really romantic. Was last fall the first time you were in touch in 50 years?"

"Yes. You see," Joann colored slightly, remembering, "I wrote Henry a Dear John letter after Jesse died. In today's lingo, I dumped him. I gave him no reason to think I'd change my mind; no crack to wedge some hope into. Henry moved on, married, had children -"

"I never fell out of love with you," he said softly, almost as if they were alone. "I did what I believed you wanted – I did my best to move on and have a good life. Carolyn was a fine lady and a good mother, and I don't regret my time with her, but after she died five years ago, I realized just to what degree I continued to hold feelings for you." Henry looked around the room, and acknowledged the presence of his audience by correcting himself. "For Joann, that is. I knew I still loved her. That love never really faded. About three months before the reunion, some classmates on the committee contacted me. I agreed to help out, and that's how it all started. Modern technology," Henry chuckled happily. "What my dad would have thought, I don't know. I emailed the love of my life, and we began corresponding before the reunion. We saw each other for the first time in 50 years at the reunion, in good old Pottersville. After that, things developed pretty quickly."

"I retired in January, and had the house sold by mid-March. It took Henry a little longer to organize his affairs, so I stayed at his place with him until we were ready to leave. We put our belongings into storage and we took off on our trip at the end of April."

"You went to visit Jesse's grave." Halia stated matter-of-factly. "Justin told me he saw you there."

"Yes. I had ended my relationship with Henry almost as a sort of penance – an attempt to assuage my guilt. It was like a pact I made with ... well, I thought it was with Jesse all those years, but really it was with myself. It was a way to go on living when I had been unable to stop Jesse's death. If I denied myself the love of my life, then maybe I could survive the grief of losing Jesse." Joann trailed off, her eyes dry, but focused on something distant and internal. Henry hugged her gently. Louise, Grace, Asha and Lukey Jane all cried openly, passing around Halia's box of tissues. Rob cleared his throat and wrapped his arms around Asha, ducking his face into her hair. Halia sat alone, silent and dry-eyed, and watched Joann.

After a moment, Joann's gaze re-entered Halia's living room, and she met Halia's eyes. "Being found by Henry started a chain of events in my life that has been nothing short of miraculous. I hope that the search you undertook brought good into your life." Reaching across the arm of the couch, Joann extended her hand to Halia, who grasped it and held on tight.

The rest of the story poured out of the three of them; Henry, Joann and Halia each taking turns in the telling. Spontaneous applause broke out when Halia described the process of identifying Henry, and Joann laughed until she was breathless when she heard Halia's description of Rachel Zimmerman, LCSW. Finally, when it seemed that there were no more loose ends to tie up, footsteps creaked on the front porch.

Bezef exploded into excited barking, until Lukey Jane corralled her and wrestled her into relative silence. The mood was broken, and everyone sat there, blinking, while Halia hurried to her feet and crossed the room.

The door opened, blocking the new arrival from

view. The voice, young, deep and musical, was un-mistakable. "Uuh, I saw Grace's car here," Kennedy Edmonds sounded shyly confused and adorable. "I was just, umm, on my way to The Eft, and umm, this woman asked me about Grace and Halia's house, and umm, … a coati?"

Ken stood in Halia's foyer, surveying the scene, as Grace burst into laughter, her hands covering her mouth. She leapt to her feet. "The coati is in the car," she explained, picking her way across the living room. "I trapped it today – early this morning – and Loni Greene was supposed to pick it up from me at the animal hospital this afternoon. You two," Grace indicated Joann and Henry, "kind of made me forget my plans! Is she here? My co-workers must have told her where I went." Grace was out the door and down the porch steps before her sentence was finished. Halia gestured for Ken to join the rest of them in the living room. A moment later, Grace stuck her head 'round the front door and offered "You guys want to see Stella before she goes back home?"

Joann and Henry joined those who knew all about Grace and Stella, filing out the front door and following Grace to the pick-up truck where Loni Greene waited. Halia brought up the rear, and as all her friends, new and old, crossed her front lawn, Halia stood on her porch, leaning against a signature green column and watched the evening light turn Preston Mountain a warm September shade of richness. Halia stayed there, alone, and took it all in.

closed tonight

**Join us this Friday evening
for a belated wedding celebration
check our website for details**

the blue eft
nellie hill road   **dover plains, ny**

9 781934 937433